The Nine Guardians

a novel by

ROSARIO CASTELLANOS

*translated from the Spanish
with a Preface by*
Irene Nicholson

readers international

This book was first published in Mexico in 1957 under the title *Balún-Canán* by the Fondo de Cultura Económica, Mexico City
© Fondo de Cultura Económica 1957

English translation copyright
© Faber and Faber Limited 1959

1992 edition by Readers International Inc, Columbia, Louisiana USA and Readers International, London. Editorial inquiries to the London office at 8 Strathray Gardens, London NW3 4NY England. US/Canadian inquiries to the Subscriber Service Department, P.O. Box 959, Columbia LA 71418 USA.

Front cover: *Carnival Figures*, painting by Mexican artist Jose Chavez Morado, 1959
Back cover: Cut-paper Day of the Dead silhouettes by Mexican artist Victor Manuel Cuellar
Cover design by Jan Brychta

Printed and bound in Malta by Progress Press Co. Ltd

CIP information for this book is on record at the Library of Congress and the British Library.

ISBN 0-930523-89-X Hardcover
ISBN 0-930523-90-3 Paperback

The Nine Guardians

Readers International titles from Latin
America and the Caribbean:

To
EMILIO CARBALLIDO
AND
MY FRIENDS IN CHIAPAS

Contents

Preface

Balún-Canán means "Nine Stars", and is the name the Indians gave to the ancient Mayan villages in the district of the State of Chiapas, in Mexico, where the novel is laid.

The home of the Argüellos is Comitán, a small town in the State of Chiapas, close to the Guatemalan border. This is rugged and remote territory which even today has received little influence from Mexico City. The novel takes place during the Presidency of Lázaro Cárdenas, between 1934 and 1940. Cárdenas, who consolidated the Mexican Revolution which had begun in 1910, was strongly anti-clerical. It was during his régime that it became illegal to say Mass, and many priests lost their lives for doing so. He also pursued a policy of agrarian reform which included the return of land to the peasants. Many large estates were thus broken up, and the families who had owned them were either ruined or forced off the land into the cities.

Besides Cárdenas himself, the only other historical figure mentioned in the novel is the Dominican priest and reformer, Bartolomé de las Casas, who did much for the Indians' cause in the years immediately after the conquest of Mexico by Spain, in the sixteenth century.

It has been thought best to leave a few Indian and Spanish words with precise shades of meaning untranslated, and a short glossary is provided.

IRENE NICHOLSON

PART I

Comitán

We shall whisper the origin. We shall whisper
the story and the tale, and that is all.
One thing only we do, and that is to return; we
have fulfilled our task, and our days are done.
Think of us, blot us not from your memory,
consign us not to oblivion.

From the Book of Counsel,
an ancient Maya manuscript

PART I

1

"And then in anger they dispossessed us, they confiscated what we had treasured: the word, which is memory's strong-box. Ever since that day they have burned and been eaten up with the great logs on the hearth. The smoke rises on the wind and crumbles away. Only the ash remains, and it has no face. All this so that you might come, and he who was younger than you are, and a breath—just a breath—might suffice you. . . ."

"Don't tell me that tale, Nana."

"So you think I was talking to you! Do you suppose one speaks to the seed of the anise?"

"I'm not a seed of anise. I'm a little girl and I'm seven years old. All five fingers of my right hand and two of the left. And when I stand up straight I can see my father's knees just in front of me. But not higher. He must, I suppose, go on growing like a big tree, and in its topmost branch a very small tiger is hiding. My mother is different. Birds wander through her hair—so black and thick and curly—and they like it there, and they linger. I'm only supposing that's how it is, that's all; for I've never seen it. I see what's as high as myself. Some bushes, their leaves nibbled by the insects, the desks stained with ink, my brother. My brother I can see from head to foot; because he was born after me, and when he was born I already knew lots of things which I explain to him now very meticulously. This, for example:

" 'Columbus discovered America'."

Mario looks at me as if I don't really deserve his atten-

13

tion, and shrugs his shoulders indifferently. I'm choked with rage. As usual, I take all the blame.

"Don't wriggle so, child, I can't finish combing."

Does Nana know I hate her when she combs my hair? No, she doesn't. She doesn't know anything. She's Indian, she doesn't wear shoes, and has no other garment under the blue cloth of her *tzec*. She isn't ashamed. She says the ground hasn't any eyes.

"Done! Now for some breakfast."

But eating's a beastly affair. In front of me the plate, staring up at me unblinking. Then the long stretch of table. After that. . . . I don't know. I'm afraid that beyond it there may be a looking-glass.

"Drink up your milk."

Every afternoon at five a Swiss cow goes by tinkling her little tin bell. (I've explained to Mario that Swiss means fat.) Her owner leads her, tied to a rope, and at every corner he stops and milks her. The servants come out of the houses and buy a mugful each. And badly behaved children like me—we pull faces and spill it over the cloth.

"God will punish you for wasting it," says Nana.

"I want coffee. Like you. Like everyone."

"You'll turn into an Indian."

Her threat frightens me. From tomorrow there'll be no more spilt milk.

2

Nana leads me through the street by the hand. The pavements are flagstones, polished and slippery. The street is cobbled. Little stones are arranged like petals in a flower. From between the joints grows short grass which the Indians tear up with the points of their machetes. There are carts drawn by sleepy bullocks; and ponies that strike sparks with their hoofs; and old horses tied to posts by their halters. All day they remain there, heads hanging, ears sadly twitching. We've just passed one. I held my breath and pressed close to the wall, afraid that any minute the horse would bare its great yellow teeth—and he has such lots of them—and bite my arm. I'd be ashamed, because my arms are very skinny and the horse might laugh.

The balconies are forever staring into the street, watching it go uphill and down and the way it turns the corners. Watching the gentlemen pass with their mahogany canes; the ranchers dragging their spurs as they walk; the Indians running under their heavy burdens. And at all times the diligent trotting donkeys loaded with water in wooden tubs. It must be nice to be like the balconies, always idle, absent-minded, just looking on. When I'm grown up. . . .

Now we begin climbing down Market Hill. The butchers' hatchets are ringing inside, and the stupid, sated flies are buzzing. We trip over the Indian women sitting on the ground weaving palm. They are talking together in their odd language, panting like hunted deer. And suddenly they let their sobs fly into the air, high-pitched, without tears. They always frighten me though I've heard them so often.

We skirt past the puddles. Last night came the first shower, the one that brings out the little ants with wings that go *tzisim*. We pass in front of the shops smelling of freshly dyed cloth. Behind the counter the assistant is measuring with a yard-stick. We can hear the grains of rice pattering against the metal scales. Someone is crumbling a handful of cocoa. And through the open street doors goes a girl with a basket on her head, and she screams, afraid that either the dogs or the owners will let fly at her:

"Dumplings—come buy!"

Nana urges me on. Now the only person in the street is a man with squeaking yellow shoes he can't have worn very often. A large door is wide open, and in front of the lighted forge stands the blacksmith, dark from his trade. His chest shows bare and sweating as he hammers. An old maid opens her window just wide enough to watch us furtively. Her mouth is clamped tight as if she'd locked some secret in. She is sad because she knows her hair is turning white.

"Say how-do-you-do, child, she's a friend of your mother."

But we're already some distance off. The last few steps I almost run. I mustn't be late for school.

3

The classroom walls are whitewashed. The damp makes strange shapes on them, which I turn into pictures when they punish me and put me in the corner. Otherwise I sit in front of Señorita Silvina, at a low, square desk. I listen to her as she talks. Her voice is like the little machines for sharpening pencils: troublesome, but useful. She speaks without emphasis, simply laying out the catalogue of knowledge before us. She allows each of us to make our choice of what we prefer. From the very beginning I picked on the word *meteor*, and ever since it has been a great burden upon me, because I think it must be sad to have dropped out of the sky.

No one has ever been able to discover which grade each of us is in. Though we are very different, we are all jumbled together. There are fat girls who sit on the back bench so they can eat peanuts without being seen. There are girls who go to the blackboard and do multiplication

16

sums. There are girls who never do anything except raise their hands and ask if they can go to the lavatory.

It goes on like that for years. Then suddenly, without warning, the miracle happens. A girl is called aside and told:

"Buy yourself a sheet of cardboard. You're going to draw the map of the world."

The girl returns to her desk, grave and responsible, puffed up with her importance. Then she struggles earnestly with the continents; some turn out much bigger than others, and the oceans are quite smooth. Later her parents come to fetch her, and they take her away for ever.

(Other girls never achieve this magnificent apotheosis, but drift about as dazed as homeless ghosts.)

At noon the servants arrive with a rustle of starched cotton and a scent of brilliantine, carrying cups of *posol*. We all sit in a row on a bench on the veranda and drink, while the servants poke at the bricks with their toes.

We spend the play-hour in the patio, singing rounds like "Oranges and Lemons", or discussing such things as the angel with the golden ball or the devil with seven cords, or singing:

> *Let's to the orchard go*
> *Where the bull and the bullfinch play. . . .*

The teacher looks on indulgently, sitting under the bamboo trees. The wind drags out of their branches a perpetual soughing and creates a rain of green and yellow leaves, and the teacher sits there inside her black dress, as small and as lonely as a saint in its niche.

Today a lady came looking for her. The teacher shook the little bamboo leaves out of her skirt, and they spoke together for a long time on the veranda. The teacher seemed more and more distressed as the conversation went on. Then the lady took her leave.

The sound of a gong brought playtime to an end. When we were all in the classroom the teacher said:

"Dear children: you are too innocent to know anything about the dangerous times it is our fate to be living in. We must be prudent, and then our enemies will have no chance to harm us. This school is our only heritage, and its reputation is the pride of the town. There are people who are conspiring now to seize it out of our hands, and we have to defend it with the only weapons we possess: order, composure, and, above all, secrecy. What goes on here must not be spoken of beyond these walls. Let's have no chitter-chatter in the street. If we can do that, we'll be all right."

We enjoyed hearing her put so many words together at one time, so quickly and without faltering as if she were reciting from a book. Confusedly, in a way we could not altogether understand, Señorita Silvina was asking us to take a pledge. We all stood up as a sign we had consented.

4

Whenever the Indians of Chactajal come to the house it's a sign there's a fiesta on the way. They bring sacks of maize and beans, bundles of salt beef and cones of brown sugar. Then the granaries are opened and the rats run about again, fat and sleek.

Lounging in the hammock on the veranda, my father receives the Indians. They approach one by one and offer their foreheads for him to touch with the three middle fingers of his right hand. Then they return to the respectful distance where they belong. My father talks to them about the business of the farm. He knows their language and their customs. They answer respectfully in words of one syllable, laughing briefly when they're supposed to.

I go to the kitchen where Nana is heating coffee.

"They've brought bad news, like the black moths."

I sniff in the larder. I like to see the colour of the butter and to touch the bloom of the fruit, and peel the onion-skins.

"It's witches' doings that's afoot, child. They gobble everything up—the crops, peace in the family, people's health."

I've discovered a basket of eggs. The freckled ones are turkeys'.

"Just look what they've done to me."

Pulling up her *tzec*, Nana shows me a soft reddish wound disfiguring her·knee.

I stare at it, eyes wide with surprise.

"Don't say anything about it, child. I came away from Chactajal hoping they wouldn't follow, but their curses reach a long way."

"Why do they hurt you?"

"Because I was brought up in your house. Because I love your parents, and Mario, and you."

"Is it wicked to love us?"

"It's wicked to love those that give orders and have possessions. That's what the law says."

The cauldron rests quietly on the coals. Inside it the coffee has begun to boil.

"Tell them to come. Their drink's ready."

I go away, sad because of what I've just heard. My father dismisses the Indians with a gesture, and lies on in the hammock, reading. I see him now for the first time. He's the one who gives the orders and owns things. I can't bear the look of him and run to take shelter in the kitchen. The Indians sitting by the hearth are holding their steaming mugs very gingerly. Nana serves them with such measured courtesy one would think they were kings. On their feet they wear sandals—and thick cakes of mud; and their breeches of unbleached cotton are patched and dirty, and their food-bags are empty.

When she's finished serving them, Nana sits down too. Solemnly she stretches both hands to the fire and holds them there a while. They talk, and it's as if a circle had closed around them. I break it in my suffering:

"Nana, I'm cold."

She draws me to her lap, as she always has done ever since I was born. It is warm and tender, but it has a wound. A wound, and it's we who've opened it.

5

Today they've been up and down Comitán with music and comic turns. A small, ricketty *marimba*, rattling like a skeleton; and behind it a swarm of barefoot urchins, curious Indians, and servants hiding their shopping baskets under their shawls. At every corner they stop, and a man stands on a box, cups his hands into a megaphone, and shouts:

"We offer you today a splendid circus performance! The world-famous contortionist, Don Pepe. The Irish loop executed with the utmost difficulty by the sisters Cordero. Trained dogs and clowns and snakes, all at popular prices for the amusement of the discriminating public of Comitán."

A circus! I've never seen one in my life. It must be like those coloured picture-books my brother and I look at before going to sleep. It must be bringing us people from far-away lands so we children can get an idea of what they're like. Maybe there's even a railway train we can get acquainted with.

"Mama, I want to go to the circus."

"A circus indeed. A few poor people dead with hunger who don't know how to make their way back to their own village and begin walking the tightrope."

"The circus, I want to go to the circus!"

"What for? To see some little ragamuffins, probably with worms, losing their parents' respect by going about covered with paint and making themselves a laughing stock."

Mario wants to go too. He doesn't argue. He simply yells till they give him whatever he wants.

By seven at night we are all in the front row—Mario and I clinging to Nana's hands. We are wrapped in overcoats and mufflers, and we wait for the show to begin. It's in the large patio of the only inn in Comitán. The drovers lodge there with their mules (that's why it always smells of fresh manure), the government employees without their families, the girls who have run away from home and are wandering about "on the loose". They have placed a few wooden benches in the patio, and a fence to mark the place reserved for the "ring". The only audience is ourselves. Nana has put on her new *tzec*—the one stitched with lots of coloured ribbons—her frilly blouse and bright Guatemalan shawl. Mario and I sit shivering with cold and excitement. But we see not a sign of preparation. People are going to and fro as usual: the boy with fodder for the animals; the young girl who creeps out to iron some trousers and who is all muffled up so everybody will be sure to know she's ashamed to be seen in that place. But no contortionist, no foreigner to show us what his country's like, no train.

Slowly the minutes go by. My heart beats faster as it tries to set the clock a good example. Nothing.

"Let's go, children, it's getting late."

"Not yet, Nana. Wait a bit. Just a little bit longer."

The man who sells the tickets is dozing at the street door. Dear God, why does no one come? We're waiting for all of them. For the girls who put lumps of lead in the hem of their skirts so the wind won't lift them; for their sweethearts who wear caps and stand at the street corners whistling; for the fat women with woollen scarves and heaps of children; for the men with gold braid on their jackets. But nobody comes. They must be drinking chocolate at home without a twinge of conscience, while here in the patio we can't begin—and all because of them.

The ticket-man bestirs himself and comes towards us.

"Seeing there's no people we'll return the price of admission."

"Thank you, sir," says Nana, taking the money.

Why thanks? What about the Irish loop? And the snakes? And the trained dogs? We didn't come here just so a sleepy man could keep our money for a while and then return it.

"No people, no show."

It sounds like when one's punished unfairly. Like when one's made to drink lemonade with a purge in it. Like waking in the dead of night and finding nobody in the room.

"Why did no one come?"

"It's not a time for fun, my child. Can't you get the feel of it? There's a smell of storm in the air."

6

"They say that in the forest there's an animal called *dzulúm*. Every night he goes prowling through his kingdom. He goes to where the she-lion is lying with her

22

cubs, and she gives him the carcase of a calf she's just killed. The *dzulúm* takes it, but doesn't eat it, because he doesn't prowl from hunger but from the will to command. The tigers run away with a crackling of dry leaves when they smell him near. The flocks wake with a tenth of them gone, and the monkeys, shameless things, howl with fear in the treetops."

"And what's the *dzulúm* like?"

"No one's ever seen him and lived to say. But I've a feeling in my bones he's handsome, for even educated people pay him tribute."

We're in the kitchen. The embers are scarcely flickering under their coating of ash. The candle flame tells us which way the wind blows. The servants jump when a thunderclap echoes far away. Nana continues talking.

"Once—it's a long time ago—we were all in Chactajal. Your grandparents chanced upon an orphan girl whom they treated as their own daughter. Her name was Angelica. She was like a lily on its stem, and so gentle and obedient to her betters, and so meek and thoughtful toward us who looked after her. She had no end of suitors. But she seemed not to notice them, or perhaps she was waiting for another. So the days went by, until one morning a new thing dawned. The *dzulúm* was prowling about the edge of the farm. The signs of it was the damage he left on all sides and a fear that dried the udders of the beasts giving suck. Angelica knew it, and when she knew it she trembled like a thoroughbred mare that sees a shadow pass. From that moment she had no peace. The needlework dropped from her hands. She lost her happiness and wandered here and there as if she were searching for it in every corner. She was up betimes to drink spring water because she was burning with thirst. Your grandpapa thought she was ill and fetched the best medicine-man in the district. The medicine-man came and asked to speak to her alone. Heaven knows what things must have been said, but the man came out in a fright, and that very night he went back home without a by your leave. Angelica was all eaten up like a candle wick. Afternoons she went roaming in the fields, and got back when dark had fallen with the hem of her skirt torn to shreds by the briars. And when we asked where she'd been, she only said she couldn't find the way and she looked at us as if pleading for help. And we all crowded about her but couldn't hit upon the right word. Until once she didn't come back."

Nana picks up the tongs and stirs the embers. Outside, for some time now, a rainstorm has been battering against the tiles.

"The Indians went looking for her with big pine torches. They yelled aloud, and hacked open a path, following her tracks. But suddenly the trail faded out. Days and days they searched. They had the bloodhounds with them. But they found not so much as a bit of Angelica's dress, not a scrap of her body."

"Did the *dzulúm* carry her off?"

"She set her eyes on him, and she followed him like she was bewitched, and every footstep beckoned to the next one, on and on, to the road's end. He went ahead, beautiful and strong, with his name that means a yearning to be dead."

7

This afternoon we're going on an expedition. From very early the servants have been washing their feet, scrubbing them against a stone. Then they take from their chests the mirrors with celluloid frames and their wooden combs. They grease their hair with scented pomade; they plait it with red ribbons, and prepare to go.

Comitán

My parents have hired an automobile a...
for us at the door. We settle ourselves inside, all b..
who doesn't want to come because she's afraid. She sa,
the automobile is the devil's invention, and she's hidden
in the back yard so as not to see.

Perhaps Nana's right. The automobile is a monster that
puffs and blows smoke, and as fast as it pulls us along it
keeps jumping ferociously on to the pavement. It has a
sense of smell that is all its own, which guides it toward
the posts and railings and gets them into a tangle, but they
swerve neatly aside, and we're able to arrive without too
many bruises at Nicalococ Moor.

It's the time of year when families bring their children
to fly kites. The sky is full of them. There's Mario's. It's
made of blue and green and red tissue paper and it has a
very long tail. There it rides above us, humming as if it's
about to rip into shreds, more debonair and bolder than
the rest, with lots of line so it can climb and swerve and
not another kite can reach it.

The grown-ups lay bets. The little boys run, dragged
by their kites that seek out the most favourable gusts of
wind. Mario stumbles and falls, and his knobbly knees
are bleeding, but he doesn't let go of the string and he
gets to his feet regardless, and runs on. We girls watch
from our places, apart from the boys.

What a vast moor it is, a plain without flocks where the
only animal that plays is the wind. And how it rears, and
sometimes knocks over the birds that have come timidly
to rest on their rumps. And how it whinnies! It's so free,
and so bold!

Now I know that this is the voice I've been hearing
ever since I was born. It's my constant companion. I've
known it come in winter, armed with knives that are
sharp and long, to stab through our flesh that's suffering
with cold. I've felt it in summer, drawing lazily ever

Comitán

nearer, yellow with pollen, with a flavour of wild honey between the lips. It announces the night with barks of anger, and it grows tame at noon when the town clock strikes twelve. It knocks on the doors and upsets the flower vases and muddles the papers on the desk and plays tricks with the little girls' frocks. But until today I've never been to its homeland where its will runs free, and I stand here with lowered eyes because (Nana's said so) that's the way humility looks at bigness.

"How stupid you are. You pay no heed just when your brother's kite's winning."

He is proud of his success. Out of breath, with burning cheeks, he comes to hug my parents.

It's growing dark. It's time to go back to Comitán. The moment we're back home I look for Nana to tell her the news.

"You know? Today I've met the wind."

She doesn't stop working. Thoughtful and unsmiling she goes on husking corn. But I know she's happy.

"That's good, child. Because your people possess Nine Guardians, and the wind is one."

8

Mario and I are playing in the garden. As usual the gate is open wide. We see Uncle David lean on the hinges. He's slightly off balance. His drill jacket is stained with grease and dirt, and his white hair is rumpled as if he'd been sleeping in straw. His shoestrings are undone. He's carrying a guitar.

"Uncle David, how nice of you to come."

(Our parents have suggested we call him Uncle though he's no relation. That way he feels less lonely.)

"I don't often pay calls. Where are the grown-ups?"

"Gone out. They left us alone."

"And aren't you afraid of thieves? The palmy days are over when sausage-meat was so plentiful the strings of it could be used to tie up the dogs. Times are different now. With the new customs there come new songs."

We've been moving toward the hammock. Uncle David manages after a struggle to squeeze himself into it. Now he's our own height and we can inspect him at close quarters. What a lot of wrinkles there are on his face! With the tips of my fingers I try to count them. One, two, five . . . but at that point his cheek sinks into a hole, because he hasn't any teeth. From his empty mouth comes a smell of over-ripe fruit that sickens and upsets me. Mario grasps Uncle David by the feet and tries to rock him.

"Quiet now, children, I'm going to sing."

He tunes his guitar, strums it harshly, and lets his voice rip, wavering and insecure:

> *The tithe-days are over*
> *For rancher and drover. . . .*

"What's tithe, Uncle David?"

"It's the work the Indians are obliged to do and the masters aren't obliged to pay."

"Oh!"

"Now that's over. If the master wants them to sow the grain, or put the cattle to graze, it will cost him a pretty penny. And you know what will happen? All the farmers will be ruined. Then we'll all be the same as the poor."

"All?"

"Yes."

"Us too?"

"You too."

"And what shall we do?"

27

Comitán

"What the poor do. Beg. Go to the other man's house at mealtime just in case he'll allow you to be his guest."

"I don't like it," says Mario, "I want to be what you are, Uncle David. A hunter."

"Not me. I want to be the mistress of the other man's house and invite the ones that come at mealtimes."

"Come here, Mario. If you're going to be a hunter, it's just as well you should know what I'm going to tell you. The quetzal is a bird that doesn't live just anywhere. Only about Tziscao. He makes his nest in the hollow tree-trunks so as not to damage his long tail-feathers. For if he sees that they're dirty or torn he dies of a broken heart. And he always perches high up. In order to bring him down, you whistle like this, imitating his mate's call. The quetzal turns his head, trying to discover where the whistle comes from. And then he flies in that direction. Now's the moment to take good aim, right at the bird's breast. Shoot. When the quetzal drops, pick him up, pull out his entrails, and stuff him with a special preparation for which I'll give you the recipe, and that will preserve him. They look quite lifelike and they sell well."

"You see," Mario defies me, "it's not difficult."

"It has its risks," adds Uncle David. "Because Tziscao's the place where the lakes are of many colours, and that's where the Nine Guardians live."

"Who are the Nine Guardians?"

"Don't be so inquisitive, child. The old people know, and that's why they call the place *Balún-Canán*. They give it that name when they talk among themselves. But we, little people, it's better we keep quiet. And you, Mario, when you go hunting, don't do as I did. Ask, find out things, because there are trees and orchids and birds that one ought to respect. The Indians have singled them out specially to appease the guardians' mouths. Don't touch them or they'll bring you bad luck. Nobody warned me about that when I went into the mountains of Tziscao for the first time."

Uncle David's puffed and spongy cheeks quiver and contract. I rasp across the silence with a sudden chord from the guitar.

"Sing some more."

Uncle David's voice, shakier and more out of tune than ever, picks up his new song once again:

> *The tithe-days are over*
> *For rancher and drover. . . .*

9

Mother always gets up very early. From my bed I can hear her hurriedly gulp down a cup of coffee. Then she goes out into the street. Her feet tap the pavement briskly, and as I follow her with my thoughts she climbs the steps of the arcade, passes the barracks, and takes the San Sebastián road. Then the shape of her vanishes and I don't know where she goes. Many times I've asked her to take me along, but she always puts me off saying I'm too small to understand and that it's bad for me to be up early. So, as usual when I want to know anything, I go and ask Nana. She is on the veranda sitting in a leather chair mending clothes. On the ground is a calabash full of threads of many colours.

"Where did Mother go?"

It's noon. In the kitchen somebody is chopping vegetables on a board. Nana selects threads for her work and pauses before answering.

"She's gone to visit the crookback."

"Who's the crookback?"

"A very poor woman."

"I know what the poor are like," I exclaim crossly.

29

"You've often seen them knock at the street gate with their sticks for the blind; and wrap the *tortilla* left over from breakfast in an old net bag; and cross themselves and kiss the money they're given. But there are others you've never seen. The crookback lives in a house made of shingle, on the edge of the village."

"And why does Mama visit her?"

"To bring her a little happiness. She looks after her like a younger sister."

What she tells me still isn't enough to satisfy me. I still can't understand. But I've learned not to be impatient, and I cuddle close to Nana and wait. Her words will come in good time.

"At first," she says, "before Santo Domingo de Guzmán and San Caralampio and the Virgin of Perpetual Succour, they were only four in number, the lords in heaven. Each one sat on his chair and rested. For the earth had already been made, just as we see it now, its lap heaped high with bounty. The ocean had already been made, before which everyone who sees it trembles. The wind had already been made to be the guardian over all things. But man was not made yet. Then one of the four lords, the one dressed in yellow, said:

" 'We'll make man, so that he may know us and his heart may be consumed with gratitude like a grain of incense.'

"The other three agreed with a nod, and went to look for moulds in which to work.

" 'What shall we make man of?' they asked.

"And the one who was dressed in yellow took a lump of mud and with his fingers drew in the face and the arms and legs. The other three watched him and gave their consent. But when the little clay man was finished and was put to the test of water, he crumbled away.

" 'Let's make a man of wood,' said the one dressed in

red. The others agreed. So he who was dressed in red lopped off a branch and with the blade of a knife he marked the features in. When the wooden man was made he was put to the test of water and his limbs floated; they didn't fall to pieces, and his features were not rubbed out. The four lords were satisfied. But when the manikin was put to the test of fire he began to crackle and lose his shape.

"The four lords spent a whole night in parley until one of them, the one who was dressed in black, said:

" 'My advice is that we make a man of gold.'

"And he untied the gold he kept knotted in his hand-kerchief, and between the four of them they modelled him. One pulled out his nose, another stuck in his teeth, another drew the snail-shell of his ears. When the golden man was finished they tested him in water and in fire and the golden man came out even more beautiful and re-splendent than before. Then the four lords looked at one another satisfied. And they set the gold man on the ground, and they waited, hoping he would recognize them and give them praise. But the gold man did not move, he didn't even blink: he was quite silent. And his heart was like the stone of the sapodilla, very hard and very dry. Then three of the four lords asked the one who had not yet given his opinion:

" 'What shall we make man of?'

"And this last one, who was dressed neither in yellow nor in red nor in black, for he wore a garment that had no colour at all, said:

" 'Let's make man out of flesh.'

"And with his machete he cut off the fingers of his left hand. And the fingers jumped into the air and fell into the midst of things, and never suffered the tests of water and of fire. The four lords could scarcely make out what the men of flesh looked like, because distance had

shrunk them to the size of ants. The effort they made to
see the men of flesh inflamed the four lords' eyes, and
with so much rubbing of them they grew drowsy. The
one with the yellow robe yawned, and his yawn opened
the mouths of the other three. And they fell asleep, for
they were tired and old. In the meantime on earth the
men of flesh scurried to and fro like ants. They had already learned which fruit is good to eat, with what big
leaves they could protect themselves from the rain, and
which animals don't bite.

"One day they were astonished to see standing in front
of them the man of gold. His glitter struck them between
the eyes, and when they touched him their hands turned
cold as if they had touched a snake. They stood there
waiting for the man of gold to speak. The time came to
eat, and the men of flesh gave the man of gold a morsel.
The time came to go away, and the men of flesh carried
the man of gold with them. And day by day the hardness
of the heart of the man of gold was softened, until the
word of gratitude the four lords had placed within him
rose to his lips.

"The lords woke up to hear their names pronounced
among the psalms of praise. And they looked to see what
had happened on earth while they were sleeping. And they
approved what they saw. And from that moment they
called the man of gold rich and the men of flesh poor.
And they ordered things in such a way that the rich man
should care for the poor and shelter him, since it was the
rich man who benefited by the poor man's acts. And the
lords so ordered it that the poor should answer for the
rich before the face of Truth. That is why our law says
that no rich man can enter heaven if a poor man does not
lead him by the hand."

Nana falls silent. Carefully she folds the clothes she has
been mending, picks up the calabash with the coloured

threads, and gets to her feet to be going away. But before her first step can take her from me, I ask her:

"Who is my poor man, Nana?"

She stops, and as she helps me to my feet she says:

"You don't know yet. But if you watch carefully, when more years and understanding are upon you, you will recognize the poor one that is yours.'

10

My bedroom windows are shut because I can't stand the light. I'm trembling with cold under the covers, yet I'm burning with fever. Nana bends over me and lays a damp handkerchief on my forehead. It doesn't do any good. It will never be able to remove the memory of what I've seen. That memory will stay here inside me, as if it were carved in stone. There's no way to forget.

He came from a long way off, from Chactajal. Many miles across mountains hard to scale, moors where the wind howls, endless stony wastes. And there was the man spilling blood, lying on a stretcher carried by four of his companions. They arrived panting, altogether beaten by the exhausting journey. And the dying man had breath enough to last him over the threshold into our house. We hurried to look at him. A blow from a machete had almost chopped off his hand. The rags that bound it were stained with blood, and he was bleeding from other wounds too, and his matted hair clung to his head in cakes of sweat and blood.

His companions set him down in front of us, and there he died, muttering some word that only Nana and my father caught, and which they won't reveal.

Now he's laid out in the stable. They've put him in a pinewood coffin, too short for his height, its joints badly made and the blood seeping through them. Slowly out of one little drop forms and swells another, until by sheer weight it spills and falls down to the earth and the manure, which devour it noiselessly. And the dead man is there alone. The other Indians went straight back to the farm because they are needed for work. And who else will keep him company? The servants don't think he's good enough for them, and Nana is looking after me.

"Did they kill him because he's a sorcerer?"

I've got to know. That word he said, it may be the only thing that can take away the stain of blood that's fallen across the day.

"They killed him because your father trusted him. Now there's dissension among them, and they've broken the peace like a stick across the knee. Evil stirs one man against others. Some want to go on as they've done till now, in the shadow of the big house. Others prefer to have no master."

She goes on talking but I'm no longer listening. I see my mother walking quickly, very early in the morning, stopping in front of a house made of shingle. Inside is the crookback sitting in her rush chair, her hands limp in her lap. My mother has taken her some breakfast, but the crookback screams when Mother lays at her feet the bleeding entrails of a freshly killed ox, still throbbing.

No, no, no, that's not how it is. It's my father who's lying in a hammock on the veranda, reading, and he doesn't see that around him are skeletons leering with silent laughter, never-ending. I run away terrified, and I find Nana washing our clothes on the banks of a swirling red river. She is on her knees, beating the linen against the stones, and the noise of it muffles the echo of my voice. And I'm weeping in the silent air while the river rises and my feet get wet.

Comitán

11

Mother takes us to pay a call. Very formally we go—Mario, she, and I—to the house of her friend Amalia, the old maid.

When the door is opened to us it is as if the lid had been lifted from a scented cedar chest where faded ribbons and illegible papers are folded away.

Amalia comes out to greet us. She has a cosy grey woollen shawl thrown over her shoulders, and her face is like petals that have been pressed in a book and have faded. She smiles sweetly, but we all know she is sad because her hair is turning white.

On the veranda there are lots of flowerpots with begonias, that queer type of palm they call "quetzal tail", and other plants that thrive in the shade. On the walls there are canary cages and wires for vines to climb up. On the wooden pillars, nothing. Just their roundness.

We go into the drawing-room. Such lots of things! Enormous mirrors that seem, by the way they tilt forward from their nails, to be bowing and paying their respects to anyone who passes by. They stare like old people, the pupils of their eyes veiled and distant. There are casual tables with porcelain statuettes. Fans. Portraits of gentlemen who have died a long time ago. Tables inlaid with mahogany. A reed screen. Rugs. Embroidered cushions. And in one of the windows, sunk deep, only just peeping from her chair, an old lady is staring intently into the street.

"Mama keeps much the same since she lost the use of her mind," says Amalia by way of excuse.

Mario and I go very close to the old lady and study her with attention. She is tiny, bony, and has a hump. She doesn't notice our presence.

Comitán

Mother and Amalia sit on the sofa and gossip.

"Look, Zoraida, I'm embroidering this napkin."

The old maid takes a piece of snow-white linen from a little rush basket.

"It's to cover her face when she dies."

With a vague gesture she points to the seat where the old lady is sitting.

"God be praised, I have everything ready for her funeral. The gown is of very fine twill with lace insertions."

They continue talking. At a certain moment their girlhood slips into the conversation. It's as if the lemon trees in the patio were to enter with their whiff of sweet blossom to stir this stuffy atmosphere. They fall silent and look about them with a stunned expression as if something very beautiful had dropped out of their hands.

The old lady is sobbing, so silently that only my brother and I can hear. We run to tell the others.

Solicitously Amalia approaches her mother's chair. She has to bend right down to hear what the old lady is muttering. She wants them to take her to Guatemala, she says between sobs. Her daughter makes a gesture of compliance and pushes the chair to the next window. The old lady is pacified, and looks out into the street as if she had never seen it before.

"Come, children," the spinster invites us, "wouldn't you like some sweets?"

As she selects the candies, taking them from their glass bowl, she asks:

"And what truth is there in all these rumours going about?"

Mother doesn't know what she's referring to.

"They talk of agrarian reforms, that they're seizing the farms from the owners, and that the Indians have risen against their masters."

36

The words tumble over one another breathlessly, as if haste could make them harmless. She blinks as she waits for the reply. Mother pauses, wondering what to say.

"Fear exaggerates everything."

"But in Chactajal. . . . Didn't they just bring an Indian to your house all slashed up by the rebels?"

"That's not true. It wasn't like that. You know what happens at their fiestas. A drunken orgy started, and ended in a fight. It's not the first time."

Amalia studies my mother incredulously, then remarks suddenly:

"Anyhow I'm glad we sold our ranch in good time. All our property is here now in Comitán—houses, fields and all. It's safer."

"For a woman alone like you it's all right. But men don't know what to do with themselves when they're not in the country."

We've eaten the candies. A clock strikes. Is it as late as that already? They turn on the lights.

"Haven't the children grown? It's time to think of their first communion."

"They haven't had any instruction."

"Send them to me. I'll prepare them. I'd like them to be my godchildren."

She pats us in a friendly way with her left hand while the right one straightens her whitening hair. Then she says:

"If Mother hasn't died by then, that's to say."

12

We have a number of fairs every year in Comitán, but none so gay and lively as that of San Caralampio. He is renowned for his miracles, and flocks of pilgrims come from long distances to pray before his image. It was carved in Guatemala, and shows him kneeling, with a long white beard and a glow of saintliness, while over his head the executioner has poised his axe for the death blow. (It's known the executioner was a Jew.) But nowadays people have to remain outside the church door, which is closed like the rest of them by government orders. That isn't sufficient reason to put off the fair, so in the *plaza* round the church they are setting up stalls and switchbacks.

Hawkers come down from San Cristobal loaded with wares: dried fruit; pickles; badly made rag dolls with their cheeks painted a scandalous red to leave no doubt they're from the cold lands; clay shepherds with thick ankles; legs of mutton made of cotton wool; caskets of varnished wood; coarse-woven cloth.

The peddlers—well wrapped in woollen blankets—spread their merchandise on rush mats on the ground. With the hoarse voices of men who smoke strong tobacco they proclaim their wares to the multitude. They haggle at length about prices. The rancher with his bright new satin jacket is stupefied by the wealth spread before his eyes. After deep thought he pulls a homespun kerchief from his pocket, unties the knots where he hides his money, and buys a pound of hazel-nuts, a bundle of leaf cigars, and a miniature violin.

A little way off the Lotto-man is shouting:

"The pole-star of the north."

People glance at their cards, and if they have it they put down a grain of corn.

"Auntie's umbrella."

The prizes are displayed on stands. Glass objects that have no very well-defined shape; rings with the special property of turning everything near them green; silk handkerchiefs so diaphanous they blow away like thistle-down at the least puff.

"Death, dire and dreadful."

"Lotto!"

General excitement. Everyone envies the lucky man, who smiles complacently while the dispenser of bounties invites him to choose whatever he fancies most from such wonderful things.

Nana and I have been sitting here for hours, and so far we haven't won a thing. I feel sad, and very remote from the gifts. Nana gets up and says:

"Stay still. I won't be long."

I watch her go. She makes a sign to the stall-man and they whisper together. She hands him something and he bows as if he were thanking her. Then she comes and sits down beside me again.

"Mr. Plum parading."

I can't find him on my card, but Nana picks up a grain of corn and puts it on one of the pictures.

"Is that Mr. Plum?"

"That's him."

I never knew Mr. Plum was a fruit.

"The dandy of Gay Paree."

There's a catch in that one too.

"The heart of a woman."

"Lotto!" calls Nana, and the stall-man claps delightedly.

"What prize will you have?" he asks me.

I choose a ring because I want my finger to turn green.

We wander about among the crowds. They shove us and tread on our toes. Very high up, above my head, their words and laughter float. There's a smell of cheap scent, clothes just ironed, and old brandy. Chicken in hot chocolate sauce is boiling in enormous earthen casseroles, and punch spiced with cinnamon is kept bubbling on the hob. In another corner of the *plaza* they have erected a

Comitán

platform and spread it with fresh cypress for dancing.
There are couples embracing the way *ladinos* do, while
the *marimba* plays thick and drowsy music.

But this year the Fair Organization Committee has
outdone itself. It sent to the very centre, to the Capital,
for a thing never seen before: a Ferris wheel. There it
stands, large and shining, with its thousands of electric
bulbs. Nana and I want to take a ride in it, but there's
such a crowd we have to wait our turn. In front of us
there's an Indian. He gets to the gate and asks for his
ticket.

"Hey you there, upstart Indian, speaking pure Castille.
Who'd have been giving you leave?"

For there are rules. Spanish is our privilege. And we
use it with a "your honour" to our superiors, with a
"thou" to our equals, and with a "ye" to the Indians.

"Indian dumbcluck. On up with you now, and don't
get riled."

The Indian takes his ticket without a word.

"Get yourself a drink and stop drooling."

"An upstart Indian's on the Ferris wheel. It's Anti-
Christ!"

We sit in a kind of cradle. The attendant fastens the
safety bar. He starts up the motor; we rise slowly sky-
ward and for a moment are suspended there. All Comitán
is within our grasp like a brood of chicks! The dark roofs
where moss sprouts in the damp. The whitewashed walls.
The stone towers. The endless moors. And the bogs.
And the wind.

All of a sudden we gain speed. The wheel turns giddily.
Faces swim together, things go higgledy-piggledy. Then
a scream of terror comes from the crowd below. At first
we don't know what's happened. Then we see that the
safety bar of the Indian's seat has come unfastened and he
has been thrown forward. He manages to catch hold of

the end of the pole, and there he hangs while the wheel goes turning, on, and on, and on.

The attendant switches off the current, but the wheel goes by its own momentum. When it stops at last, the Indian is left hanging high up, sweating with exhaustion and fear.

Little by little, so slowly that to our eyes it seems an eternity, he climbs down. When he is close enough to the ground, he jumps. His face is ashen. Somebody passes him a bottle of Comitán home-brew, but he spurns it ungraciously.

"Why did you stop?" he asks.

The attendant is furious.

"How do you mean, why? Because you fell and you'd have been killed, you damfool Indian."

The Indian looks at him offended and grinds his teeth.

"I didn't fall. I unfixed the stick. I like riding that way best."

A burst of merriment greets his words.

"Listen to what he's up to now."

"Nice fellow!"

The Indian senses the scorn and mockery round him. He meets the challenge.

"I'll have another ticket. I'll ride as I please. And don't you be giving me short measure!"

The lookers-on are intrigued by what's about to happen. They whisper and laugh and wink with their hands over their mouths.

Nana pushes her way through the crowd, dragging me after her, and I keep looking back to the place we've left. I can't see what's happening, and protest. She goes on regardless, very fast, as if a pack of hounds were after her. I want to ask her why, but the question sticks in my throat when I see that her eyes are cloudy with tears.

13

Our house is in the parish of Calvary. They closed our church the same date as the rest.

I remember that day of mourning. The military destroyed the altar with shot and made a bonfire in the middle of the road to burn the wooden planks. The broken bodies of saints writhed in flames, and the rabble were squabbling and snatching the crowns they had torn from the statues. A drunken man set his horse prancing, striking sparks among the ashes. Ever since we've all been waiting to be punished.

But the statues of the Calvary were saved. Their great age and the centuries of devotion protected them. Termites are eating them now in a padlocked church.

The Municipal President has agreed, though grudgingly, that each month a lady of the district should take on the task of cleaning the church. It's Mother's turn now and we go with a bevy of servants carrying all the brooms, mops, pails of water, and dusters needed for the job.

The key grates in the rusty lock, and the door turns awkwardly on its hinges just wide enough to let us through, then closes again.

How desolate it is inside! The high, bare walls. The wooden choir-screen crudely carved. There is no altar but in the central position are three enormous crucifixes draped in purple cloth as they are during Lent.

The servants set to work, chasing the spiders with brooms from the corners and breaking the precious webs spun so secretly and patiently. A bat soars up, flying from this intrusion into his private kingdom. The light dazzles him and he beats against the walls and can't aim straight at the holes where the panes are broken. We chase after him, frightening him with feather brooms, turning him

42

silly with our cries. At last he escapes and we stand there frustrated and come back to our senses.

Mother calls us to order. We sprinkle the floor before sweeping it, but still the dustclouds rise and are starred by the light. Mother begins cleaning the statues with chamois leather. She removes the cloth from one of them, and a hopelessly martyred Christ appears hanging from a cross whose joints have come all unstuck. His bones are very nearly prodding through his yellow flesh, and the blood flows freely from his hands, his open side, and his nailed feet. His head droops lifeless on his breast, and there, too, the crown of thorns sets little spurts of blood flowing down.

The sight is so sudden that it leaves me transfixed. I stare at the image a moment in mute horror. Then like a blind creature I rush at the door and push it violently, beating it in desperation with my fists. But in vain, the door won't open and I'm trapped. I'll never get out, never. I've fallen into the black pit of hell.

Mother runs after me and shakes me by the shoulders.

"What's the matter with you?"

I can't answer. I struggle in her clutches, out of my mind with fear.

"Answer me."

She slaps me in the face. Her eyes are flashing with fright and anger. Something inside me snaps and yields, beaten.

"It's like . . ." I say, pointing to the crucifix, "it's like the Indian they brought to our house, all cut up with the machete."

14

The rains have set in and the roads to Mexico City are closed. Cars are bogged down in the mud, and planes fall, beaten by the storm. Only the droves of mules go on trafficking among the neighbouring hamlets fetching and carrying goods and passengers and mail.

We lean out of the balconies to watch them come. They trail in the wake of the she-ass who gallantly tinkles her bell. They arrive unshod, with sore backs; but they come from far and they bring news and things from other parts. What joy it gives us to know that among the firmly strapped boxes and the bundles rolled up in rush mats come the canvas mailbags striped in three colours, filled with newspapers and letters! We're so cut off in Comitán in the rains. We are so far away, always. Once I saw a map of Mexico, and to the south, where we live, it came to a full stop. After that, not even a wheel track, just a line to mark the frontier. People go away, and when they go, they write. But their words reach us so many weeks later that by the time we get them they're faded and have no scent, like withered flowers. On this occasion the postman hasn't brought us a thing. Father will re-read the newspapers from the time before.

We're in the drawing-room. Mother is crocheting an altar-cloth for the oratory, with a single hook and coarse, crude thread. Mario and I stare out into the street, our faces glued to the pane. We see a man coming toward us, one of those that wear waistcoats and gold braid. He reaches the front door and stops. Then he knocks.

"Come in," Mother says without stopping her work.

The man appears in the drawing-room door.

"Good afternoon."

Father gets up to receive him.

"Jaime Rovelo! To what do we owe this pleasure?"

They embrace, delighted to see each other. Father offers his friend a chair and sits down himself.

"You won't find it so good, César, when you know what brings me."

He is sad. His greying moustache droops sadly down.

"Bad news?" Mother asks.

"Can there be anything else in these times?"

"Come now, Jaime, don't exaggerate. There are still little doves to be caught here and there."

She doesn't succeed in altering his expression. Father observes him with a curiosity in which alarm is not yet mingled. The man can't find a way to begin. His hands tremble slightly.

"Did you receive today's paper?"

"No. As usual it's suffered some mishap on the way. And in spite of everything we've got to trust the post."

"It reaches me punctually. I had a letter today from Mexico City."

"From your son?"

"Such a handsome boy. And so industrious. He's just taking his law degree, isn't he?"

"Yes, he's already working in chambers."

"How pleased you must be, Don Jaime, to have started him on a career!"

"One never knows what it will lead to. The devil disposes, so the proverb goes. As I was telling you, I had a letter from him today."

"Not bad news?"

"The Government has passed another decree against us."

He takes a letter from his waistcoat pocket, unfolds the sheets, selects one, and passes it to Mother.

"Please read it. Here."

"A law has been passed by which proprietors of farms with more than five families of Indians in their service must provide facilities for teaching, by establishing a school and paying the salary of a rural master."

Mother folds the paper and smiles scornfully.

"Who ever heard of such a thing? Teaching them to

read when they're not even able to speak Spanish!"

"Go on, Jaime, you almost scared me. When I saw you arrive with that hang-dog look I thought there really had been some disaster. But this isn't important. You remember when they fixed the minimum salary? Our hearts went into our boots. It was the end of everything. And what happened? We're slippery lizards and they can't catch us as easily as all that. We discovered a ruse by which we didn't have to pay."

"No Indian's worth seventy-five *centavos* a day. Nor even a month."

"Besides, I ask you, what would they do with the money? Only get drunk."

"What I'm saying is that we can fix things now as we did before. Let's see the letter."

Father reads it silently.

"The law doesn't say that the rural teacher must be appointed by the authorities. So we have a loophole. We can choose the one that suits us. Don't you see the game?"

Don Jaime nods, but his expression doesn't change.

"Here I'm solving the problem for you and you're carrying on as gloomy as before. Is there more to this?"

"My son thinks it's a reasonable and necessary law; that Cárdenas is a fair President."

Mother jumps, and says passionately:

"Fair? When he tramples on our rights, when he seizes our properties? And to give them—to whom? The Indians. He doesn't know them; he's never been near them and found out how they stink of filth and drink. He's never done them a favour and been rewarded with their ingratitude. He's never given them a job to do and taken the measure of their laziness. And they're so hypocritical, so underhand, so deceitful!"

"Zoraida," says Father reproachfully.

"It's true," she cries, "and I'd a thousand times rather

never have been born, than be born among such a race of vipers!"

I search out my brother's eyes. Mother's voice frightens him as it does me; the red glow on Mother's cheeks frightens us both. On tiptoe, without the grown-ups noticing, we creep out of the room, and we silently close the door behind us so that if Nana should chance to pass that way she won't hear what they're saying.

15

"*Ave Maria!*" a woman is calling at the gate. She is old, fat, shabbily dressed, and carries a bundle under her shawl.

With a flutter of starched fustian the servants hurry to let her in, and they offer her an armchair on the veranda. The woman sits, out of breath. She lays the bundle on her lap and with a handkerchief wipes the sweat that trickles down her face and throat. She doesn't get up when Mother comes to greet her.

"Doña Pastora, how marvellous to see you here. You know the house is yours."

Mother sits by her side and eyes the bundle avidly.

"I've brought lots of things. I know your taste now, and I remembered you when I was buying."

"Let's see, Doña Pastora."

"Just like this, in front of them all?"

The servants are crowding round and the woman doesn't seem pleased.

"They're people of trust," Mother argues.

"It's not the way things are done."

"It's up to you, Doña Pastora, you're the one to say. . . . Get back to your work, girls. But first make sure the street gate is firmly locked."

Comitán

It's noon. Heavy with its own fragrance, the wind is sleeping in the garden. Sounds come from far away: plates slapping against water in the kitchen; the chocolate-grinder's droning song. How quiet the clouds are up there!

The woman unties the knots of her bundle, and out of the drab cloth bursts a cascade of colours. Astonished and delighted, Mother exclaims:

"How exquisite!"

"They're real Guatemalan weaves. Don't be thinking they'll run at the first wash. They'll last you a lifetime exactly as they are now."

There are counterpanes striped red and yellow; bright embroidered shawls round which the Greek key-pattern marches solemnly and where humming-birds fly in a blue heaven, and the tiger lays his tiny velvet paw, and the butterfly has ceased forever to flutter.

Mother chooses this, and that, and something else besides.

"Nothing more?"

"I'd like to take them all, but times are hard. One can't spend as before."

"I've got something else you'd fancy."

Doña Pastora takes a little case from her blouse. She opens it, and the jewellery shines out. Gold twined into necklaces; filigree ear-rings; finely worked lockets.

"They're very expensive."

"You know where I come from, Zoraida. You know I have to cover the cost of the journey and the risks."

"Yes, Doña Pastora, but. . . ."

"Don't the things please you? After all the trouble I took to choose them?"

There is a veiled threat in her voice. Mother is almost groaning, she wants the jewels so much.

"César says we mustn't buy more than is needed, that

the affairs of the ranch. . . . I don't understand. Only . . . there's no money."

The case closes with a dry snap. Doña Pastora puts it back in her blouse. She picks up the things that have been discarded. She ties the knots once more. Mother watches, as if asking forgiveness, and at last Doña Pastora relents.

"Tell your husband I can sell him what he'll be wanting."

"What?"

"A secret."

"A secret?"

"A place on the border. There are no guards. It's easy to cross at any hour. Tell him if he pays I'll show him where it is."

Mother smiles, thinking it's a joke.

"César's not going into competition with you, Doña Pastora. He's not thinking of smuggling."

Doña Pastora looks at Mother and repeats with emphasis:

"Tell him what I said. Because the time will come when you will have to run away."

16

For some days at school we've been expecting an unwelcome visitor. Today, just as Señorita Silvina was explaining that wasps' eyes are polyhedral, there was a knock at the door. She looked cautious, and said:

"It might be him."

She rose and took down the picture of San Caralampio which was always nailed to the wall above the blackboard. A square patch was left which it was impossible to conceal. Then she ordered one of the pupils to open the gate. While the girl was crossing the patio the teacher gave us our instructions:

"Remember my advice. Be very discreet. There's no need to speak of the ways of the school to a stranger."

Now the stranger stood in front of us, tall and serious in his black cashmere suit.

"I'm the Inspector from the Ministry of Public Education."

He spoke with the accent of a native of Mexico City. The teacher blushed and lowered her eyes. This was the first time she had ever carried on a conversation with a man. Confused, she just managed to stammer:

"Get up, girls, and say how-do-you-do to the Inspector."

He stopped her with a commanding gesture and we didn't have time to obey.

"Let's dispense with these hypocrisies. I came here for another purpose. I want you to show me the documents authorizing you to run this school."

"Documents?"

"Or does it function secretly like a brandy factory?"

The teacher was caught off her guard. She had never been spoken to like this before.

"I have no documents. My grandparents gave me my first lessons. Then my parents. Now. . . ."

"And now it's your turn. And since your grandparents' time every generation has been spitting in the face of the law. Anyway, I can't imagine what you can teach when I see how ignorant you are. I'm sure that you are not aware, either, that education is a task reserved for the State, not for private individuals."

"Yes, sir."

"And that the State provides free education for its citizens. Make a note of that: free. Whereas you charge."

"A pittance, sir. Twelve *reales* a month."

"Highway robbery, but never mind, we'll pass that over. What is your plan of study?"

"I teach what I can, sir. Pothooks, the three Rs."

The Inspector cut her short and went up to one of the girls in the front row.

"You there, give me the copy-book."

The girl did not move until the teacher had given her assent. Then she pulled a copy-book from under her desk and handed it to the Inspector. He began turning the pages, and as he read an ironical smirk twisted his lips.

" 'Lesson about things'. Would you do me the favour, Miss Teacher, of explaining precisely what subjects come under this heading?"

Señorita Silvina, so shy and *petite* in her black dress, seemed like a mouse caught in a trap. The Inspector's uncompromising eyes shifted contemptuously away and turned back to the copy-book.

" 'Forces and levers'. Indeed! I can assure you that in the capital we've not yet heard of these discoveries in pedagogy. It would be a good thing if you would enlighten us."

The teacher's knees trembled, and for a moment we thought she would fall. She staggered to her chair and sat down. There she was, quiet, pale, and remote.

" 'History and heat'. What a beautiful association of deas! But we can't stop to go into that; there's another matter to be considered. Does the building comply with the sanitary regulations for a school?"

The teacher's voice burst out quick and sharp.

"Need you ask? You can see it's an old skeleton that's about to fall round our ears any minute."

"Charming. And you'll be crushed to death, happily, victims that have been sacrificed to God. For I'm willing to wager you're Catholics. Right?"

Silence.

"Aren't you Catholics? Don't you pray every day at the beginning and end of classes?"

Comitán

A girl stood up at the back of the room. She was about thirteen, fat, clumsy, with a bovine expression, one of those who would never draw the map of the world—so the teacher had decided; she was too dull, too slow-witted.

"We pray an Our Father, an *Ave Maria*, and the *Gloria*. On Saturdays a whole rosary."

"Thank you, child, you've given me the information I required. You may sit down."

None of us dared turn and look at her. We were too ashamed.

"All the rest might have been overlooked, but this is the last straw. I promise you, Mistress Teacher, that I'll go straight back from here and make sure this little dugout of yours is closed down."

When the Inspector had gone the teacher hid her face in her hands and began to sob fitfully, and savagely. Her shoulders—so scraggy and narrow, and so helpless—were bent double, weighed by intolerable suffering.

We all turned to the girl who had told on us.

"It's your fault. Go and ask her forgiveness."

The girl made a tremendous effort to understand why we were blaming her. She wouldn't budge from her place. But those who were round her dragged her to her feet and pushed and shoved her toward the teacher, where she stood quite still, her arms hanging limp. She saw the teacher weeping, yet seemed to feel no remorse. The teacher raised her face, and with reddened eyes, still moist, asked:

"Why did you do that?"

"You taught me always to speak the truth."

17

Father said that when the newsboy came we weren't to

let him go away: he wanted a word with him. We kept him on the veranda till Father had finished breakfast.

The newsboy had an alert, likeable face. Father received him kindly.

"Sit down, Ernesto."

"Thank you, Don César."

But the boy remained standing with his bundle of newspapers.

"Here's a chair. Or are you pressed for time?"

"It's only that . . . I don't want to be disrespectful. We're not equals, and. . . ."

"They don't set much store by such distinctions nowadays. Anyway I believe we're related, aren't we?"

"I'm the illegitimate son of your brother Ernesto."

"I've heard something of the kind. You're as white-skinned as he was, you've got blue eyes. Did you ever know your father?"

"I spoke to him a few times."

"He was a good and honest man. You bear his surname, you ought to be so too."

Ernesto lowered his eyes to hide his emotion. He sat facing my father, trying to hide his worn soles.

"Are you happy where you work?"

"They treat me well. But the pay hardly stretches for Mother and me."

"You seem intelligent, advanced for your age. You should aim higher."

Ernesto's expression brightened.

"Have you been to school?"

"Only up to fourth grade primary. Then Mother took ill."

"But you learned to read well and to write?"

"That's how I got this job."

"Wouldn't you like to change it for one that's less exacting and better paid?"

"There's no need to ask, sir.

"I'm your uncle. Don't call me sir."

Ernesto gave Father a suspicious glance. He didn't want to accept the cigar he was offered.

"It's a simple matter. You know the law now insists we must have a rural teacher on the farm."

"Yes, I've heard so."

"But as everything in Mexico works topsy-turvy, it's ordering us to use an article that's in short supply. So we have to look about us where we can. And as there's no pool of rural teachers to draw on, we've no alternative but to improvise. From the start I'd been thinking you'd do."

"Me?"

"You can read and write. That will fill the bill. As to the rest. . . ."

"I can't speak *tzeltal*, Uncle."

"You don't have to. You'll live with us in the big house. We'll provide you with food and clothes of course, and we'll make sure your mother lacks nothing. She's ill, you say?"

"She went out overheated after ironing and the cold air got her. She went blind. A neighbour looks after her."

"We could leave her enough money for her expenses while you're away."

"How long would it be?"

Now that Ernesto found himself on surer ground he recovered his composure. He felt proud to be there, sitting in front of a gentleman with a waistcoat and gold braid, talking like his equal and smoking his cigars. Besides, he felt he was wanted. His value shot up in his own eyes.

"The length of time depends on the circumstances. If you're not happy you can come back when you please. I guarantee you'll like it though. Chactajal has a good climate, and we'll treat you well."

"About the pay. . . ."

"We won't haggle over that. And look here, you don't have to rush into a decision this very day. Go back home, think it well over, discuss it with your mother. And if it suits you, let me know."

"When do we go to the ranch?"

"Next week."

18

As I don't go to school now, I'm cooped up in the house all day, and I'm bored. I trail after the servants, into the pantry, to the bedrooms, the dining-room. I watch them at their chores. I get in their way by sitting on the chair they're just about to brush, and make them impatient rumpling the quilt they've just spread.

"Off with you, child, buy a *real*'s worth of Get-Thee Hence!"

I get up and go out alone on to the veranda. The donkey-men pass to and fro emptying their water-barrels into the big earthen jugs in the kitchen.

Nana is toasting coffee. She pays no more heed to me than to the puppies, though they bark and bark.

I open a door. It leads to Father's study. I've often rummaged before in the unlocked drawers. There are piles of letters tied with old ribbon. There are photographs of bearded, faded yellow gentlemen, of pale young girls with their hair falling loose, of naked babies going for a swim across the carpet. I know them all by heart. Papers covered with figures, but I don't understand them. Lots of books on the shelves. They are so large that if I take one out they'll notice it has gone. But here's an unbound booklet. It's small and hasn't many pages. Inside there's some handwriting, and people such as Mario sometimes draws.

Comitán

I hide the book beneath my pinafore and slip stealthily out of the library. There's no one about. I reach the back yard without being seen. There, in the shade of a fig tree, I begin to read.

"I am my tribe's elder brother: I am its memory.

"I was there with the founders of the sacred ceremonial cities. I am of those who departed and never looked back. I guided their pilgrim steps. I opened their path through the forest. I brought them to this land of atonement.

"Here, in the place called Chactajal, we built our huts, here we wove the cloth of our garments, here worked the clay for our use. Far from others, we did not brandish the spoils of war in our fists, nor furtively count the gains of our trafficking. Assembled about the tree after the day's tasks were done, we called upon our gods of peace. Oh, we rejoiced, for we believed that our lives had found favour in their eyes. But they, in their councils, had terror in store for us.

"There were omens. Drought and death and other misfortunes, but our soothsayers were unable to say when so doleful a fate would befall us. They only adjured us that each should look into his own heart and examine it, and should twist the claw of greed, and slam the door on the adulterous thought, and stay the quick footsteps of vengeance. But who is there that can stop the cloud in whose womb the lightning writhes? They came, who were destined to come.

"Haughty and hard of manner and strong of voice: such were the instruments of our chiding.

"We slept not upon javelins; but we lay upon the weariness of a day that was filled with labour. Our gaze did not lurk in ambush, but we opened it wide on dread. And we had learned very well, from ancient days, the occupation of victims.

Comitán

"We wept for the captive lands, we wept for the maidens defiled. But between ourselves and the god's broken image there could not even be weeping. No bridge of lamentation, no flight of sighs. Pecked at by vultures, mocked by the hyena, thus we behold them now who had been our protectors, whom for centuries we had borne submissively on our backs. All this we saw, and yet in truth we died not.

"They preserved us for humiliation and servile tasks. They set us apart like darnel from the grain. Fit for burning, fit to be trampled, thus were we made, little brothers.

"Behold how the men of Castile spread round about them the light of their fair complexions. Behold them here, able in exacting tributes, powerful to punish, impaled within their language as we reigning in our silence.

"First came the one they called Abelardo Argüello. He caused us to lay the foundations of the big house and spring the chapel vault. In his time a great desolation covered our faces. And dawn found the newborn child smothered under its mother's body. For we no longer wished to prolong our suffering further.

"José Domingo Argüello was the name of the one who followed. He broadened his lands till river and forest let him advance no more. He marked the boundaries of the pastures and created the foaling-grounds for the animals. He died, thrown from his horse during a gallop, before he had reached the peak of his ambition.

"Josefa Argüello, his daughter, sombre and commanding, instituted the custom of the whip and the use of the stocks. She empowered a sorcerer to keep us bound to her desire, and no one could cross her but a great harm always befell them. By her orders many mahogany and cedar trees were felled, and she caused all the furniture of her house to be made in these timbers. She died without issue, consumed by her own spinsterhood.

57

Comitán

"Rodulfo Argüello we never knew. He delegated his authority to others, and with other men's hands squeezed the last drop of our sweat. That was when they sent us to Pacayal to clear the forest and prepare for sowing the cane. From Comitán we carried on our backs the sugar-mill for the crushing. Fine sires were also bought to improve the breed of the herds.

"Estanislao Argüello, the widower, had a gentle nature. In his time much livestock escaped and ran wild in the hills. And though we salted the salt-licks, we never succeeded in making the cattle come down again so that we might brand their hides. Our quinine rations were raised, and it was ordered that the women should not perform rough tasks. The widower died late in life, of a sickness.

"An orphan, one 'picked up by the wayside' as they used to say in those days, was the heir, because she had attended the death agony: Otilia. Other more legal relatives contested the inheritance, and it was then that the outlying lands could no longer be preserved. And so the meadow called 'Tiger Corner' was lost. Also the 'House of the Thunderbolt'. Otilia, who was skilled in embroidery, decorated the cloak that covers the Virgin in the chapel. At her request the Curate of Comitán came to baptize the children and marry the couples already living together. Since the time when Otilia stood godmother to us, we have all borne Christian names. Through marriage she came to adopt the surname Argüello. Her bed brought forth only male children, and she left her estate divided among her sons, so that we, too, were dispersed under the authority of several masters. And it is here, my younger brothers, that we meet again. In these words we are once more joined together as in the beginning; just as many branches unite at the trunk of the silk-cotton tree."

Comitán

A shadow deeper than the leaves of the fig tree tumbles across me. I look up. It is my mother. Hastily I try to hide the papers, but she has picked them up and is absorbed in studying them.

"You mustn't play with these things," she says at last. "They are Mario's inheritance. The male child's."

19

Yesterday the supplies for the journey arrived from Chactajal. The animals are resting in the stable. They woke with their manes and tails already curled and in pigtails. And the servants say that last night the jangle of silver spurs could be heard on the cobbled streets. It was the Spectre, the awful thing that wanders through fields and hamlets marking the foreheads of beasts with a sign of ill-omen.

A little while ago Ernesto came to leave his belongings. Only three changes of clothes. He wrapped them in an ordinary rush mat and tied them with rope.

Nana won't go to the farm with us, she's afraid of sorcerers. But she's looking after the preparations for our departure. Earlier on she sent for the woman who grinds chocolate. Together they've been weighing the cocoa and measuring out the sugar and other ingredients to mix in with it. Then the woman went to the room specially prepared for her, and before locking herself in she warned:

"Nobody must come where I work. For there are those that have burning eyes and leave evil wherever they look, and then the chocolate curdles."

On the other hand the woman who makes the candles doesn't hide her task. She works in the middle of the patio in the full light of the sun. She melts the wax in a huge copper cauldron over the fire. She sings as she hangs the wicks on to the wooden wheel bristling with nails. Then with a big ladle she pours the melted wax from the cauldron over the tapers. At each turn of the wheel more and more wax clings to the wicks, and the candles begin to take shape.

In the clay oven the servants are baking bread. It comes out yellow and covered with a crust only a little darker, smelling of abundance, of blessings, and of riches. They pack it in huge panniers, laying it carefully so that it doesn't crumble, and covering it with white napkins stiff with starch.

Here are the irons cheek by jowl with the coals, so that both are fused like lovers in a single heat: till a hand pulls them apart. Then the sheets steam, for the damp hasn't gone out of them yet. They send out their scent of cleanliness, the memory of interminable siestas under the sun, of long lapping in the wind.

At the far end of the back patio they're dismembering a pig they killed very early this morning. The lard is boiling now, and lets off a thick, filthy smoke. Nearby the dogs are licking the blood the earth hasn't yet swallowed up. The dogs with their greedy tongues are untiring in their search for scraps and go growling between the workmen's legs.

The house is a beehive of sounds and occupation. Only the Indians are quiet, squatting on their haunches on the veranda, scratching for fleas. It worries Mother to see them idle. But there's no task they can be given on these occasions. Then she has an idea:

"See thou . . . how art thou called? Go to the home of the girl Amalia Domínguez. She needs a donkey-boy to bring water. And thou, too, ask for the house of Jaime Rovelo. There's a forest of weeds in his patio needs uprooting."

Comitán

The Indians get to their feet in their docile way. They sling their foodbags over their shoulders: with a lump of *posol* and fried pancakes, which is all they've brought from the ranch. For they know that where they're going they won't get anything to eat either.

20

Nana takes me aside to say good-bye. We are in the chapel. We kneel before the statues on the altar. Then Nana crosses my forehead and says:

"I come to deliver my little child to thee, Lord, thou art witness that I can no longer watch over her now that distance will divide us. But thou who art here, and there also, protect her. Make her paths straight so that she may not trip or fall, so that the stone turns not against her to hit her, that no wild beast springs out on her to bite her, that the lightning shall not redden the roof that gives her shelter. For through my heart she has known thee and has sworn to be faithful to thee and has revered thee. For thou art the powerful one, and strong.

"Have mercy on her eyes that they look not about them like birds of prey.

"Have mercy on her hands that they close not on their prey as the tiger's, that they open to give what they possess, that they open to receive what they need, as if obeying thy law.

"Have mercy on her tongue, that it loose not threats, as the knife looseth sparks when blade clashes against blade.

"Purify her entrails, that from them may arise actions, not like the crawling weed, but like great trees that shelter and bear fruit.

"Protect her, as up to now I have protected her, from

breathing scorn. If any should come and bow before her face, may she not vaunt herself and say: I have bowed the neck of this foal. May she also stoop to pick that precious flower which it is given to few to gather in this world, and which is called humility.

"Thou didst grant servants unto her. Grant her also the spirit of an elder sister, keeper, and guardian. Give into her keeping the scales in which actions are weighed, that her patience outweigh her anger, that her compassion outweigh her justice, and that her love outweigh her revenge.

"Open her understanding, broaden it so that truth may find ample space there, that she may pause before raising the whip, knowing that every lash that falls prints a scar on the chastiser's shoulder. May her acts be like ointment poured into wounds.

"I come to deliver my little child to thee. I give her to thee. I commend her to thee, so that every day, as the pitcher is carried to the well to be filled, thou mayest carry her heart into the presence of the good things she has received from her servants, so that she may never be found wanting in gratitude, so that she may sit at her table, where hunger has never sat, that she may bless the cloth that covers it and that is so beautiful, that she may feel the walls of her house real and solid about her. This is our blood, and our work, and our sacrifice."

On the veranda we hear the coming and going of the muleteers, of the servants helping to close the trunks. The horses are already saddled and are pawing the bricks in the forecourt. My mother's voice calls my name as she searches for me.

Nana gets to her feet. Then she turns to me and says:

"It's time for us to say good-bye, my child."

But I stay on the ground and cling to her *tzec*, weeping, for I don't want to go.

Comitán

She loosens my hold gently and raises me up to her face. She kisses me on the cheeks and makes the sign of the cross on my mouth.

"You see, what with all that praying it's as if I'd gone back to the times I gave you suck."

21

It is already broad day when we leave Comitán. Father and Ernesto ride ahead on horseback. My mother, brother, and I in sedan chairs carried by Indians. We go at the pace of the slowest. The sun pricks through the canopy hung over our heads, made of Guatemalan cloth. The air is thick and hot under the cloth, and suffocates me.

The moors are long in passing. And when they do, the mountains rise with their hundred flinty knives and their rugged paths. I measure the height we're at by the panting of the Indian who carries me. Level with us go the pines. They catch the wind with their hands so crowded with fingers, and by the time they set it loose again it is anointed with wholesome resins. Among the rocks grows a sturdy blue flower that sends out a sharp scent of pollen where the bee buzzes drunkenly. The earth is thick-grained and black.

Somewhere in the forest the lightning flashes. As if answering a shepherd's whistle, the dark woolly clouds heap and pile above us. Father shouts an order in *tzeltal* and brings his whip down on his horse's croup.

The Indians quicken their pace. We must reach Lomantán before the storm is upon us. But we're only just over the crest of the hill when scattered drops begin to fall. At first it's only a light drizzle, and we're sure it won't last. But soon it gathers strength and rivulets of water spill over the upturned brims of our hats and trickle between the folds of the rubber capes that aren't large enough to cover us.

At last in the distance we see a settlement of rude palm-roofed huts made of wattle and daub. Scenting strangers, the thin, mangy dogs all dripping with water come out to bark. The commotion rouses the people, who lean out of their doors. They are Indians. Meek-looking women who proffer their breasts to the grasping mouths of new-born babies; pot-bellied, barefoot urchins; toothless old men with yellow complexions.

Father goes ahead and reins in his horse in front of one of the huts. He talks to the man who seems to be the owner. But to my father's arguments the other answers with tranquil sullenness. Father points to us all, soaked in rain. He explains that we need a fire to warm our food and somewhere to shelter. From his pouch he takes some silver coins and offers them. The Indian has understood our plight but doesn't want to help. In spite of what he sees, he goes on flatly refusing with his sad, absent, expressionless face.

We have no alternative but to go forward. We push on now through the mist that leads us a game of blind-man's-buff. The horses slither down the soft slopes, or their hooves strike on the stones with a sharp, unpleasant sound. The Indians grope their way cautiously, step by step.

About seven in the evening we reach Bajucú. The pine-flare is alight in the sheepfold. On the veranda of the big house, on long wooden benches, sit women wrapped in thick black shawls.

"Good evening, mistress," says my father dismounting. "Will you give us lodging?"

"The *patrón's* in Comitán, and he took the keys to the rooms. But you can pass the night here if you like."

After a cup of coffee we settle ourselves on the veranda.

Comitán

Our rubber capes serve as pillows. We lay rush mats and sheepskins on the brick floor. We are so tired we're asleep before the pine-flare dies.

22

The air is clean when it wakes, just breathed from the mouth of God. Presently it fills with the clatter of day. In the stable the cows snuffle their warm vapour over the calves' flanks. In the fowl-run the turkeys prink their feathers while the ugly, sad females scratch for any little worm. The hen is sententiously laying eggs, sitting on her nest like a throne.

The beasts are saddled. We leave Bajucú early, for the journey is long. Leisurely we go, lulled by the even gait of the Indians and the horses. In the thickness of the trees the birds stir very slightly, as if they were the brightest and greenest of all the leaves. Soon one sound dominates all the rest and casts its spell over the spaces round. It's the river Jataté, announcing its presence from a long way off. It flows in spate, dragging lopped-off branches and dead cattle: thick with mud, slow in its lordship and power. The rope-bridge spanning it broke last night. There's not even a rough canoe to cross in.

But we can't stop. We must press on. Father takes me in his arms and sits me on the pommel of his saddle. Ernesto looks after my brother. Both men spur their horses and lash them with their whips. The horses neigh, frightened, refusing to go forward. When at last they plunge into the water they send cold spray splashing all about them. They swim with their eyes wide with terror, pitting their strength against the current which is forcing them downstream. They avoid the logs and the scum and keep their upper lips stubbornly above water. On the far bank Mario and I are deposited in charge of Ernesto. Father goes back to help those left behind. By the time we're all together again, we're ready for lunch.

We light a fire on the beach. We take the provisions from the saddlebags: slices of smoked ham, fried chicken, hard-boiled eggs, and a swill of local brew because of the fright we've had. We set to with an appetite, then stretch out in the shade awhile for a noon-day doze.

Over the ground moves a long column of ants, very industrious, carrying crumbs and slender bits of grass. The sun rides high over the branches, turning them gold. One can almost weigh the silence in one's hand.

Just when did we first hear that noise of trodden leaf-mould? As if in that state half-waking, half-dreaming, we saw a fawn standing in front of us. Hunted by goodness knows what greater danger, he came, and he pulled up short at the very edge of the tablecloth, trembling with surprise and fear, his flanks quivering with weariness, his scratched eyes moist, his ears alert. He wanted to turn and escape, but Ernesto had already pulled his pistol from its holster, and he aimed at the animal's forehead, from the midst of which the antlers were only just breaking through. There he lay stretched, the hooves full of mud from his death race, the skin glistening with his last sweat.

"It was his death he was looking for."

Ernesto doesn't want to take the glory for himself, but it's quite clear he's proud of his achievement. He cleans the barrel of the pistol carefully with a handkerchief before putting it away.

Mario and I edge timidly toward the spot where the deer is lying. We did not know it was as easy as that to die and to lie quiet. One of the Indians just behind us kneels, and with the tip of a stick prises open the fawn's eyelid. There is the iris, all snuffed out and opaque like a puddle of stagnant water where things have already begun to rot. The other Indians also stoop to look at that naked eye; and they see something deep within it, because when they stand again their expressions have changed. They move away, and go and squat on their haunches some distance off, avoiding us. From there they watch us, whispering.

"What are they saying?" Ernesto asks, beginning to feel wretched.

Father puts out the embers, stamping on them with his strong boots.

"Nothing. Superstitions. Untie the horses."

His voice is thick with rage. Ernesto doesn't understand. He persists:

"The deer?"

"It can rot where it lies."

From that time the Indians have called the place "Where our Shadow Rots".

23

The next stop is Palo María, a cattle farm belonging to my father's first cousins. There are three of them: Aunt Romelia, the solitary one who shuts herself up in her room whenever she has migraine; Aunt Matilde, a spinster who blushes when she's spoken to; and Aunt Francisca.

They've lived on the ranch for years, ever since they were orphaned and Aunt Francisca took charge of the household. They seldom come to our town. When they do, we watch them ride in side-saddle on their three white mules, twirling the dark silk parasols that shade them from the sun. They stay with us several days, visit their doctor, order dresses from the seamstress, and when they go calling they listen (Aunt Romelia with delight, Aunt Matilde shocked, Aunt Fràncisca haughtily) to whatever gossip happens to have Comitán by the ears. When they go they give Mario and me a silver *peso* each. They warn us to be good, and then we hear no more of them except for brief and infrequent letters.

This time it's we who are the guests. As they weren't expecting us, their exclamations of welcome are interspersed with orders to the servants, who scatter in all directions to prepare supper and to air and clean the rooms we'll be using. In the meantime we sit on the veranda and have a drink to celebrate.

"It's a pleasure to have you with us," says Aunt Matilde, her eye fixed on Ernesto.

"Why don't you play us a tune on the piano?" asks Aunt Romelia. Confidentially she adds: "Matilde knows a waltz called 'In the Shade of a Mangrove Tree'. It's charming, full of arpeggios. Unfortunately I can't bear listening to music any more. At the first arpeggio my migraine starts up."

"Haven't Dr. Mazariegos's medicines done you any good?"

"Dr. Mazariegos is a fund of professional knowledge, but my case is complicated, César, very complicated."

She is proud of her ill-health and shows it off like a trophy.

"Have you finished yet, sir?"

Aunt Matilde takes Ernesto's glass.

"Don't call him sir. He's your cousin, son of my brother Ernesto."

"Really?"

Aunt Matilde can't hide her displeasure. Aunt Francisca comes to the rescue.

"How nice to know you're one of the family."

"Even if I'm only a bastard?"

Comitán

Ernesto's voice is harsh and defiant. Aunt Matilde blushes and drops the glass. She runs into the house, hiding her face in her apron.

"You see what your cousins are like, César," says Aunt Francisca. "They cry if they hear a mosquito buzz, they're nervous and take aspirins. And it's my job to find a broom and sweep up the broken glass."

After supper my mother, who is very tired, goes off to bed. Aunt Romelia and Aunt Matilde follow. We stay in the dining-room a little longer. The gas lamp hanging from the ceiling hums as if it were devouring the insects that keep coming to life again and circling round it.

Aunt Francisca says:

"I thought this year you wouldn't be going to Chactajal, César."

"Why not? I always go to supervise the grinding of the corn and the branding."

"I thought if you did come it would be alone. Why have you brought the family?"

"Zoraida wanted to come, and since the children aren't at school. . . ."

"It's not wise. The things that are happening on the ranches aren't fit for children's eyes. I'm even wondering whether it wouldn't be best if my sisters went to Mexico City. You see what a state Romelia's in. She's perfectly well, but it comforts her to think she's suffering from every imaginable disease. That's my excuse for sending her. As to Matilde, she's not really on the shelf yet, don't you agree, Ernesto?" Aunt Francisca gets no reply. She goes on: "She ought to have a little diversion."

Father takes his cousin's hand in his.

"And you?"

She draws her hand away firmly without violence, and stands up as if to cut the conversation short.

"I stay here. Where I belong."

69

24

We reach Chactajal at sunset. Round the silk-cotton tree in the yard the Indians are waiting. They come near so that we can touch their foreheads with our fingers, and they give us their "tithes": hens well hobbled so they can't escape, fresh eggs, and little measures of corn and beans. It's our task to receive them gratefully. Father orders a carafe of brandy and a bolt of cloth to be shared out among them. Then we go to the chapel to give thanks for our safe arrival. They've decorated it as if for a feast-day, with garlands of ricepaper and with sedge strewn on the floor. On the altar the Virgin shows off her silk dress embroidered with seed-pearls. At her feet a large gourd filled with fruit emits a hundred mingled scents. Mother kneels and recites the mysteries of the rosary. In one, single, anonymous voice, the Indians give the responses.

After prayers we sit on the benches round the walls. One of the Indians (a chief, probably, to judge by the respect the others pay him) puts a gourd full of *atole* into Mother's hands. Mother just tastes the liquid and then passes it on to me. I do the same and hand it to the next, and so on till we've all put our lips to the same spot.

In a corner of the church musicians are tuning their instruments. There is a drum and a reed flute. Meanwhile the men lined up on the left prepare to select their partners for the dance. They giggle and snicker. The girls wait in their places with their hands folded in their laps. They are ready to receive the red kerchief thrown by the men, provided, that is, they accept the offer to stand and dance. Or if they refuse the invitation they let it drop, casually, as if by accident.

The music is sad and sharp and harsh as the air seeping

through a dead man's bones. Its sorrowing presence is powerfully felt among us. The couples get up and stand for a moment quite still, face to face, just the right distance apart. The women lower their eyes and their arms hang limp at their sides. The men bend forward, their hands behind their backs. They scarcely lift their feet from the ground as they dance, and they go on hour after hour, shifting their weight from foot to foot, calling insistently upon some unknown being who does not reply.

The sedge loses its sheen and its fragrance. The candles are all consumed. I lay my head, heavy with sleep, on Mother's shoulder. They carry me in their arms to the big house. Through a chink in my eyelids I see the glare of the pine-flare burning in the yard, and the palms hiding the pillars of the veranda. And, in the shadows, the hostile gaze of those who don't want to join the festivities.

I go on listening from my bed—I've no idea how long —to the monotonous rhythm of drum and flute; the crackle of burning logs; the crickets chirping deep in the grass; and, now and then, the howl of a wild beast forlorn in the forest thickness.

"Who's there?"

I sit up trembling. In the darkness I can't make out the features of the shape that's standing quite still in front of me. I think I can discern the form of an Indian woman, ageless, without a face.

"Nana!" I let out a short cry.

The shape draws closer and sits on the edge of the bed. It does not touch me, nor breathe softly on my cheek, nor stroke my hair as Nana always does to lull me to sleep, but these words blow into my ear:

"I'm with you, child. And I'll come when you call as the dove when the corn-seeds are scattered. Sleep now. Dream that this wide land is yours, that you are shearing oh so many peaceful sheep; that the harvest is full in the granaries. But beware that you do not wake with your feet caught in the stocks and your hand nailed to the door. As if it had come to pass that your sleep were an iniquity."

PART II

Chactajal

———— ✤ ————

All moons, all years, all days, all winds, take
their course and pass away. Even so all blood
reaches its place of quiet, as it reaches its power
and its throne.

> *From the Chilam-Balam of Chumayel,*
> *an ancient Maya manuscript*

This is what is remembered of those days:

The wind of daybreak tears the mist from the moor. Its strands are broken and they rise and scatter while, silently, the great expanse is laid bare, out and out to the sodden grasses and the twisted, lonely trees, to where the ribs of the mountain rise and the River Jataté shows clear.

In the middle of the plain is the big house, a solidly built construction of thick walls capable of withstanding an attack. The rooms are strung in a row like beads, by some clever architect, so it seems. They are dark, for there are only narrow windows through which the light can filter. The roof-tiles are blackened by rain and time. The three verandas have wooden railings. Standing there, César was pointing out to Ernesto the sheds serving for kitchen and granaries. Beyond the farmyard are the cattle-pens.

"Grandmother Josefa had the cattle-pens built when she was too old to go out to the fields any more. While she sat on the veranda she could watch the branding. The cattle filed past her and were counted."

"She didn't trust the men."

"Who would? The managers are a bunch of scoundrels. The last I had is still rotting in jail."

César was feeling happy after a large breakfast. At that fresh morning hour of nine when each man was in his place performing his appointed task with perfect precision, he felt inclined to benevolence, even toward those who had tried to spoil his happiness. Like that estate manager, for instance.

Chactajal

"He almost left me penniless. I was in Europe. Very young. They sent me—like all the sons of the well-to-do families in Comitán—to study for a career. I have no head for such things and I never took a degree. But I did enjoy myself! Imagine at that age, with money and to spare, and in Paris! As long as my parents lived, all went splendidly, but afterwards came bad times and I couldn't keep body and soul together. Under cover of all that revolutionary humbug the manager was cooking accounts. I got home only just in time to save the ranch."

Ernesto wasn't interested in business affairs. He'd no idea what his uncle was talking about: mortgages, distraints, claims.

"And was it easy to settle down in Chiapas again, after living abroad?"

"You can't imagine how one misses one's home when one's abroad. Even in Paris I used to get them to send me coffee, chocolate, and sacks of sour *posol*. No, no, I'd never exchange Chactajal, not for all the Parises in France."

César wasn't a rolling stone. Wherever he might wander, he would always find his way home. And wherever he went, he'd always be the same. He might get to know the world, but that fact could never lessen his sense of self-importance. Of course, he preferred to live where others shared his opinion, where to call oneself Argüello was not a way of becoming anonymous, where his fortune was equal to or greater than those about him.

For the first time Ernesto was entering into intimacy with one of those men whom he had envied and admired so long from a distance. Greedily he drank in every word and gesture. César's clinging to custom, his abysmal ignorance of outside affairs, seemed to Ernesto only one more sign of strength and invulnerability. Ernesto was sure of one thing now: his place was with the bosses, he was of the same caste. To hide the emotion this discovery roused in him he pointed to the building that rose some distance away and asked:

"Is that the chapel where we prayed last night?"

"Yes. Did you notice that the Statue of Our Lady of Health is of carved wood? An Indian brought it on his back from Guatemala. It's very miraculous."

"They've been ringing the chimes since dawn."

"To wake the peons. My father used to tell me that in the old days when the Indians heard the chimes they used to come hurrying out of their huts, to meet here under the silk-cotton tree. The overseer used to be waiting for them with their rations of quinine and a whip in his hand, and before sending them off to their work he'd give them a few good beatings. Not as a punishment, but to pep them up. And the Indians used to fight among themselves for front place, because by the time the last of them had taken his turn the overseer was worn out and didn't lash so hard."

"Don't they do that any more?"

"Not any more. A certain Estanislao Argüello forbade it."

"Why?"

"Father used to say he was a man with very advanced ideas, but I think he just noticed that the Indians liked being whipped, so there wasn't any point in it. But certainly the other ranchers were furious. They said his bad example would be infectious, and that the Indians would not respect them any more if they didn't force themselves to be respected. So the bosses took over the whipping task themselves. Many Indians from Chactajal went to other farms because they said they were treated with more respect."

"And Don Estanislao?"

"Wouldn't budge. The neighbours wanted to do him a

bad turn and picked a quarrel on a question of boundaries. But they came up against a stone wall. The old man was a very competent lawyer and kept them at bay. It wasn't till later, in my parents' will, that Chactajal was divided. Pity. But there were so many heirs there was no way out."

"You can't complain. You got the *hacienda* buildings."

"I'm the eldest. I also got the Indians to do the work."

"I've counted their huts. There are over fifty."

"A lot are derelict. They say that the first Argüello who came and settled here found quite a big village, but little by little it's been shrinking. There's a lot of malaria and dysentery, and illness is decimating the Indians. Others stray away maybe. They steal off into the woods and escape. In any case I gave some of the families to the other Argüellos. All told, there's not more than twenty left."

He looked toward the settlement. Smoke was rising from only a few of the huts. In others there was no sign of life.

"The empty huts are tumbling down. You'll be thinking those who say this is the end are right, because you're green and inexperienced. But we've cried to heaven often enough before for worse troubles: for epidemics, and revolutions, and bad harvests! But good times come back and we go on living here and we're still masters."

Why shouldn't it be the same now, precisely now, when Ernesto had come? He had a right to a time of plenty and of ease. He too, like all the Argüellos.

A lad came from the stables leading two spirited, light-footed animals by the halters. They were saddled ready for the fields. César and Ernesto went down the steps from the veranda to the farmyard. They mounted, and at a slow trot put the house behind them. The boy ran ahead to open the big gate and clear the way. They had no sooner reached the path that wound among the huts than the beat of hoofs roused the skinny dogs, who scratched their scabs and fleas and barked hugely. The women, kneeling on the ground to pound the grain, stopped their tasks and sat quietly with arms rigid, as if rooted into the stone of their mortars, their slack breasts hanging loose in their blouses. They watched the two men pass through the open hut gates, or through the gaps in the walls packed with dung and liane. The naked, snub-nosed urchins with their distended bellies, playing in a tangle in the mud all of a heap with the pigs, turned to stare at the riders, their eyes blinking curiously.

"There are the Indian women to do your bidding, Ernesto. We'll be looking out for one of these brats to turn up with your complexion."

The joke irritated Ernesto. It seemed to put him on a level with his inferiors. He answered curtly:

"I've my bad moments, Uncle, but not bad taste."

"You say that now. Wait a few months and you'll be singing to another tune. Beggars can't be choosers. I'm talking from experience."

"You?"

"Why so surprised? Yes, me. Like everyone. I've a sprinkling of children among them."

It was doing them a favour, really, because after that the Indian women were more sought after and could marry where they liked. The Indian always recognized this virtue in his woman, that the *patrón* had found pleasure in her. And the children were among those that hung about the big house and served there faithfully.

In forming his judgment, Ernesto did not range himself on the side of the victims. He didn't consider himself one of them. His mother's case had been different. She wasn't an Indian. A humble village woman she might be, but white. And Ernesto was proud of his Argüello blood. The masters had a right to plant their seed where they

79

pleased. Whatever dark and primitive sense of justice Ernesto might have possessed was smothered by custom, by the usualness of events which nobody else's conscience considered a reproach, and above all, by the admiration in which he held this man who rode on in front with such insolent self-confidence. As if he were anxious to help César keep his secret, he asked:

"Doña Zoraida knows?"

But Ernesto's complicity wasn't required.

"What, about my children? Of course."

One would have had to be very stupid to ignore so evident a state of affairs. In any case every rancher's wife was resigned to the fact that her husband was the farm's chief stud-bull. Was there by any chance a saint watching over Zoraida, that she should be an exception? Besides, there was nothing to be upset about. Children such as these, women like these, had no meaning. The legal ones were all that counted.

They'd left the settlement behind. Scrub and hostile creepers flanked the path. Thorns stuck into the heavy cloth of their trousers, and scratched the smooth surface of their leather leggings. César spurred his horse lightly so that it would more quickly reach the clearing in the undergrowth.

"This is the Graveyard Field. They call it that because when we were setting up posts for the wiring a grave turned up full of skeletons and potsherds. A crazy *gringo* chasing butterflies, so he said. . . ."

"Oh yes, the one they nicknamed Mister Peshpen."

"Butterflies fiddlesticks! What he was really after must have been oil, or mines, or something of the kind. So Mister Peshpen became enthusiastic about his discovery. He wanted to go on digging, because the books say that all this district is an archaeological region and we might discover very important ruins. But the only ruin there was likely to be was my own, if we'd started abandoning our work to dig holes. When Mister Peshpen saw I wasn't going to give in, he pestered me for some papers I have in the house in Comitán, written by an Indian."

"An Indian really wrote them?"

"And in Spanish, just to be classier still. My father ordered them to be written to prove how old our properties are, and their extent. Things being as they are, you'll realize I wasn't going to part with a document like that, however interesting and rare it might be. To console Mister Peshpen, I had to give him the potsherds we dug up. He took them to New York, and from there he sent me a photo. They're in the museum."

They rode on. Before them stretched a meadow full of tall grass rocked on the wind. The horns and flanks of the cattle dotted here and there in the distance, grazing, were only just visible above it.

"So these fields are new."

"I ordered them to be fenced. Not so much for their location—because there are others better—but to set up landmarks between my land and the others'."

"Which direction did my father's lie?"

"Your father received his legacy in money."

"Didn't he work here, ever?"

"Money gives no return, and it can't last, is what I've always said. He wasted it in less time than it takes to tell: in bad business and bouts of drinking. He was broke when he died."

"If he'd had time—they say he was a very able man— he'd have set himself on his feet again. If it hadn't been for that unfortunate accident. . . ."

César gave Ernesto a quick, furtive glance. Was the boy being simple, or calculating, talking like that?

"It wasn't an accident. It was suicide."

Ernesto reined his horse. He'd heard the rumour, but it

had never seemed to him credible. Now the brutality of the statement stunned him.

"He killed himself? Why?"

"He was up to his neck in debt and no way out."

"But he'd just married a very rich girl, one of the Grajales from Chiapas."

"She wouldn't release a penny to help him."

"The low bitch!"

"She discovered that Ernesto had only married her for her money. The girls of the hot lands aren't as tame as ours. She couldn't forgive him. But later when she was left a widow she went herself to look for the creditors and pay them."

"Did he die without a will?"

"He left a letter with his last requests."

"Didn't he mention me?"

"No. Why?"

"I'm his son."

"Not the only one. In any case he never recognized you."

César said this without meaning to offend. To him his brother's behaviour was so natural that he didn't even trouble to find an excuse or a way of softening the statement. But if he'd looked behind him he would have seen Ernesto's face, with a purple mark as if he'd just been struck. He was trembling all over with rage, but he couldn't contradict César's statement because what he had said was true. No, he didn't belong to the race of the masters after all. Ernesto was only a bastard of whom his father had been ashamed. For whenever he had tried to approach him, following his mother's advice and his own desires and needs, he'd been sent away with a few pence as if he'd been a beggar. Yet in spite of everything he had loved that man, who had never consented to be anything more than a stranger to his son. Ernesto rebelled against

82

this weakness of his own heart, which sanctioned his father's cynicism and indifference, the ease with which he threw off his responsibilities: a shrug of the shoulders was enough. He was glad to hear about his father's marriage, and that the girl had such a surname and such wealth. He would never be able to forgive that foreigner—a girl from Chiapas, from the hot land—that she'd let his father die. His father's life mattered far more than jealousies or a woman's fury. He, his son, so abject, would have been glad to be near him and help him. He, who had more reason for resentment than anyone else. But it was too late to change anything now. And so Ernesto continued chained to the shadow of a dead man; to the dead man's brother who had that same note of authority when he spoke, who used the same gestures; who kept himself at the same disdainful distance as the other.

They had reached a small corral. They reined in their horses under a tree. From there they could hear the call of the cattlemen rounding up the herd—"*Tou, tou, tou,*" ever nearer—the barking of the sheepdogs growing more insistent when they wanted to bring in a calf, which tossed its head and tried to break loose from the rest and run away on its own. Crowding together, bellowing, blinded by the dust they threw up in their charge, the cattle entered the corral.

"Fine cattle this batch—crossed with zebu. Give good meat, and the bullocks will stand a lot of work. But they're fierce, and the cattle-buyers shun this lot like the plague. Watch how they fight."

The bulls locked horns in a violent, unresolved struggle. They seemed fierce and out for blood. Their hooves pawed the ground threateningly, and they bellowed with warm, hoarse breath.

The cattle-men were emptying sacks of salt into the wooden troughs. The animals jostled to lick it with their

83

Chactajal

thick sandpaper tongues. The cows, persistently chewing the cud, opened wide their huge, wondering eyes, searching for their heifers, pushing them gingerly forward to taste the pinkish, crystalline grains.

César shouted to one of the cow-men.

"Hey ye, watch that little calf, the black one with the star on its forehead: looks like it had maggots."

Guided by César's signals, the cow-man found the animal. Spitting into his hands, he gripped his lasso and set it rocking through the air. The calf was quivering close to its dam, and never noticed the moment when the lasso fell about its throat. The cow-man ran to the nearest stake, made the rope fast, and began to pull. The calf was bellowing with tongue out, struggling; but not for long. Another cowboy hobbled its legs to throw it. It twisted as if seized by convulsions, but couldn't break loose. The dam looked on, lowing sadly, but the stampede of the other animals swept her from the spot.

The calf had an open wound in one rump, and maggots were swarming there. The cowboy squirted creosote into it and rubbed it, mixing in dung. The calf looked strangely inexpressive as it bore the operation. Only the rattle in its throat betrayed its suffering. Ernesto couldn't bear it any more, and looked the other way so as not to see. The movement did not escape César, who said sardonically:

"You're a bad rancher like your father. Come on, because when the castrating of the bulls begins you're going to faint."

Cold sweat broke out on Ernesto's forehead. His cheeks were pale. Between clenched teeth he managed to splutter:

"It's nothing. Not used to it."

But he didn't insist that they stay, and when César's horse ambled on, his own followed quietly.

"I want you to see the cane fields. This year's harvest is coming on well."

84

Chactajal

The cane stalks rose in a close green haze, rasping the air with their leaves' sharp edge.

"There's the mill."

Under a lean-to roof was the oldest type of crusher, the kind still turned by animals.

"If we need to, we can always impress an Indian for the job."

César had heard of newer and faster machines of course. He'd seen them on his travels. But as this one still gave good yield, he saw no reason to change.

"It's time to go home. They'll be waiting for us to take *posol*."

The hand holding the rein swung hard across. The horses sniffed the stable and trotted happily.

Ernesto was thoughtful. César asked:

"What do you think of Chactajal?"

Ernesto couldn't answer yet. The roof of his mouth was still dry with the way his stomach had turned at the sight of the pens. The smell of mixed manure and creosote was still pungent in his nose. The dust was stinging his eyelids. But worse, there was the shame of having appeared unworthy, ridiculous, and weak before César.

"Chactajal's the best *hacienda* for miles round. Ask anyone if anywhere near there are better studs than those you've seen. As to seeds—they send them to me specially from the States. I'll show you the catalogues. It's a 'thanksgiving land': if you sow one, it will return you a hundred in benediction. The big house goes without saying. There's not another to compare with it in all the cold country. As they're built in these parts, it's well done."

"Yes, one can see that."

Ernesto agreed but with a feeling of distaste. How childish César was, insisting on the value of his property as if he were trying to sell it. Ernesto was certainly no buyer. The mention of wealth brought other things to his mind, movies he'd seen in the cinema in Comitán. The rich were the people who lived in palaces, who gave orders to liveried flunkeys, who ate exquisite viands off golden dishes. But here there was only an old house. There were leaks in Ernesto's bedroom, and all night rats and possum ran in the rafters. As for the flunkeys, one might as well ignore them entirely. Maidservants and boys, all were Indian. Ragged. There was no way at all to make them understand. They hurried to obey orders, but as they didn't understand they obeyed all wrong. The plates were of pewter, battered with use. The meals were no better than his mother made in Comitán. Ranch food, they used to say proudly, offering no excuses, when they carved the salt beef and served the fried plantain.

So this was what it was to be rich. Still, Ernesto wasn't one to be disappointed in his relatives. No, indeed, he was satisfied. Naturally he would have liked to enjoy one of those movie-existences, but not at the price of humiliation. Honest-to-goodness wealth as on the ciné screen would have opened a still greater rift between him and the Argüellos: even as it was, his family admitted him with difficulty and many reservations, but at least he could identify himself with them and draw near them just because of their needs and privations. The same blood, the same name, the same set of customs. In what respect was one superior to the other?

They'd reached a fence. Ernesto, deep in his own thoughts, made not the slightest move to dismount. César waited a few moments, drumming his fingers on the pommel of his saddle. When he spoke his voice was full of impatience and irritation.

"What are you waiting for? Get down and open."

Ernesto came to, blinking. He measured the gulf that separated him from this man, and, his mouth bitter with saliva, he obeyed.

Chactajal

2

These wicker rocking-chairs are already very old, and
how the woodworm have eaten them! We ought to buy
a modern suite like the one Don Jaime Rovelo has in his
drawing-room—"Pullman", they call it. But César
evades the subject every time I bring it up. He says it's
not that he's mean, but that this furniture's a legacy from
goodness knows whom and that it ought to be treasured
as a relic. Oh! He's going to scold me when he finds the
portraits are covered with dust and the flies have done
their little cakewalk across them. This very day, before I
forget, I'm going to tell the maid to pass a cloth over
them. She's Indian, a bit slow in the head. . . . If only we
had the ones from Comitán. They're really hard-working. But César didn't want us to bring any. Because of
the cost, I suppose. So one's got to make do with what one
has. It's easier driving a donkey. . . . But I'm not going to
start acting housemaid now. We weren't like that at
home. What should we be doing with hoarding such
bric-à-brac as if it were gold in a napkin? We were always
too poor for that anyway. Mother was left a widow when
I was five. What a task she had to bring me up! Making
palm hats and shirts of unbleached cotton for the donkey-
boys. Never a day went by that someone who'd come
to collect what was owing didn't hammer at the door. If
it wasn't the rent, it was the vegetable woman. Mother
always received them very friendly, quite as if they were
visitors. She told them the straits she was in and promised
to pay when the money managed to get itself saved up.
But we never did save any. Once, I remember—I was
already one for the boys and liked to put on a bit of side,
it was when the peddlers came down for the San Caralampio fair—I fell in love with some sandals I saw on a

stall. They were leather sandals, the hide well tanned, and they cost three *pesos*—a fortune. Every day I passed to take a peep at them, terrified they might have been bought already. I don't know what moved my god-mother's heart, but she suddenly became specially gener-ous and gave me five *pesos* pocket-money. I rushed off to the stall where I'd seen the sandals. With the two *pesos* left I bought a pair of coarse black cotton stockings with clocks. The day I wore them for the first time I'd have given a lot if the streets could have been glistening clean and not so stony, I trod very gingerly so that my sandals wouldn't get scratched and dirty. It was the last night of the fair. There was a serenade of wind instruments, and I went down to sit on the church stoop. I stuck my feet out all I could so that people would see my new shoes. They pinched me and squeaked, but they were so pretty. Amalia, who was always jealous of me, nicknamed me "Sandalaria" and started the rumour I never took my shoes off even to sleep and that when I died they'd bury me in them. Then I began a three days' prayer to Santa Rita de Casia, who intervenes for things that are quite impossible, and asked her to fix me up the miracle that now and then—but not always—the sandals would turn into boots and Amalia'd think I owned two pairs. But before I'd ended the three days' praying some men came to impound all we'd got and they took away everything, even the sandals. They left us, as you might say, with nothing but a rush mat. We had to go and live in a single room. Mama slaved day in and day out to make a bit more so that we shouldn't suffer such tribulations, and at night she told her rosary and put everything into the hands of Divine Providence and went off to sleep sound as a dormouse. I was the one who used to pass the night awake and overburdened, worrying in case perhaps the man who brought us the straw for the hats wasn't trusting

us any more. My face used to fall with shame when I had
to go and talk to him and ask him to wait because we
were expecting a money order, which was a lie, for who'd
be sending us money orders when there was no one to
help us, anywhere? So when César took notice of me and
spoke to Mama, for his intentions were honourable, I
saw heaven opening before me. Zoraida de Argüello. I
like the name, and it suits me. But I was frightened of
marrying a man so tall and so proper, and who'd got
used already to living alone. For he'd had no sweethearts,
not real sweethearts that is, not regular ones. Affairs he'd
never lacked, otherwise he'd be no man, but I was the
only girl he'd marry. My bridal gown was a joy to behold, embroidered with coloured beads as was the
fashion then. César ordered it from Guatemala. He was
rich and wanted to make a splash. But how topsy-turvy
the world behaves. Now he says he's short of money and
he even makes me give back the things I buy. I have to
ask his permission first. How I blushed with shame in
front of Doña Pastora! I went pale and red by turns as I
invented tales that the weaves I'd chosen turned out not
to be Guatemalan at all. "Let your mouth be the measure
of that," said she, and she threw the money down on to
the pile of sheets and refused to take them back. Oh!
Mother never lived to see such things. While she was alive
I was careful she lacked nothing. Even her supplies of
chocolate I bought myself, scraping from what César
gave me to spend. And little by little I paid off all her
debts. The poor soul's last years were easier, though it
always hurt her to see me like a hen bought on the
market. And César's family thinks I'm not good enough
because my surname is Solís, the lesser Solís family, and
so I'm just a nonentity. But they couldn't say anything
against my honour. When I married I was young and
middling pretty. Afterwards came my bad turns and I

simply shrivelled up living with such an intent, serious man who's like a holy sepulchre. Being older than me, he puts on airs and it almost makes me want to speak to him formally, but in front of him I'd be a slobbering ass to show it. Why should I be handing him my arm to twist? If he wants to pet me or come near me he's got to plead for it even now. I don't know how women can be so soft in the head as to marry just for the need of a man. Even supposing life were for ever. After Mario was born I was very poorly. Not another child, Doctor Mazariegos ordered. Pity, because I'd like to have had lots of children. They cheer a house up. César says why do we want more? But I know if it weren't for the two we have he'd have left me long ago. He's bored with me because I have no small-talk. And he was educated abroad. When we were courting he used to visit me in a frock coat, and he liked to explain to me the phases of the moon, which I never did understand. Now he talks to me hardly at all. Yet I don't want to be living apart like Romelia does. One's a hanger-on everywhere then, and fits nowhere. If one dresses up nice and goes out into the street they say one's being a coquette. If one shuts oneself in they think one's up to some monkey-business. Thank God I've two children. And one's a boy.

3

At dusk the family congregates on the veranda of the big house.

The flocks of sheep come slowly home, and in the barn the cows are lowing disconsolately at being parted from their heifers. The murmur of men at work grows less. Tools are returned to their place of rest. In the stable the harness, saturated in horse-sweat, is put out to air, and the wind picks up an acrid smell as it blows past. The tame, sullen beasts of burden are grazing wherever they please. Smoke rises from shack and kitchen, blurring and veiling the evening light still more.

"Like a cool drink?" Zoraida asks.

Ernesto with his elbows propped on the balustrade is gazing out at the distant sky. He shakes his head. From the hammock where he is lounging, César makes a sign to say he'll have one.

"Try to get some food into you, Ernesto," he says, "you've scarcely eaten all day."

It's true. Since that first conversation with his uncle in Comitán, Ernesto has been jittery and he can't sleep well, he turns restlessly in his dreams, and suffers nightmares. The incidents of the journey to Chactajal (the deer he shot so thoughtlessly) have stolen his peace. And it's worse now that he has settled into a disagreeable and stupid routine. He has no definite work to do, and for that very reason he is loaded with all kinds of jobs that are tiresome and humiliating. César washed his hands of him after the first day, considering him useless for farm work. So he has been in the big house at the mercy of Zoraida's foolish and unpredictable caprices. For there's really no point in dusting and polishing the furniture over and over, it will never acquire a less down-at-heel look. But at least a job of that sort is tolerable. What he can't bear is when he has to act as nursemaid, for Ernesto mistrusts children instinctively. He thinks they're cunning, clever, wiser in many things than their scrubbed little faces reveal. Those eyes, so penetrating and so new, have an unerring way of exposing the more shameful secrets and stupid weaknesses of the grown-ups. Ernesto feels a strange uneasiness at being thus observed and subjected to scrutiny. If anyone looks at him critically he begins to tremble out of all control, and an irrational violence seizes him that can only be quieted by fighting back against the one who is censuring him. He has no idea how he managed to control himself the first time the two children pointed to him as if he'd been a comical and rather badly constructed toy, shouting, "Bastard, bastard!" Of course the children had no very clear idea of the meaning of the word. They were repeating it mechanically, parrotwise, because they'd heard it said. But they had a way of mimicking the scornful tone and the wry grimace that always goes with such language.

"*San tat, patrón.*"

With their frayed straw hats wheeling between their fingers, the Indians have been filing up. From their huts, from the moment they were allowed to knock off work, they've been coming to pay their respects to César. They shuffle up to him one by one. First come the ancients surrounded by an aura of respect. They offer their foreheads to the touch of César's hand—a hand from which some kind of magic blessing must surely come. Then they pass on to Zoraida, but only as a matter of courtesy; and the ceremony is repeated in front of her. After that they squat, backs against the veranda pillars.

From his shirt pocket César pulls a bundle of leaf cigars and invites them to smoke. Solemnly the Indians accept as if performing a ritual. In the ever-deepening dusk the burning cigar-tips flicker like fireflies.

"Tell them to begin the preparations. It's almost time for the nine-day prayer to Our Lady of Health. They must sweep the chapel well and pick wild flowers to decorate it."

César repeats the instructions in *tzeltal*. The Indians listen seriously and give their assent. When the *patrón* finishes talking, it's their turn. They recount the details of the day and then lapse into silence, waiting for their master's approval, advice, or scolding. César knows how to suit his voice to the occasion, how to choose the right words. He hands out approval in measured doses so as not to seem too grudging, so that his commands shall have power and his scoldings inspire fear. He knows each man personally. Together they've suffered many dangers and shifts of fortune, and now the men are proving their loyalty. Because times are hard for those who rule, and the government itself is actually inciting the Indians against their masters, handing them over rights the Indians don't deserve and can't use. Loyalty is worth a lot these days when set against the betrayal of some of the others. For many of the men whom César had once counted as his—his own sons among them perhaps—have risen in rebellion. They insist on the minimum wage, refuse to render tithes as they used to, and abandon the farm without a by-your-leave. Of course they're being lured by lumber merchants, strangers who simply want their own businesses to prosper, who have dangled a hook to the Indians and taken them off to be hands in the sawmills or coffee-pickers on the coast. They go, the dullest-witted among them, thinking of profit and unaware that no one returns from those climates alive. They're not worth pitying. They spin the rope for their own hanging. On the other hand to those who stay behind César shows a special deference which is not far removed from gratitude. Nevertheless he keeps his old sternness and severity, and when it comes time to inspect the results of their labours his gesture and voice must necessarily be despotic. It's in his blood, and it's the example he has always seen in neighbour and friend. But in these leisurely talks he knows how to be cordial, as he swings lazily in his hammock, tired from the day's work and satisfied it's done. He entertains the Indians with the tales of his travels as if they were little children: the things he's seen in great cities; the advances of a civilization they don't understand, whose benefits they've never enjoyed. The Indians drink it all in greedily, marvelling. But all they hear is to them only a myth. The world evoked in César's stories is beautiful to be sure, but they wouldn't lift a hand to grasp it, for to them it would be like sacrilege.

Zoraida is bored. The scene she is witnessing is the same as the last and the last but one. She finds it disturbing to contemplate the dark faces all alike and the sound of the language she can't understand. In despair she gets out of her rocking-chair and leans on the balustrade beside Ernesto.

"Do you understand what they're saying?" she asks, pointing to the group of Indians.

"No."

"They're so uncouth they're incapable of learning Spanish. The first time I came to Chactajal I wanted to teach the woman who looked after my baby. Not a word could she get into her head. She couldn't even pronounce the *f*. And yet there are people who say they're the same as us."

Us: the exclusive circle Ernesto is not allowed to violate is broken. But his satisfaction is only partial, for he'd rather it had been César who broke it, for César is the man and the Argüello.

Night has fallen. The Indians begin to rise and take leave. A boy crosses the yard, carrying a torch of burning pinewood to light the beacon. A cold and hostile wind is blowing. A wild monkey squeaks sorrowfully, far away. Zoraida shudders.

"Let's go in. I'm shivering."

In the dining-room, lit by the flickering yellow candles, two maids are laying the table, a heavy affair of rough cedarwood, its feet placed in little clay pots filled with water to stop the ants from crawling up. Seeing the

Chactajal

family enter, the maids hurry to finish laying and go away to serve dinner. While everyone takes his appointed place, Zoraida supervises the correct placing of plates and silver; she changes things about, shaking her head disapprovingly.

"Ernesto, put Mario's napkin straight, please. It's crooked."

The servants enter with a dish of piping-hot beans, the tureen full of hot *tortillas*, and the coffee-pot.

Zoraida serves. They eat in silence. Insects fly in and out of the dark and smash against the mosquito netting. Suddenly the door opens and an Indian appears. His features can hardly be seen in the fluttering candle-light.

Ernesto has just raised his spoon, spilling over with bean broth, to his mouth, and now he is waiting for the Indian to bow with the customary respect. But seconds go by, and the Indian makes not the least movement of submission. Ernesto carefully replaces the spoon on his plate. Zoraida turns a vexed face to César, mutely begging him for an explanation. César speaks to the intruder, asking him something in *tzeltal*. But the Indian replies in Spanish.

"I didn't come alone. My comrades are waiting on the veranda."

Zoraida starts violently back as if an insect had stung her with its poison. What disrespect is this? A low Indian presuming first to burst in without leave to where they are sitting, and then to be speaking in Spanish! And using such words as "comrades", words that not even César, for all he's been educated abroad, is accustomed to use. She gulps down some coffee to wet her dry throat. She expects a prompt answer that will put the man in his place. But César (how odd men are, they always behave unexpectedly!) seems in no hurry. He listens patiently, crumbling a bit of cheese over his beans, while the Indian continues:

Chactajal

"They appointed me, Felipe Carranza Pech, to speak in their name."

"You went to the farms of Tapachula, didn't you? And you nearly came to grief for good and all. How skinny you are. Malaria has wasted you. I thought you weren't going to come back even if you did survive, since you went without paying your *tata's* debts, not to mention your own. . . ."

"I came to see my family and fields."

Zoraida is on the point of laughing sarcastically at such a presumptuous and possessive manner of referring to things that aren't his. But a gesture from César stops her.

"I'll take you back, on condition. . . ."

Felipe doesn't attend to what the *patrón* is saying. He's watching Ernesto. He's quite unaware that he is breaking in on César's admonition when he says:

"My comrades sent me to ask if this is the teacher from Comitán."

Ernesto goes to César's side. He says:

"I'm the one. What do you want with me?"

"My comrades sent me to ask when you'd be starting school."

Ernesto looks wild-eyed toward César as if asking for help. With finicky exactness César is peeling an orange. He doesn't deign to raise his eyes to the Indian, but asks:

"You're very interested in the matter?"

"Yes."

"Why?"

"I want the law to be kept."

Not true. She's dreaming. It's one of those troubled dreams that embitter the nights when she wakes shaking and scared because she has dreamed that somebody's running off with her children. She is compelled to put on the light then, and get up, and hurry barefoot to the children's room to convince herself they're there and that nothing has happened. But now the nightmare doesn't end. And it's she, Zoraida, in the midst of this senseless conversation, listening to the Indian's untiring and inflexible voice hammering away at a single statement:

"The law demands it."

César loses his patience at last and bangs violently on the table.

"What school is it you want opened? I've done my part bringing the teacher. The rest's up to you."

César waits for a faltering reply, for sudden humility, for a proposal of truce. But Felipe's expression doesn't change. And his voice is no different when he says:

"I'll speak to my comrades so that we can all decide together what has to be done."

The door creaks as it opens to let the Indian out. Ernesto gets up, very pale, facing César.

"I warned you in Comitán. I'm not going to give any classes. I don't want to, and I don't know how, and you can't force me."

César pushes away his coffee-cup disgustedly.

"It's cold," he complains to Zoraida, who carries it off to the kitchen. When they're alone, César looks scornfully at Ernesto and says with hypocritical gentleness:

"You're turning out to be the kind that hollers before he's trodden on."

Then, drily:

"You're not the one to issue orders here, but me. And if I order you to earn your keep giving classes, you'll give them."

Zoraida comes back.

"I daren't go into the kitchen. I'm afraid. They're all crowding the veranda. There are lots of them, César."

"Good. Ernesto was just complaining he wouldn't have enough pupils."

The children run to the door and squash their noses

97

against the mosquito netting. But by the time they look out there's not a soul on the veranda.

4

They were sitting on the earth floor round the fire. From time to time one of them took a handful of copal and threw it on to the coals, and the air spread out, burning and aromatic.

"That's what they told me at the big house."

Felipe fell silent, waiting for the others to chew the matter over. The fire lay stars on his face and gave it a red glow.

Kneeling on the ground in a corner of the hut Felipe's wife poured out a jug of bitter *atole*. She got up and gave it to her husband. He touched the edge of the jug with his lips and passed it to the next, who then had authority to speak.

"Our grandparents were builders. They created Chactajal. They built the chapel where we see it now. They sowed grain. They fixed the boundaries of the cattle-pens. It wasn't the *patrones*, the whites; they merely ordered the work to be done and saw it completed. It was our grandparents who did it."

Everyone nodded to show that he who spoke, spoke well. So he went on:

"Years have fallen on the house, yet the house still stands. Thou'rt witness, *tata* Domingo."

The old man agreed:

"It happened so because the white man's authority moved the hand of the Indian. Because the white man's spirit upheld the Indian's labour."

The others were silent, lowering their eyes as if they did not want to see the hut that sheltered them.

Chactajal

The thin wattle walls, crookedly laced with tendrils, were insufficient to protect them from the cold, which used to enter and nibble at them like a wild beast. And when hail sent its pebbles against the thatch, the roof broke. For the Indian is helpless to do better if the white man's will is not behind him.

From the shadow he sat in, someone sighed:

"There's none like them!"

Felipe rocked with laughter. His wife watched him terrified, thinking he'd gone off his head.

"I'm remembering what I saw in Tapachula. There are whites so poor they beg and drop with fever in the streets."

The rest hardened their eyes, unbelieving.

"It was in Tapachula that they gave me the paper to read, and it speaks well. I understood what it says: that we're equal to white men."

One of them jumped up violently.

"On whose oath is that said?"

"On the oath of the President of the Republic."

The other, with a vague fear, asked again:

"What is the President of the Republic?"

Felipe described what he'd seen. He had been in Tapachula when Lázaro Cárdenas went there. Cárdenas had gathered them all beneath the main balcony of the town hall. There he had spoken, promising to return them their lands.

Someone timidly asked:

"Is he a god?"

"He's a man. I was close to him."

(He'd shaken hands, but Felipe couldn't tell them that, it was a secret.)

The others sidled away from Felipe, seeking the shelter of the dark.

"The President of the Republic wants us to receive in-

struction. That's why he sent the teacher, that's why a
school has to be built."

Tata Domingo objected:

"The President of the Republic wants; but has he
power to order it so?"

Proudly Felipe declared:

"He has more power than the Argüellos and the
owners of all the farms around."

Felipe's wife slipped silently to the door. She couldn't
go on listening.

"And where may thy President be?"

"In Mexico City."

"What's Mexico City?"

"A place."

"Further than Ocosingo?"

"And further than Tapachula."

The cowards removed their masks now:

"Let's give no ear to Felipe. He's laying a snare for us."

"If we follow his counsels the *patrón* will whip us."

"Nobody needs a school!"

They bunched close in the shadows as if in need of
protection, as if wanting to run away. For Felipe's words
herded them as the sheep-dog's bark herds the strayed
yearlings.

"It's not I who ask that a school shall be built. It's law.
And there's punishment for anyone who doesn't obey."

"But the guardian of the law is far, and the *patrón* is
here, watching us."

"Today I stood before César, and I spoke in his own
tongue. Look: no harm has befallen me."

"He'll be thinking the stocks have a use."

"He'll be goading the dogs to pursue us!"

"Why should harm fall on us all? The *patrón* doesn't
know which of us went with Felipe."

"The *patrona* left the room once, and then returned."

Chactajal

"But how could she recognize our faces in the dark?"

The fire was almost out. With his fingertip Felipe drew signs in the ashes. Not raising his eyes, in a flat voice, he confessed.

"I said to César: 'These are my comrades.' And I didn't omit the name of one of those who went with me. And I added: 'If one should return to the big house tomorrow it will be with a tasty morsel of false reconciliation. Have a care you don't eat it.'"

Their lips clamped down in surprise. They knew now that what they had done was not to be undone, that they could never retreat.

"Those that wish to go, go. I'll continue alone."

Felipe got to his feet as if inviting them to be off. One of them made a sign to *tata* Domingo to intercede.

"Where can we go now, lad, except where you lead us?"

"I don't want to lead you except toward all our good. There's no reason for fear. Count our number. Thou, *tata* Domingo, with thy three grown sons. And Manuel with his brother, and Jacinto with the men of Pacayal. And Juan who's enough by himself. And as many more if we call them. César's not even got law on his side."

"Whatever thou sayest, Felipe, that shall be our law."

"You'll obey me in all things. I know what's wisest to do. We'll build the school. After each man has done his day's work, so César has nothing against us, we'll build the school. We'll gather the materials ourselves."

"Who will tell us that it is to be done thus, and thus?"

"He who knows."

"*Tata* Domingo."

"I'm very old, lad. It's long since I've done such work. Memory doesn't help me."

"And your sons? Didn't you pass on to them what you know for an inheritance?"

"My sons are servants at the big house. They've quarrelled with me."

"Drop it, Felipe. Another time it will come to pass."

They were in a hurry to go away, happy to have postponed the fulfilment of the project. But Felipe stopped them.

"If there's no one among us that's capable, I'll go looking in other farms and villages. I'll go tomorrow and look. But before I go I'm asking you to bind our will fast."

He went for a bottle of brandy and said as he uncorked it:

"Whoever drinks now, it will be a sign of a pledge."

They all drank. The strong liquor stirred up the fury in each one's breast. So they were bound then with a triple oath.

After the last had gone, Juan returned and found Felipe still squatting by the ashes with doubts in his head.

Felipe couldn't feel confidence in the men he'd picked. The first time he'd spoken to them, coming back from Tapachula, he had found them in discord and near to rebellion. But they walked in darkness still, as he had done before his travels. He told them what he had seen, but it wasn't in order to comfort them, or to lie. Again and again he had to repeat it, so as to break down their sense of inferiority. There was no need to wait for the resurrection of their gods, who had deserted them in the hour of trial, who had allowed their offerings to be thrown as waste scraps to the farmyard animals. How many of them had waited with their eyes closed, yet had never seen them come! No. He had known a man— Cárdenas; he had heard him speak. (He had shaken his hand, but that was his private secret and strength.) And he knew that Cárdenas was meting out justice and that the time had ripened for justice to be fulfilled. He had re-

turned to Chactajal to bring the good news. What else
should he return for? To find the fences round his crops
broken down, and the pigs rooting in the seedbeds, and
other animals trampling with their hooves among the
broken maize stalks? No; he had returned because he
knew it was necessary that one among them all should
put himself in the place of elder brother. The ancients
had had one man to guard them on their pilgrimages, to
counsel them in their dreams. This man had left them the
constancy of his wayfaring, a constancy which they had
rejected too. And since their leader had abandoned them
there had been years and years of stubbing their feet
against stones. No one knew the way to placate the
enemy's power. In times of tribulation they used to visit
the dark caves, laden with gifts. They used to chew bitter
leaves before saying their prayers; and once when they
had grown desperate they chose the best among them and
crucified him. Because the white men keep their God
thus, nailed hand and foot to stop his anger from being
unleashed. But the Indians had watched it rot, that
martyred body they had tried to set up as a safeguard
against misfortune. Then they had grown very quiet, and
more than quiet: mute. When Felipe spoke to them they
hunched their shoulders with a gesture of unconcern.
"Who gave authority to this man?" they asked themselves. Others spoke Spanish, like him. Others had gone
far away and come back again, like him. But Felipe was
the only one among them who could read and write. He
had learnt to do so in Tapachula, after meeting Cárdenas.

The woman came and covered the embers till next day.
Noiselessly, not to disturb Felipe's thoughts, she went and
lay down in a corner. Her closed eyes feigned sleep, but
under her lids images happened, tumbling one over the
other. The dance in the chapel when Felipe had chosen
her, throwing the red handkerchief on to her lap. There

were the afternoons when she returned from the river, her *tzec* still dripping water, and Felipe watched her frowning as he sat on a log by the way. And then the negotiations between the two families. The year of testing had passed, each of them serving in the house of the other's parents. She had done her best, for it was good that Felipe should be her husband. Whenever she ground the corn the dough of the *posol* came out finer and more tasty. (Surreptitiously she used to mix in almond nuts bought from the peddlers; she carried them hidden in her blouse. But her parents-in-law did not know this when they praised the lightness of her hand.) She knew ways to make all the eggs from a single nest burst into yellow chicks.

Felipe sowed the grain and looked after the farm animals. And all this time they did not speak, because they kept the custom of courtship scrupulously, so as not to be estranged from blessings. They used to see each other at feasts, but exchanged no word; they used to meet accidentally on the roads, but they did not stop, and in the encounter only their garments touched, ever so slightly.

At the end of a year the parents met again. They were in full accord that Felipe was clever and Juana fit for work, and they agreed to the match. But they argued the question of the dowry at length. Finally Felipe's family said they would accept her together with a yearling bull calf, a measure of corn, and a bushel of beans. All this she delivered to her in-laws. Felipe bought the carafe of brandy for the wedding feast, and saw to it that she left her golden ear-rings and her coral necklace to pay his parents for the time during which they had given her lodging. Then they went to live together. And many months later, when the curate came to solemnize the nine-day prayer to Our Lady of Health, they married.

Juana had borne no children. A sorcerer had dried up

her womb. In vain she pounded the herbs the women recommended, and drank the potions. In vain she went on certain nights of the month to embrace the silk-cotton tree in the yard. Shame had fallen upon her. But in spite of everything, Felipe did not want to leave her. Whenever he went away—for he seemed to be a rolling stone— she stayed sitting with clasped hands as if she had said good-bye to him for ever. Yet Felipe always returned. But this time, coming back from Tapachula, he wasn't the same any more. His mouth was full of disrespectful words and bold opinions. She, being humble and still full of gratitude to him, did not repudiate him in front of the rest but kept her thoughts silent and secret. She feared this man whom the lands of the seacoast had thrown her back, bitter and harsh as salt, a trouble-maker, restless as wind. And in the depths of her heart, in that deep place where thoughts never reach, she longed for him to be off once again. Far, far away. And that he'd never come back.

A cold gust made her open her eyes, scared. The door slat banged against the lintel, and there in the centre of the hut was *tata* Domingo, head bowed, as if prepared to receive Felipe's orders.

5

"*Patrona, patrona,* here come the peddlers."

With an apron over her head, the servant ran into the chapel.

"In a minute," Zoraida answered without enthusiasm. "Are you coming, Ernesto? If you feel like buying anything, tell them to charge it to our account."

"You go ahead. I'll catch up in a minute."

Zoraida went out into the yard. The other women had

Chactajal

gathered there already, leaving maize half-shelled in the granary, chicks peeping with hunger in the fowl-run, joints of salt beef in the kitchen where the cat could get them. Zoraida knew this but didn't scold them for it. When the peddlers come, custom can go by the board.

Shaping their unbleached cotton hoods into blinkers as a protection against the sharp reflection of the sun, the women fixed their eyes on the road. The peddlers were coming down the last slope. It was possible to count as many as eight mules laden with heavy bales wrapped in rush matting. The women clapped delightedly.

"You there, have you money?"

"I've been saving up all year."

For in those huge bundles of sacking the peddlers were bringing an inexhaustible treasure-trove: brass kettles with fat and shining paunches; grinding-mills with fine large handles, brilliantly polished copper cauldrons. For the girls, coral chokers, broad ribbons, bolts of cotton and percale, powders for mixing love potions. For the children there were candies dyed red with an aniseed in the middle, bald monkeys on sticks and nervous jumping jacks. The men could buy machetes with blades that shuddered like snakes, and woven sashes and palm hats inset with mirrors.

"How far d'you suppose they'll have come?"

"From Ocosingo, perhaps."

"From San Carlos."

"Further than Comitán."

For these peddlers (natives of the district of Custitali in San Cristóbal, from which fact they derive their name, Custitaleros) wander the length and breadth of Chiapas. They are picturesque, with their singsong accent and their halting pronunciation; and they are as useful as carrier ants.

A boy hurried to open the big yard door. The peddlers

106

slid off the haunches of their mules and crossed the thresh-
hold. Wrapped as usual in their thick woollen blankets,
they advanced with much hard stamping to shake the
dust from their shoes. With a stick they removed the burs
clinging to their clothes, then sidled up to pay their respects to Zoraida. They asked to be allowed a small
corner and leave to sell their wares. In their wake came a
woman riding a fine white mule. She had wrapped up her
head and veiled her face with a transparent scarf. The
cloth of her dress was of good quality. When he saw that
she was about to dismount, one of the peddlers proffered
his interlocked hands as a stirrup. Timidly and clumsily
she placed her feet there, and then on the ground, and
stepped forward hesitantly. Her limbs had lost supple-
ness and were swollen from so many miles of travel. She
tottered slightly as if she were drunk. Zoraida was watching her closely. Something about her seemed familiar.
Knitting her forehead, she tried to recollect what it was,
and suddenly she exclaimed in a tone of mingled surprise,
alarm, and scolding:

"Matilde!"

Matilde it was. When she heard her name called, she
stopped dead. As the shawl did not seem to be sufficient
disguise, she hid her face in both hands.

A peddler went up to Zoraida.

"With your leave, *patrona*, we'll hand the lady over to
you."

Another explained:

"When we were passing through Palo María the girl
Matilde looked for a chance to speak to us."

"She offered us money if we'd bring her to Chactajal."

"We set out at midnight."

"None saw us go."

"In case they should follow, we said we were going to
Las Delicias."

"God and the Most Holy Mother can vouch for it, we've looked after her as if she were our own."

"We haven't come to render an evil account."

"Is it true what they say, Matilde?"

Matilde nodded. She couldn't speak yet.

"Ask her if we accepted a cent of the money she offered."

"We're Christians, *patrona*."

"Very well. I'll see you're rewarded."

Zoraida cut the conversation short. While Matilde, leaning on Zoraida's arm, climbed the steps from the yard on to the veranda, the farm-boy set the chapel bell swinging to announce that the peddlers were about to unpack their wares. Ernesto heard the bare, quick patter of Indian feet as people hurried to the big house. He hesitated a moment, then followed.

Zoraida led Matilde into the drawing-room and forced her to lie on a wooden bench. An Indian from among the servants—annoyed because she had to be here while the others negotiated with the peddlers—brought a cup of orange tea.

Zoraida put her arm behind Matilde's head to prop her up.

"Drink this, it will do you good."

Matilde made an effort to take a sip.

"No. I've got a lump here. It's days since I could swallow."

She let her head fall back as though it had become disjointed.

Matilde's eyes followed the Indian out of the room. She didn't speak till the woman had gone.

"Are your people to be trusted, Zoraida?"

"Utterly. Why?"

"Because if Francisca discovers I'm here, she'll kill me."

Zoraida couldn't help smiling.

"Francisca must be displeased that you've come without permission. But as to killing. . . ."

"Yes, she'll kill me!"

Matilde screamed in a sharp, disagreeable voice. Zoraida got to her feet.

"You're very nervous. Rest a while. We'll speak later."

Matilde held her back, tugging peevishly at her sleeve.

"Don't go. Don't leave me alone. I'm afraid."

"Afraid of what, child?"

Matilde looked at her surprised, as if the question were too silly to need a reply. But she said:

"I'm afraid of Francisca."

"Of Francisca?"

"Don't repeat what I say as if you thought I were raving, because I'm not mad. Francisca hasn't been able to make me mad!"

Zoraida sat down again beside Matilde.

"Why have you quarrelled?"

"It's not a law suit or anything. You know I've always respected and loved her."

(Francisca had taken the place of their mother, who had died when Matilde was born. And from that day all parties and amusements had ended, together with Francisca's engagement to Jaime Rovelo. Francisca had devoted herself to looking after Matilde. She used to watch over her all night long when she was ill. She bought her the most expensive toys, and the prettiest dresses. She herself taught Matilde how to read, because in Palo María there was no one else to do it. For years they had lived on the farm, working in order to be rich so that Matilde could buy whatever she pleased and so that she could offer her husband a fine dowry. But as it turned out, Matilde's soul was like an empty jug, reasonably content with whatever went into it. She was tied to her sister's apron strings, and when she reached the appropriate age she said she didn't want to marry but that she wanted to live with Francisca always. They had lived together contentedly until Romelia, estranged from her husband, had returned home to come like a wall between them. She set them on edge with her everlasting, uninterrupted chatter and the terrible headaches she suffered. Francisca tolerated and humoured her sister. Age had not made her more reliable, less of a chatterbox, or less frivolous. But when the talk started about agrarian reforms and new laws, and the Indians angrily claimed their rights, Francisca began to consider sending her sisters away. Romelia jumped at the idea of going to Mexico City, but in order that the trip should not appear too much like an escape she complained more than ever of indispositions, and insisted that she would have to consult specialists in the capital. Matilde refused to go with her. How could she abandon Francisca at such a time, so fraught with dangers? Yet it appeared that now, only a few weeks later, Matilde was running away from Francisca as though she had been her worst enemy.)

"This kind of difference blows over. You'll make it up. I'll ask César to act as peacemaker between you."

Matilde disagreed vehemently.

"If it's a burden on you to have me here, I'll go. There's sure to be some charitable soul who'll take me in. But to return to Palo María—never. Do you hear? Never!"

(It was the first time Matilde had spoken in such a tone. She had always been over-humble, submissive, and docile, yet now she was rising against Francisca like a fighting cock. Why? There had never been disputes over money. A man . . . no, it wasn't possible. After her break with Jaime, Francisca had rebuffed whatever suitors had turned up. She used to say in that outspoken way of hers, not sparing even her own defects, that they couldn't be after her for anything but her money, for she'd never been pretty, and now she was old into the bargain. And Matilde had never had a young man. Perhaps she'd fallen in love for the first time and Francisca was opposing the match. . . .)

"It's no longer possible to live in Palo María. The Indians give themselves such airs."

"You've jumped from the frying pan into the fire."

"But César's here, and he's all of a man."

"You're surely not going to suggest that Francisca isn't one. Why, she's always worn trousers, and carried a machete into the bargain."

Matilde's lips puckered in a gesture of bitter mockery.

"Trousers and machete. D'you know what she did? She set up the stocks in the middle of the yard. And at the point of the whip, she put the Indians in them and left them happily there in the sun. Those that couldn't bear it, died. But not just like that. Before they died Francisca seized them and. . . ."

"What?"

Noticing Zoraida's morbid anticipation, Matilde turned her flushed cheeks to the wall.

"Nothing. I'm ashamed to say."

Zoraida got up, frustrated.

"But the woman must be out of her mind! To do such a thing now, when the situation's so delicate."

"The Indians came to the big house and threatened us. Do you think Francisca was frightened? She told them if they didn't like her treatment they could go."

"Easily said. And what will you all live on if the Indians abandon Palo María?"

"Francisca doesn't care. She hasn't been out to the fields since. She's dismissed all the cow-men. From the veranda of the big house we've been watching the buzzards swooping to eat the cattle that are dying of worms, and the little newborn calves that are falling ill because there's no one to vaccinate them."

"But my darlings, where's it all going to end?"

"Francisca never goes out of the house now. She ordered all the rooms to be draped in black. Then she herself drove the nails into a coffin and painted it black and put it where her bed stood before, and there she lies, and she doesn't sleep, I've seen her. She can't sleep."

(Those endless nights of wakefulness. Matilde locked into her room, alert to the slightest noise, trembling even at the flutter of bats in the creaking rafters. And Francisca pacing up and down the veranda wrapped in a black shawl. Then came that cry of terror, a pursuit through the patio amid the mad barking of dogs and the frightened neighing of horses. At dawn they had gone out—the servants and Matilde—to look for Francisca. They had found her still as death at the foot of a gorge, battered by stones and scratched by thorns. When she came to herself she said she'd had a vision. The rumour ran among the Indians that the *dzulúm* had dragged her there, and if he hadn't taken her off altogether it was only because she'd made a pact to serve and obey him.)

"That about the *dzulúm's* just a tale."

"Ask Francisca. She says she saw him. They spoke."

"Those are just tales to scare the Indians."

"The Indians come and ask her advice. And when she tells one of them that such and such a thing will happen, it happens."

(There'd been a man called Emilio Jatón. She had said to him: "You'll not reach home safe and sound." And on the way a fearful anguish seized him and a heart attack of some sort, and he fell down in a faint. With the help of four of them they had carried him to his hut. There he lay for weeks, prostrate and near to death on his rush mat until finally they had sent a little offering of food to the *patrona* and had begged her to come and cure him. Then Francisca had prepared a drink and had given it to him to take. The Indian recovered as if by the touch of a hand. He was working now by the week in the big house. . . .)

"May Holy Saint Caralampio have mercy on us!"

"I begged, on my knees I begged Francisca that we should go to Comitán. We have money saved up, we could buy a house or a shop. But Francisca replied that if I said such a thing again she'd do harm to me too."

(Francisca's eyes had been glassy when she made these threats. Since that moment she had watched Matilde suspiciously, had driven her away so that she could recite runes and curses alone.)

"How calm you were to put up with it! When you tell· César, he's going to be cross with you for not having come at the beginning."

"How could I? It's not my house."

"You've more right to be here than I."

It hurt Zoraida to say this, but it was true. The house had belonged to Matilde's grandparents, so that she was neither a foreigner nor an outsider. Whereas Zoraida. . . .

To hide her chagrin, she said:

"Come with me. We'll see they get a room ready for you."

They opened the door. Ernesto was standing there, quite unashamed of having been caught eavesdropping. He returned Zoraida's inquiring gaze without flinching, just as if they hadn't caught him listening there at all. What a hypocrite. A bastard he certainly must be!

6

"It's very sad to be an orphan!" How many times they had told Matilde so, stroking her head pityingly!

Chactajal

"This girl will be dragged up any way God wills, like fodder for the horses, because her second mother, Francisca, is still very young and she'll marry. And the child will become a stumbling block. And if Francisca doesn't marry? Then it will be worse. There'll be no man in this family to keep order."

Matilde would go away with her head hanging and one word buzzing about her ears: orphan. They were bad, those visitors. They said all that because they supposed she was alone, that she had no one. They knew that the only portrait of her mother—the one in the drawing-room—was hung so high that Matilde couldn't reach to see it, even if she climbed on to a chair. And from down below the glass broke up the rays of light into reflections that blurred the face and made it unrecognizable. But she had a secret and a refuge. She had discovered it one day by chance in the playroom. There was a large cupboard, and inside, swinging on their hangers, with balls of naphtha in them to keep them from the moths, were her mother's clothes. That was where Matilde went whenever she was sad, whenever Francisca scolded her for some mischief, or whenever visitors came predicting trouble. She stayed there for hours at a time while the others shouted for her, searching in the orchard or the kitchen or the cattle-pens. For hours on end she stayed there, breathing the smell of disinfectant, buffered from outside threats, well protected by the cushion of darkness. There she lay sleeping, a little cocoon in a corner, exhausted from having wept so long. Once a hand on her shoulder had wakened her. It was Francisca. Without a word she had taken Matilde in her arms and kissed her eyelids, still damp. But the same afternoon Francisca had ordered the cupboard to be cleared out and she gave the clothes away to the poor.

"Matilde, my dear, I need a cone of sugar."

Chactajal

With a startled movement, Matilde undid the bunch of keys she carried pinned to her belt—Zoraida had handed them over to her the day she arrived in Chactajal because she herself had been busy preparing for the nine-days' prayer—and went to the larder. Matilde had taken charge of the housekeeping. She ordered the meals, and gave out the food to the kitchen. She looked after the cleaning of the rooms. And she herself undertook the mending of the clothes.

How Francisca would have laughed to see her. Matilde had always been lazy. She liked lying in the hammock from morning till night, swinging there day-dreaming. (It was always a party. Matilde was sitting under a glass lamp. The rustle of her dress spilt round her. In her hand was a wineglass. There was music. An orchestra was playing a waltz, and couples were dancing. First she looked at his feet, shod in patent leather, then at his suit of good cashmere, and the white shirt, and the neatly knotted tie. But just as she was about to look into his face, some cry or other, a flutter of the sparrow-hawks hovering over the hen-coop, a door banging in the wind, something, anything, woke her. This man's face—and he had to turn up eventually because she was fated to be his—was always hidden from her just as her mother's had been.) But here in Chactajal it was different. She was in a strange house and had to be very obliging. Set out to please and you'll be at ease, so wise people say. Matilde did her best to fulfil the tasks given her. She was afraid they would disdain her for taking what she hadn't earned. At first she cherished the hope that Francisca—shocked at finding her gone—would come to her senses and look for her. Away down the road she seemed to see the figure of her elder sister, with her dark silk sunshade. But Francisca accepted the separation with never a word of protest or the least attempt to discover where

Chactajal

Matilde was living. When Francisca found herself alone, she shut herself into the black-curtained rooms of Palo María and refused to see or speak to anyone except those Indians who recognized her powers and came to her for advice. Travellers, annoyed because she had not given them hospitality, spread her reputation as a witch: it ran from farm to farm, to Comitán and even as far as San Cristóbal.

"Poor child, Matilde, to be ending up as maid-of-all-work when you were once a *patrona*."

Matilde smiled resignedly. The world is clad and shod in changes of fortune such as these, in just such sudden, inexplicable betrayals. Think of it: that a servant should talk to her as an equal, with compassion, and that Matilde should have to be grateful for it, because she'd never been so alone and uncared for.

"The dead man and the jailed stink after three days, Matilde dear."

It was true. Matilde lived on edge, ready to run off and escape at the slightest hint her presence might not be wanted in that house. But there was nowhere to go. The only thing it was possible to do was to try and make herself so scarce that she ceased to be a nuisance to the others. Mealtimes—which was when they all met—were a torture to her. She made the excuse of having to supervise the serving in order not to sit with them at table. At first this seemed exaggerated behaviour and they insisted she should join them. But afterwards it became a natural habit for Matilde to eat in the kitchen later, with the servants. Even there the food choked her so that she could not swallow it. She would push her plate away discouraged.

"Why should you be eating your heart out for nothing? You'd best ask Don César to blow you one, and so you'll find out what he wants of you."

Matilde took this advice. One afternoon when they were all taking a siesta on the veranda, she approached them with a bottle of brandy.

"César, as you're the man of the house, the head, I've come to ask you a favour."

"Yes?"

"I'm tired of being here. It's time you blew on me so my shame can go from me and I can rest in peace."

César answered gravely that he had nothing against her in his heart. He took the bottle Matilde offered him, uncorked it, and filled his mouth with a swill of the strong liquor. Matilde shut her eyes and received it full in the face as he spat. The alcohol stung her eyelids, but she had wiped out her shame. He had reconciled her with the people of the house, and now that she knew their intentions toward her she could rest in peace. She spent the afternoon with her cousins, and they all went bathing together in the river. When they were home again they sat in the farmyard singing, while Ernesto played the guitar. He had a good voice.

From a little cedar box she had brought with her from Palo María, Matilde took a handful of herbs. Hiding them under her apron she went to Ernesto's bedroom. She could not possibly leave the task of cleaning this room to the servants. They were too slipshod. They left dust in the cracks between the bricks, muddled the papers, or forgot to change the water in the vases. Matilde took the sheets laid out on the windowsill in the sun, shook them vigorously, and spread them on the bed. She laid the blankets on top, and put the bunch of herbs under the pillow.

"What made you invent such a lie?"

"Ernesto!"

Surprise made Matilde blush. Her voice was only just raised above its normal pitch. She was trying to show a sense of offended dignity and severe pride, but she had had no time to take her hand from the pillow, and she was trembling as if she had been caught doing something wrong.

"What lie?"

"That you came to Chactajal because you were running away from your sister. You weren't running away from anything. You came to find me."

Now she was sure that Ernesto had seen her put the herbs under the pillow. She was so desperate about it that she plucked up courage to reply:

"What right have you to come and insult me? I've never confided in you. I. . . ."

"Don't speak to me in that tone of voice, Matilde."

"And you're being too familiar besides."

"Why not?"

Matilde stamped her foot on the ground crossly.

"We're not equals."

"What's the difference? You're here because you have to be, like me."

"It's true I'm in an unfortunate position. But there are things no misfortune can take from me."

"Such as?"

"I . . . I'm an Argüello!"

"So am I."

"But ill-begotten."

She had answered instinctively and thoughtlessly, not meaning to offend. Now she stopped short, horrified at herself for having been capable of speaking such a word. But really it wasn't her fault. Ernesto had forced her into it. In what way had she provoked him that he should come pestering her like this—violently, brutally, hatefully?

"I was born in shame. It's not my fault, but I was born in shame. The priest didn't want to let me go to his school, because I was the child of an evil thought. My mother had to go to him grovelling before he would agree to take me. Even then he didn't let me sit with the others. I had a corner to myself, because the women complained that their children were allowed to mix with rabble. I was cleverer than they, I got the best marks, but at the end of the year the prize wasn't mine. It went to someone else, to Jaime Rovelo's son. Because I'm a bastard. Have you heard the way the children shout it? Bastard! Bastard!"

This speech touched Matilde. More gently she answered:

"Let me go, Ernesto."

"Don't you think what I'm saying is funny?"

"No."

"So it's true."

"What?"

"That you love me."

Matilde began to weep and Ernesto drew her to his breast. Her hot, flowing tears soaked his shirt.

"Yes, it's true. I couldn't have been mistaken. I saw it from the first, from the way you looked at me."

Matilde loosed herself slowly from Ernesto's grasp.

"You're crazy. Let me go."

"Why?"

Matilde went to the window and in the tone of one who is exposing herself naked, she cried:

"Can't you see? Look at me, look at me well, at these wrinkles. I'm old, Ernesto, I might be your mother."

She moved away to screen herself from the light. She pulled herself together and with her back to the wall like an animal pursued, she waited. Ernesto had no idea of the pain in her words, of the self-laceration of such a confession. He saw only that his will was being thwarted. He realized that this woman was escaping from his clutches, that he hadn't been able to subdue her, that he'd failed.

Chactajal

"Don't speak my mother's name. Don't dare compare yourself with her!"

Matilde's face was stiff and utterly pale. Her obstinate silence made Ernesto burn still hotter.

"You think you're better than she is, more honourable. Why? Because you'd rather dry up as an old maid than sacrifice yourself for a son's sake. She's sacrificed herself for me, and I'm not ashamed she's my mother. I'm not ashamed to be seen with her in the street though she's poorly dressed and barefoot and blind."

Ernesto let himself drop into a chair. With his handkerchief he wiped away the sweat running down his forehead. Was he going crazy? Why had he let himself carry on like this? What need was there for this woman to see the conflict that had been torturing him since he was born? She would only go afterwards and tell the others, and they would laugh at him. He lifted his eyes, blazing with animosity. Matilde had turned her back so as not to look at him. She said:

"Under your pillow there's a bunch of herbs. They're so you'll sleep well and have sweet dreams."

She turned toward the door, but Ernesto took one leap and caught up with her.

"You put them there. Why?"

Matilde avoided his gaze.

"Because I don't want you to suffer."

Ernesto's lips rested against her cheek and one by one her wrinkles were smoothed away. She became young again as she used to be. As when she sat under the glass lamp with a tumbler of wine in her hand. The footsteps, muffled by the music from the orchestra, drew close. She looked first at the shoes. They were old. The trousers, patched; the shirt-collar open. No tie. And then the face: Ernesto's face. Her hand let the wineglass drop and it fell to the floor, broken.

Chactajal

7

"We shall choose a place for the building, high on a hill. Blessed because it looks upon the sun's birth, blessed because favourable constellations of stars are ruling over it, blessed because in its entrails under the earth we shall find the roots of a silk-cotton tree.

"We shall dig and injure our mother earth, and to appease the groans from her mouth we shall spill the blood of an animal in sacrifice. The cock shall be mightily spurred and shall drip blood from the wound in its throat.

"We have said: it shall be the work of us all. Behold our work, created by each man's giving. The women came here to show the manner of their love, hidden as deep as the foundations. Here the men proved the measure of their strength, which is like the supporting pillar and the lintel of stone and the wall before which the wind stops its headlong stampede. The ancients poured out their science here, invisible as the empty space the vault has consecrated, trusty as the vault itself.

"This is our house. Here the memory we have lost shall come to be like the maiden redeemed from the river's rage. And she shall sit among us and teach us the doctrine. And we shall listen to her reverently. And our faces shall shine as when the dawn lays its light upon them."

That was the way Felipe wrote down how the school was built, for those who came after.

8

The day of Our Lady of Health dawned cloudy. The chapel bell had been ringing since sunrise and its doors were open wide. Indians entered with offerings: bunches

121

of wild flowers, measures of incense, harvest tithes. All these were brought and laid at the Virgin's feet, which were almost hidden by the ample broad folds of her dress embroidered with seed-pearls that shone in the candle-light. The trek to and fro of bare feet withered the cypress spread on the floor. Its ever-weakening scent rose and mingled with the sweat of the crowd, with the bitter smell of milk from the newborn babies and the whiffs of brandy clinging to objects, to people, and to the air itself. Effigies of more saints wrapped up like mummies in yards and yards of coarse cotton leaned against the wall or lay on the ground. Out stuck their disproportionately small heads, the only part of their bodies that were not swaddled in cloth.

The women, coiled on the ground, were rocking their snivelling babies smothered under *rebozos*. Their high-pitched, piercing voices began a monologue which, since it was directed at the images whose swathing bound them and reduced them to impotence, acquired a harsh inflexion as if they had been blaming or reproving a dull-witted servant, as if their role were that of conquerors before the vanquished. Then the women turned distracted glances towards the niche which held the lovely Lady of Health in thrall. Supplicating, they laid bare their wretchedness and suffering before the enamelled and unmoving eyes. Their single, communal voice became the voice of a whipped dog, of a cow that had been cruelly separated from its calf. They shouted aloud for help. In their own dialect, liberally interspersed with Spanish words, they complained of hunger, sickness, and of the ambushes the sorcerers laid for them. Little by little the voices were overcome with exhaustion and faded off into a hoarse murmur, as of water trickling among stones. One might have thought the sudden spasms that shook these women's breasts were sobs, only that the pupils of their eyes, fixed stubbornly on the altar, were shrouded in a dry and mineral opacity.

The men staggered into the chapel and knelt beside their womenfolk. With their arms stretched out crosswise, they succeeded in preserving a balance their drunkenness made otherwise almost impossible, and their swollen tongues stumbled over the muddled prayers, one word at enmity with another. Noisily they wept, beating their heads with their fists, and then, tired out, drained as it might be by haemorrhage, they slid into unconsciousness. Between snores, out of dreams, they uttered threats. Then their womenfolk bent over them and with the fringes of their *rebozos* wiped away the sweat that soaked the men's temples, and the viscous threads of saliva that trickled from the cracks between their lips. Hours and hours the women stayed there, quietly, watching them sleep.

The big house turned its back on these ceremonies and refused to witness them. The *patrones* pretended to know nothing so as not to appear to connive, by their presence there, at a cult the curate had condemned and had labelled idolatrous. For many years past these demonstrations of the Indians had been forbidden, and now that relations between César on the one hand and Felipe's faction on the other had become so strained, César did not wish to make them still worse by imposing his own will in a matter about which he was, in his heart of hearts, indifferent, and which to the Indians meant the perpetuation of an age-old custom. By the final night, when César and all his family would attend the prayers for the ninth day, there would be no trace of the events of the days before. The effigies wrapped in their coarse cotton would have been put away once more in the corners where they lived the year round. Fresh branches would replace the trampled cypress, and the guttering candles would be exchanged for others with new wicks freshly burning. But now in the precincts of the chapel the Indians, free for a while from their master's eye, sent up their barbaric prayers and went through the motions of a simple ritual which was a distorted inheritance from pagan times. It was a heavy-hearted gesture of unity and supplication, a request for truce such as a child might make, trembling under the invisible power that lays its cloak over all things.

Zoraida was pacing impatiently up and down the big house veranda. Suddenly she stopped, facing César.

"Are those Indians going to howl like monkeys all the blessed day?"

César paused a few moments deliberately before taking his eyes from the newspaper he was reading for the umpteenth time. He answered:

"It's their custom."

"No it isn't. Can't you remember? Other years they've gone into the forest and we used to hear them far away. But they don't respect us any more. And you take it without turning a hair."

"I know the grease my cattle's made of, Zoraida."

"They wouldn't dare do this if Felipe weren't preaching rebellion."

César sighed resignedly and folded his paper. Zoraida's tone demanded more attention than the vague, marginal kind he had been conceding her up till now. As if he had been explaining to a child, and a stupid one at that, César replied:

"We can't do anything. These things are—how shall I put it?—details. They annoy you, but if you were to bring an accusation before the judge, they wouldn't be considered a crime."

Zoraida arched her eyebrows in a gesture of exaggerated surprise.

"Ah! So you've thought of going to the judge." Then sarcastically:

"This is a new departure. You've always managed your own affairs before."

César flung the paper to the floor in irritation.

"That's just it: before. But can't you see the situation's changing? The Indians dare provoke us now because they are ripe for anything. They only want a pretext to come toppling round our ears, and I'm not giving it to them."

Zoraida offered a disdainful smile whose intention did not escape César.

"I don't care what you think, I know what I have to do. And stop fidgeting, you set my nerves on edge."

Blushing with shame, Zoraida stopped. César had never allowed himself to talk like that, especially in front of outsiders. In her pride she was ready to expostulate and excuse herself, but she did not feel sure any more of her power over this man, and the fear of making herself ridiculous kept her silent.

Matilde had witnessed the scene between her cousins with growing embarrassment. Without even a muttered excuse she now rose to go. Ernesto watched her and was about to make a move to follow, but Matilde's coldness stopped him. She didn't want to speak to him. She'd been avoiding him for days, since *that* day.

"What's your opinion, Ernesto?"

César's question brought him sharply to the present. He shrugged his shoulders non-commitally, but that didn't satisfy César, who went on:

"What I'm saying is, we have to be prudent. Only a woman would think of acting like a wild cat."

Zoraida sat down in the chair Matilde had left. Her new dress would be creased, and the knowledge of it gave her a sour satisfaction.

"It looks as if the prudent are just plain scared."

Chactajal

Ernesto spoke with malice, but César straightened himself scarcely perceptibly and asked:

"Have you heard the latest news?"

The others were silent. He went on:

"Of course, cooped up here, you can't know, but I've seen when I go to the fields. The Indians have built a hut on Crotch Hill."

"For the school?"

"Who said they could?"

Ernesto and Zoraida were vying with each other for the first word. Sunk back again in his hammock, César was enjoying the effect of his announcement. He said gently:

"Holidays are over, Ernesto."

"But I warned you in Comitán. . . ."

Ernesto would have given much to get away from this place, but he didn't want to say so or they would scoff at him for running away and being a coward.

"You can go back if you like. You can take your chance and go. Tell me, is what I'm asking you a sacrifice? I won't forget to recompense you, and that's on the word of an Argüello."

César's voice was almost affectionate, but Ernesto wasn't going to be trapped again. Delighted to be able to show his generosity and his disdain in any way possible, he declared:

"If I stay it's not because of the reward but because *I* at least keep my word."

And he stamped off, sorry that Matilde had not seen how boldly he had behaved.

César's comment was caustic:

"Poor neurasthenic!"

Zoraida didn't want to agree and thus ally herself with her husband. She remained serious and aloof. César picked up the newspaper he had dropped and went on reading. Zoraida fidgeted, rocking in the squeaky chair and sighing pointedly. These slight noises and the deliberate way in which they were made grated on César's nerves. He pretended to concentrate on his newspaper, but was very far from being able to do so. Zoraida knew this, and was pleased when a good reason for interrupting him appeared.

"It looks as if we're going to have a visitor."

César looked down the road. A rider was advancing quickly along it, disappearing and reappearing again with the rises and dips in the hills. He didn't dismount but opened the yard gate and from there called:

"Good day, sir and ma'am."

César and Zoraida rose to receive him.

"Come in. You're very welcome."

"I'd like to unsaddle my horse. Where's the stable?"

"Don't worry. The stable boy will look after that. Boy! Boy!"

César's call faded away and nobody answered. Zoraida lowered her eyelids to hide her shame, but César extricated himself from the predicament with a show of good humour, explaining:

"Today's a fiesta. . . . I was forgetting the hired men are off work. . . . You can tether your horse to that post and the saddle will sit nicely on the railing."

The new arrival climbed the steps. He shook hands with César and greeted Zoraida with a perfunctory nod.

"Isn't there a cool drink we could offer the gentleman, Zoraida? A glass of . . . what would you care for? You know what a ranch house is supplied with."

So he wanted to humiliate her in front of this man too, making her go to the kitchen to prepare a drink. He knew perfectly well that the servants were at the fiesta. Zoraida tightened her lips, resentful but nevertheless prepared to obey. The newcomer saved the situation with a refusal.

"Thanks. I just passed the stream and drank my *posol*."

With effusive attention to the stranger, Zoraida offered him her rocking-chair. But the guest refused that too. Leaning against the balustrade, his hands in his trouser pockets, he asked:

"Don't you recognize me, Don César?"

César scrutinized him. The swart face and bushy eyebrows awakened no memory.

"I'm Gonzalo Utrilla, son of Gregoria that was."

"You? But why did no one tell me? Look Zoraida, it's my godson."

Gonzalo took the measure of César with an ironical glance.

"When I last saw you, you were a bit of a thing, so high. And now you're a fine strapping man."

"All thanks to your care, Godfather."

César decided to ignore the irony in this, but his tone was more circumspect when he said:

"You left Comitán a long time ago, didn't you?"

"I became a rolling stone as they say."

"And you've not settled down yet?"

Gonzalo thought he detected a slight reserve, as of someone who is afraid he is going to be asked a favour. Proudly he hastened to clear the matter up:

"I work for the Government."

César adopted a paternal attitude, and from the heights reproached him:

"For the Government. Aren't you ashamed?"

But at once he rued his lack of tact:

"No, really I'm getting behind the times. Of course you have nothing to be ashamed of. Capable and clever people are in the Government. But in my day to serve the Government was considered rather debased. It amounted to being . . . well, a thief."

"It's a good thing your day is past and gone, Don César.

Chactajal

That's to say, assuming things wouldn't have altered otherwise. The Government gives me food. On the other hand the rich have never thought I deserved so much."

All enemies are big ones, César thought. If only he'd been kinder to this Gonzalo when he was a bit of an Indian lad! The boy used to visit them on Sundays, and would sit for hours and hours on the stoop of the great door, waiting for César to condescend to come out. It had been cupboard love, not real affection, of course, because the usual thing is for godparents to give their godsons pocket-money on feast-days. But often—he repented of it now—instead of going out personally to see the little boy and slip a few coins into his hands, César had sent the servant with a present chosen without thought and quite worthless. Once when the present was a stick of sugar, Gonzalo had refused to accept it and he had never come back. Till now.

"What exactly is your work?"

"I'm an agrarian inspector."

"And have you come to Chactajal on official business?"

"I'm doing a routine turn of the highlands. I've found a lot of irregularities in the treatment of the Indians. The bosses are still taking advantage of the peasants' ignorance. But the peasants are not without protection any more."

"And what happens when you discover these irregularities?"

"You'll see, Godfather."

"I trust not. My affairs are in order."

"Let's hope so."

Gonzalo let his words drop, precise and cutting as the blow of an axe. Disappointed that he couldn't start a friendly chat, César had to surrender.

"You'll be pressed for time. If there's any way we can help. . . . What do you have to do?"

"Talk to the Indians."

"You're lucky to come today. You'll find them all in the chapel. As I said apropos of the stable boy, it's a feast-day, the day of Chactajal's patron saint. You're really in luck."

"It wasn't luck, Don César, it was calculation."

Gonzalo started off down the steps. César caught up with him and asked:

"Won't you stay and eat with us?"

"No, I'm going on to Palo María."

As César insisted on walking along beside him, Gonzalo said almost sharply:

"I'd be grateful if you were not to accompany me, Godfather. I want to speak to the Indians quite freely."

César stood with his back to the house until the figure of Gonzalo had vanished and could no longer be picked out among the great crowd of Indians. Then he turned to his wife and ordered:

"Prepare a glass of lemonade. Get Matilde to take it to the chapel. Gonzalo's going to make a speech. He'll be thirsty no doubt."

Zoraida looked at her husband in disapproval.

"Matilde . . . how should I know where Matilde is? She's never to be found when she's wanted. But if you want to stoop so low, I'll do it myself."

César went up to Zoraida and seized her by the arm. She stiffened.

"You haven't understood me, Zoraida, you never do."

"No, I'm not a fool. I can't understand the moon's phases even if you explain them to me a hundred times. But I understand when someone insults me. I have my dignity."

"It's not a question now of dignity or surrendering to a good-for-nothing like Gonzalo. I wanted to send Matilde because I wanted her to hear what he'll say to the

Indians. We've got to keep an eye on him. He's dangerous."

The weeping, the howling of the Indians had ended. Now and then the whine of a restless child reached the house, or the sudden explosion of a rocket. Zoraida edged away from her husband.

"Gonzalo's talking to them now. Can you hear?"

"It's impossible to catch the words."

As she climbed the steps Zoraida remarked in disgust: "The sky will clear all in good time."

"Shut up!"

A sound was echoing against the chapel walls. Uncontrolled shouts, drunken exclamations, the heavy movements of the multitude. And suddenly, breaking away from the crowd and running through the yard, was Matilde with head bare, hands empty, and the general appearance of one going mad. Zoraida hurried to meet her, but Matilde pushed her aside roughly and didn't stop till she was face to face with César. She was out of breath: her phrases snapped in two.

"He told them . . . he told them they haven't a boss any more. That they own the ranch, that they're not obliged to work for anyone. And he made them a sign, raising his clenched fist."

"That was when the Indians began yelling, was it?"

"And Felipe was there," said Zoraida.

Matilde denied this.

"He came only when he heard the shouting. He doesn't like going to the chapel. But he pushed through them and went up to the man, the man who's come. . . ."

"That precious godson of mine, Gonzalo Utrilla."

"And he shook hands and began telling him they'd built a school and that you've brought a teacher from Comitán, and whether they could ask for the classes to begin. The man said yes. Then they all wanted to come in

131

a body to the big house to talk to you, but the man advised them to come tomorrow, when they'd sobered up. He says that the bosses have always traded on the Indians' drunken bouts."

"Anyhow," said César, "we must be ready in case they come. I'll get my pistol, and you'd all better lock yourselves up."

"Yes, at once."

But when César was out of earshot, Zoraida turned suspiciously to Matilde:

"What were you doing in the chapel? Why were you there?"

"Let me go, Zoraida, you're hurting. Don't look at me like that. I only wanted to pray."

Before Zoraida could ask more, Matilde had run away.

9

Waking to the noise of steps on the veranda, to the flurry with which the animals met the daybreak, each sound was enough to force Matilde out of the soft and mossy cave of her sleeping, sending her back into herself in a groping search for the place where her pain lay. Even before she had become aware of waking to a strange house, far away from Francisca, far from happy times, Matilde perceived that her waking was necessarily to suffering. In vain she pressed her lids tight, begging sleep for a moment's further truce. The violent clanging of the chapel bell, the patter of bare feet, the shouts in *tzeltal*, all conspired against her and thrust her out into that chill inclemency called her conscience. Then she would open her eyes unnaturally wide, struggling like an animal caught in a trap. Matilde would sit up, galvanized, slip to the edge of the bed, and there, her face buried in her hands, she would repeat aloud as if someone had been at hand to contradict her:

"I'll never get through the day."

It loomed before her like a great tree that had to be felled, and she had only a little hatchet with a blunt edge. The first stroke of the axe was the act of having to get up. Something not herself (it wasn't her own will for her own will wanted only to die) brought her to her feet. Then like a sleep-walker Matilde would wander here and there about the room, dressing and combing her hair. Then she opened the door, said good morning, smiled with a smile sadder than tears.

Matilde slouched out from the veranda, avoiding the groups of Indians waiting to be given their day's tasks, and making straight for the big yard gate. A choice of several paths lay before her: one to the river, one to the sugar-mill, and the largest of all to Palo María. But Matilde would have none of them and set off through the tall grass. She pushed the stalks aside with both hands using a stroke as if she were swimming. The dew spattered her cheeks and the briars clung to her dress.

Slowly the sun rose in the sky. Matilde gasped wearily for breath. She felt ill. She had left the pasture hay behind and now she was walking over the moor where the grasses clung low to the earth, red and dry. Matilde searched for the shade of a tree. There was only one. Under it she let her body drop, her arms splayed out like a cross and her hands stretched taut. "How long?" she asked herself. "How long?" Not impatiently, for her weariness had drained her, but softly, in the secret hope that the executioner who was tormenting her might have compassion on her docility and might make up his mind not to prolong the torture overmuch. Suppose the fatal day should be today? An irrational terror, the terror of a mare that shies when it sniffs danger, seized her. Until that moment her desire to die had been set loose in a land of fantasy and mere imaginings. But now she was approaching her goal, the same to which Angelica had gone long before; perhaps she was even treading where Angelica had trod. Her shoes were drenched with dew, and the dampness made her bones ache. Through her clothes the rough earth hurt her; and this resistance of objects, this weariness, this rebellion of her body was the only thing that assured her that what was happening was true and not a dream as it had so often been before. Matilde began to sweat with fear. Cold sweat soaked her armpits and copied the shape of her hands on the earth where they lay so stiffly. Matilde sat up suddenly as if to shake herself out of a nightmare. "I won't do it, I'm not capable of it," she told herself, and she went on walking, still flirting with the danger, still not taking the road back to the big house. "I'm not capable of doing it." A smile of mockery, of self-abasement, twisted her face into ugliness. "I won't do it. I'm too much afraid to suffer. I don't want to be eaten by animals. I don't want to be torn to pieces and wounded all over again. Not a drop more blood: it's horrible. It makes me retch even to think of it. Oh God! How could it have happened? No, it can't be sin. A sin when it's so pleasant, and yet that it should happen thus, in loathing, shame, and suffering. There I go! I said I'd never think of what happened again. There's no use crying over spilt milk. I want to die and that's a fact, but how? Isn't there some way to sleep always a little longer and a little deeper, until one can't wake any more? But there aren't enough pills in the medicine chest, and I can't run the risk of being left alive, for they'd cure me some horrible, painful way. I don't want them to laugh at me and point at me saying: she wanted to kill herself; like people who go into a convent and can't stand it and come out again."

The open plain across which Matilde had been straying

had been closing gradually into thick smudges of tree-clumps, until the space between each smear and the next one at last disappeared and the forest began climbing the mountain slopes.

"And suppose I were never to go back?" Matilde said, as if to repel the fear that was about to stay her tracks, that was about to turn and give her a shove so that she would run frightened back home. But fear didn't come, and Matilde went walking on, because she knew the threat of it was a lie, that it spoke of some very remote history that had happened to someone or other once long ago. Had Angelica, she wondered, been desperate like she herself was now? Or had she simply got lost without intending to? Matilde went over her own route in her mind. Yes, she'd be able to find her way back. "If I don't return I'll die of. . . . Of what do people die who get lost in the forest? Of hunger? Of cold? Of fear? The animals eat them, the ants." Matilde burst out laughing, her two hands pressed to her stomach so the laughter wouldn't hurt too much. What a face Ernesto would pull. A face as gloomy as a kitchen cauldron and all tense and out of joint. Matilde grew serious, her profile sharp and predatory as a hawk's. She pounced on this idea, to peck at it greedily like the sparrow-hawk when it sees its prey in the distance. Ernesto would suffer, would pay for what he'd made her suffer. At this point she paused a long time, deliberately, tasting the thought. Then she let it fall from her in disgust. She was in greater need now, emptier than before. She was a coward. She'd never be capable of wounding Ernesto like that, in the very bull's-eye of his heart, with a brutal and conclusive wound. She'd go on tormenting him with little pinpricks, avoiding his presence, refusing to speak to him. But how long could the situation last? Ernesto would soon grow used to Matilde's shunning him and would stop looking for her.

Chactajal

What, after all, had there been between them? They had loved one another like two animals, silently, without pledges. He must surely despise her for what had happened. He would no longer be able to respect her. Matilde had given him everything. But a man is never grateful for that, and only pays back with an insult. Loose women keep men just as long as they're young, and Matilde wasn't that any more. There would be other women waiting, less stupid than she.

Anger dropped down on her and crushed her like a stone. Matilde cried out in alarm to the birds asleep in the branches, and she wakened a crowd of confused echoes. But when all the sounds had stilled again, one childish and defenceless voice persisted. Absently Matilde set out that way.

At the foot of a tree, her face pressed against the trunk, a little girl was weeping. When she sensed steps close to her hiding-place, she shut her eyes tight and stopped her ears with her fingers. These were the only ways she knew of to protect herself from threats. But the hand that touched her was gentle and protecting; it drew her away from the rough bark of the tree trunk which had left its scar across her forehead and cheek. When she had the child before her, Matilde passed her fingers across the little face as if to erase that disfiguring adult expression. Only then did the child open her eyes and take the stoppers from her ears. Matilde asked gently:

"Why did you come here?"

The child's voice was breaking with sobs: "I want to go to Comitán. I want to go with my nanny."

Matilde drew her to her lap and began kissing her frantically and weeping with gratitude, for she had a reason now to go back; her conscience needn't accuse her of cowardice.

By the time they arrived home the child was asleep.

Chactajal

Matilde laid the little girl on her own bed, and went to the dining-room where the family had already started breakfast. Zoraida showed surprise at Matilde's pallor, her dishevelled hair and clothes; but she sat and waited, not wanting to interrupt César's cross-examination.

"How are you getting on in school, Ernesto?"

"Well."

The reply was deliberately curt because Ernesto wanted to stop any further question or comment. He was aware that behind César's apparent indifference there was not only curiosity, but even real concern to know how his nephew was shaping in his role as rural teacher. The Indians' attitude was an open secret. The day after the feast of Our Lady of Health, Felipe had arrived at the big house with a courtesy that did not conceal his firmness of purpose and his determination not to let César's arguments sway him. He came to put the school they had erected under the *patrón's* orders, so that Ernesto might start using it at once. There was no further excuse to be made, no justifiable delay, and classes had begun.

"It seems the parrot's bitten off your tongue."

Ernesto forced a smile but was disinclined to talk. During the time he'd lived with César he had learnt that conversation was impossible. César was incapable of speaking to people he didn't consider his equals. Any phrase on his lips sounded either like a command or a reproof. His jokes seemed like mockery. Besides, he always chose the worst moments for questions, when they were gathered together round the table as they were now, with the noise of plates and chewing, the creaking of the door as it swung to and fro. Perhaps earlier, before he had learnt to mistrust César's benevolence, Ernesto might have described the events of the morning, in class. Even now such a confidence might have been possible in other circumstances, but not like this, under Matilde's watchful and malignant gaze. "The devil seems to have got her by the ears," he thought.

"How many pupils have you?"

César once more. What did he gain by knowing? But César's anxiety had by now grown so deep that he betrayed it in his question, however casually formulated.

César's play-acting and all that it betrayed impelled Ernesto to answer ambiguously.

"I haven't counted."

Still more openly César persisted:

"Would there be twenty?"

"Possibly."

"Or fifteen? Or fifty? Can't you make a guess?"

"No."

"Well! And do only the children come, or the grown-ups too?"

"The first day Felipe came. I told you."

"And now?"

"Now he doesn't. I've told you that too."

The first day Felipe had come to see how the class proceeded. He had sat on the ground with the children who smelt of cheap brilliantine and shone clean. Ernesto swallowed his spittle nervously. Felipe's presence there bothered him, for he seemed like a witness or a judge. But he had to make up his mind, he had to give the class, come what may. He was sure that when he wanted to say something he'd have no voice and that everyone would laugh and ridicule what he did. Choosing a passage from the Bristol Almanac, which he carried in his trouser pocket, he began to read. To his own great surprise his voice flowed along with the words and he could even put emphasis into them. He read fast, pronouncing badly and making mistakes. He read the horoscopes, the jokes, and the homilies. The children gaped open-mouthed and understood nothing. It was the same to them whether

Chactajal

Ernesto read the almanac or anything else. They couldn't speak Spanish, he couldn't speak *tzeltal*. There wasn't the slightest possibility of mutual understanding. When the class stopped, Ernesto went to Felipe, hoping the latter would realize the uselessness of going through such motions and wouldn't insist on them further. But Felipe seemed very satisfied because the law was being obeyed. He thanked Ernesto for his kindness and promised that the children would be punctual and hard-working.

The children were attentive as long as they were still, stunned by the astonishment of the new scene that spread before their eyes. But later they began to fidget and their attention strayed. They nudged each other and then sat still. Little hypocrites! They laughed behind their ragged straw hats. They let out rude noises. Ernesto made a tremendous effort not to lose his temper. The law didn't fix the number of hours, so he cut them as short as possible.

"They won't stand the pace long. They come now because there isn't much work. But the Indians need their children to help them, and at harvest time they're not going to store the grain alone. Then there'll be no school, no nothing: first things first."

"Don't be so sure, Uncle. They seem very determined."

"It's just a flash in the pan. They're like children with a new toy. But when the novelty's worn off, not one of them will remember it. I know what I'm saying. I know them."

"I hope you're not mistaken. Because I'm fed to the teeth with the farce."

"Easy, Ernesto. The worst will soon be over. And remember, I'm not one to have wool pulled over my eyes."

"Just wait for your prize," thought Zoraida ironically. "Sacrifice yourself to him if you still think it worth while.

139

Chactajal

You haven't learnt to understand yet that the Argüellos aren't the Argüellos of other days any longer. It was a joy to serve them when they had power and their word counted. But now they move about on tiptoe, advising caution and haggling over money. We've tethered ourselves to a poor tree, Ernesto, it's a tree that gives no shade."

10

At noon they would begin preparations for the daily bathe. The hired boy saddled the animals: an old mule pensioned off long since from any more important or onerous tasks, and two quiet little donkeys. These would carry Zoraida, Mario, and the little girl from the big house, down to the river. The boy used to lead the way, tugging on the animals' halters. An Indian woman carried on her head the basket of towels and soap. Matilde dawdled behind, protecting herself from the strength of the sun with a broad-brimmed hat like a wheel.

They filed slowly past the huts, and not one kind word or greeting sped them on their way. The Indian women averted their eyes and put on a show of stupidity so as not to see them go.

They selected one of the paths. The mule stumbled and at every stone its legs bent double, so that it regained its balance only painfully. Or it would stop to uproot mouthfuls of hay which it chewed placidly with eyes half closed, frightening off the flies and gnats that bothered it with a lazy flick of the tail. In vain Zoraida urged the mule forward, beating it with her whip. Vainly she jabbed at its belly with the iron stirrup of her saddle. Not even the stable boy, tugging at the halter as hard as he could, was able to make it budge. The mule would move at last, after it had swallowed the last mouthful with niggardly care. But a few steps further on it would stop again, under the shade of a tree, where it nodded sleepily. Zoraida grew desperate and made funny impatient gestures. The children laughed, and Matilde and the Indian woman with the basket had time to catch up.

Dun-coloured sand, loose and damp, left stray stains here and there as it mixed with the red earth of the path. In the leafy trees, thicker now than before, arose a scandalous tumult of grouse spreading abroad the news of strange folk passing. And a sudden fresh, sweet gust of wind clawed the steamy warmth of the air.

They dismounted beside a boulder on the beach. The stable boy tethered the animals to a tree and went off softly whistling so as not to spy on the women's bath. The women, leading the children by the hand, vanished behind a screen of branches. From her basket the Indian pulled the shifts, faded with use, and the tangled loofahs, and the soap-root, good for washing hair.

Zoraida and the little girl walked barefoot across the crackling, crystalline sand. The stiff cloth of their shifts left a snaky track behind.

"And you, Matilde?"

Matilde huddled in her towel, shuddering, and said: "I'm not well. My blood's going to curdle if I bathe."

The little girl's foot broke the surface of the water and shot back sharply as if it had been scorched.

"It's cold."

You had to make up your mind suddenly, close your eyes, hold your breath, and plunge into that hostile thing. Zoraida beat her arms blindly about her and shook her hair hard from side to side, blinking to whisk away the drops of water running down her eyes. When she opened them again she measured the distance from herself to the bank and, changing the direction of her stroke, swam back. There was the little girl, spattered with foam and shivering.

"Come," Zoraida coaxed her.

But the child shook her head, and Zoraida had to climb out on to the beach. Her shift had squeezed itself round her body and had drawn in all the lines of incipient fat. The dripping water weighed the hem down. She led the little girl to the river and, to give her confidence, went testing the bottom as she stepped, holding the child afloat when the bed shelved suddenly down under their feet into a miniature void.

"Would you like to swim?"

The child said she would, although her teeth were chattering like castanets from the cold. Matilde went to where the water threatened to lap over her shoes, and from there stretched out her arms to hand them the wings made of two calabashes. The child fastened them to her back and, held up not so much by the wings as by the certainty she couldn't sink, she swam. Under her mother's watchful eye she swam back and forth within the limits of the pool where the water ran calm; further out the fraying current tumbled.

The Indian woman, naked to the waist, her breasts exposed to the air, bathed the little boy by pouring gourds of water over his head. She rubbed his skin with soaproot until he glittered with cleanliness. With towel outspread, Matilde waited to put on Mario's clothes. She was dressing him behind the curtain of branches when Zoraida and the little girl returned, pink in the glow of the sun, and happy.

The damp shifts lay in a coil on the ground like two large red snakes. The Indian woman picked them up and wrung them out, beating them roughly against the stones on the bank.

Matilde asked Zoraida solicitously:

Chactajal

"Would you like to drink your *posol*?"

She offered her the gourd of frothing maize gruel. But just as Zoraida was about to take it she stiffened, hand poised, attracted by a sound like many feet and voices and laughter drawing closer. The animals woke from their stupor and pricked their ears in alarm.

"What's that?" asked Matilde. Her voice trembled slightly.

"People," said Zoraida.

"My God! And they'll find us like this. Get dressed quickly and we'll go."

"Don't move an inch, Matilde. Learn to stand your ground. Whoever is coming must wait. They know nobody has a right to fetch water from the river or bathe as long as the *patrones* are here."

The Indian woman ran into the trees and hurriedly donned her shift. The fringe of the soaking-wet *tzec* dripped silently on the sand.

The sound of footsteps and voices took more definite shape. A group of Indian boys, six or seven of them, came running. Zoraida looked at them severely, then screwed up her face in disdain. Her expression stopped the Indians in their tracks, but only a moment, just where the path came to a halt. One of them began moving forward again. Reassuring himself with a loud, coarse laugh, he ran quickly down the sandy dune that dropped loose and soft to the beach. There he stopped, panting not so much from the running as from expectation. He laughed some more, slapping his thighs with his open palms. The others looked from their companion to Zoraida and back. They moved forward circumspectly till they had caught up with the leader, who was already unbuttoning his shirt with clumsy, trembling fingers.

"Let's go, Zoraida," Matilde pleaded.

But Zoraida gave no sign of having heard. The pupils

of her eyes were painfully dilated as she watched how one by one the Indian boys took off their shirts and sandals. With their homespun trousers well rolled up, they went to the water's edge and plunged noiselessly in. Water seemed their native element.

"They'll foul our pool," said Zoraida in a dreamy, far-away voice.

The boys, with shining torsos like patiently polished copper, swam and dived lithely, gliding with the current, and returned to where they had begun, as silently and easily as fish.

"You see! Now the pool's muddy."

Warned by the Indian woman, the stable boy had returned and was untethering the animals.

"Let's go, Zoraida."

Matilde had to repeat her plea. She had to shake her cousin gently to bring her back to the moment. But Zoraida stood by her mule and refused to mount.

"I'd rather walk."

Slowly they climbed the sand-dune. Each time they paused for breath, Zoraida turned her face and looked long at the river.

"Don't stare at them like that, Zoraida. They'll lose all respect for you."

They had reached the path, and had taken the first steps along it, when the noise burst behind them. Shouts, ribald laughter, the sound of water broken by the collision of bodies. And the screech of birds, and the quick unfolding of escaping wings.

Zoraida stopped.

"What are they saying?" she asked.

"Goodness knows. They're talking their own language."

"No. Listen well. It's a Spanish word."

"It doesn't matter to us, Zoraida. Let's go. Look how far ahead the children are already."

Chactajal

Zoraida pulled herself violently out of Matilde's grasp. "You go back if you want to."

Matilde dropped her hands in surrender. Zoraida had returned along the path, the better to catch the sounds.

"D'you hear now what they're calling?"

The intensity of her concentration tightened her face muscles. Matilde shrugged to indicate she didn't know and didn't care.

" 'Comrade' they're calling. Listen. And they're calling it in Spanish."

Matilde was waiting for that explosion of bad temper which by now she expected from Zoraida. Instead Zoraida curved her lips into a gentle and indulgent smile, as if she had been the boys' accomplice. There was no need to insist now that they should go back. She set out at once, her head bent and her eyes fixed on the ground. She didn't speak again, but when they reached the big house and she saw César lying in his hammock on the veranda she began screaming as if an evil spirit had seized her:

"They were naked. The Indians were naked."

11

César ordered that from then on the women and children should never leave the house unless accompanied by a man, who should see they were respected and if necessary should come to their defence. The man couldn't be César, for he was busy with jobs on the farm. Ernesto had free time when morning classes were over. Matilde was worried and about to confess to César that the events of the previous day had not reached the proportions that Zoraida's exaggeration had given them. The Indians hadn't stripped naked in front of them, or insulted them, or forced them to leave the river before they had finished bathing. But Matilde had let the right moment pass for such an explanation, and it wouldn't be believed now. She had been so dumbfounded at Zoraida's screams and her false version of events that it hadn't occurred to her to contradict them. She had watched her cousin stupefied, afraid that such a tale might have serious consequences. But nothing had happened. Zoraida had not referred to the matter again, and it seemed she had forgotten it completely. The only thing was that she didn't want to bathe in the river any more. She ordered a cellar of the big house to be turned into a bathroom. It was a gloomy place, the walls rotting with damp and ooze, and the children refused to go into it.

"It's lucky you're here, Matilde, and I can hand the task over to you. You can take them to the river as from today."

Matilde felt unable to speak, but she nodded her agreement, a gesture which had become automatic by now. She didn't know how to evade such a painful duty. She hoped that at the last moment something unexpected might happen, that Ernesto would be needed for some more urgent task and wouldn't be able to go with them. But at the hour fixed Ernesto appeared and said:

"You know I'm not going because I want to."

These were the first words they had exchanged since the day of their meeting in Ernesto's room. Matilde's heart turned over and hurt to the point of breaking, and her face flushed. She lowered her eyes and began walking silently down the path after Ernesto. Behind came the children on their donkeys and the stable boy pulling the halters, and the woman with the clothes-basket on her head.

(To speak to me like that, such impertinence. Of course he feels he has every right, because to him I'm just a low slut. And he—what does he think he is? A bastard, a hungry beggar. Just look at the shoes he's wearing. Good heavens, it seems at every step as if their soles will come unstuck.)

Matilde's eyes filled with tears. She would have liked to run and catch up with Ernesto and fall humbly at his feet and kiss them and ask forgiveness for such damaging thoughts.

(If I had money as I used to, I'd run to the shop and buy him everything he needs. How happy he'd look! I know when he's happy, because I saw it once. His expression softens as if a hand had passed over it and caressed it. To see it that way again I'd even ... but I haven't any dignity, or shame, or anything. And wherever they're kind to me, there I run, like dogs do, until people can't be bothered with them and chase them away with sticks. Yes, I'm only too ready to humble myself. But he? Look at him. There he goes walking along, not even bothering to look back. Why should he? He wants nothing from me, he said so himself. What can a man like that want from an old woman like me?)

At the word "old", Matilde felt an anguish so strong she had to stop, panting, on the point of fainting. Old. It was true. She walked on again, not with her previous elastic step but dragging her feet heavily as old people do. The sun beating on her shoulders weighed on her like a load. She felt her cheeks with her finger-tips and painfully checked the fact that her skin had no longer the firmness and elasticity and freshness of youth, that it hung loose like the skin of over-ripe fruit. And—now that she was undressing under the shelter of the foliage—her body was revealed to her too, thick and ugly and defeated. Every wrinkle hurt like a scar. Why should Ernesto look at her? A retrospective shame made her cover herself suddenly. Her chemise slipped round her, crackling like dry leaves pushed apart.

Chactajal

"How could I seem pleasing to Ernesto? He's known better than me."

Suddenly, resplendently, Ernesto's youth and beauty were before her. Again, as all the day just gone, she seemed nailed to the very central point of her yearning. Her tongue stuck drily to the roof of her mouth.

("I can't bear more, not any more," she reiterated. "Why should I go on tormenting myself, letting thoughts go round and beating my head against a wall? What does it matter to me that Ernesto's what he is, and I'm what I am, if everything is already decided beforehand? These things mustn't go on humiliating me.")

With her head held high, Matilde went down to the edge of the water, and from there, without turning, she said in *tzeltal* to the Indian who was undressing the children:

"Don't take off their clothes yet. The water seems very cold. I'll test it first."

The Indian obeyed. Matilde entered the river. The water licked her feet, curling round her ankles, and her shift blew comically upward. The cold gripped her body and she had to clench her teeth so that they wouldn't chatter. She didn't go deeper. The fish nibbled gently at her legs and fled. Her inflated chemise gave her the grotesque appearance of a captive balloon. The children pointed at her and laughed. She heard the laughter and with an involuntary gesture turned her face and smiled abjectly as she had learned to do in that house. With the smile still fixed on her face, she took another step. The water was up to her waist. The sand fell away from under her feet. Further and deeper she went, her stomach contracting with the cold, till her feet lost their grip. A quick, heavy movement, and she was off balance. But she had no intention of staying there in the deep quiet of the pool, and she swam on to where the current growled, and there she stopped struggling and abandoned herself to it. As she fell, yielding to the current, she heard a cry but could not tell if it was her own or from those left behind on the beach.

Thunder broke round her ears. She felt only the whirling water dragging and beating her against the stones. Some instinct which her wish to die had not yet overcome made her strike out with her hands as she tried to keep above water and fill her lungs with air. It was damp air, and it choked her and made her cough. But her weight kept pulling her down. Viscous algae grazed her body as they flowed past. Repugnance and asphyxia drove her back to the surface, but she emerged more briefly each time. Her hair caught in a root or a tree and pulled with a strength that made her faint with the pain.

When she came to herself she was lying face down on the beach, throwing up the water she had swallowed. Somebody was pumping her arms, and at every movement the sick feeling grew worse and the spasms continued unchecked, until they turned into one long neverending retch. At last whoever it was dropped Matilde's arms, removed her shift which was torn to rags, and wrapped her in a towel. They rubbed her with alcohol to bring life back. Her whole body ached like a wound and she knew she was still alive. A huge irrational joy sent a warm wave through her. She wasn't dead. She had never really been sure of dying or even of wanting to. She suffered, and wanted not to suffer any more, that was all, but to go on living, to fill her lungs with air on a wide plain that went on forever, to run free, to eat her food in peace.

"Matilde. . . ."

The whispering voice folded her round and a hand rested gently on her shoulder. Matilde felt the contact but didn't respond with even so much as a quiver.

"Matilde!"

Chactajal

The hand on her shoulder tightened desperately. Matilde opened her eyes, leaving her small dark paradise where she had taken shelter and where there were no memories. The crude daylight dazzled her, and she had to blink a lot before the images became orderly and clear. The blotch of blue congealed into a sky that was infinitely high and washed clean of cloud. The flutter of green turned into leaf. Close at hand, warm and full of concern, was Ernesto's face. Pain, which had survived as she had done, returned to Matilde's breast. She wanted to avoid such closeness, to run away and hide her face. But the least movement made her bones creak as if they were splitting, and a scorching heat spread across her skin. Where could she run away to, anyway? Ernesto had his arm round her. Helpless, Matilde shut her eyes again, and they were wet with tears.

"Don't cry, Matilde. You're safe now."

But the sobs gripped her from inside and broke on to her lips in a froth that tasted foul.

"Thank God you're not hurt. Scratched, that's all, and you've had a bad fright."

Carefully, with the corner of the towel, Ernesto wiped Matilde's face.

"When we heard the Indian call, the boy and I ran to see what was up. The current was dragging you. I wanted to throw myself in after you but the boy was ahead of me. I would have liked to be the one to save you. You'd rather it had been me, wouldn't you?"

Ernesto waited for the reply, which didn't come. Matilde remained silent, and the only sign she gave of being awake was the tears that kept oozing from her eyes. Ernesto brushed his lips against her closed lids and stayed like that, his mouth to Matilde's ear, so that his words should not be overheard by the children, whom the Indian woman was keeping at a distance.

Chactajal

"I've dreamed of you every night."

A blind, burning, irrational fury began running through Matilde's veins. The voice spilt like thick honey and Matilde felt sullied by its gluey consistency. She knew that the man was taking upon himself the right to speak in that way precisely because she had no strength to defend herself, because she was, as she had been before, limp in his arms. Ernesto had her cornered, and wanted to nail her again to her torture like a butterfly nailed by a pin. Oh no, this time he was quite wrong. Matilde had bought her freedom by risking her life. She opened her eyes, and Ernesto shrank from her shallow, bright, hostile, ironic glance that was like something seen in a looking-glass.

"Why didn't they let me die?"

Her voice sounded cold and resentful. Ernesto was taken aback. He didn't know what to reply to so unexpected a question. He stood up. From the height he let his words fall like drops of liquid lead.

"You wanted to die?"

Matilde had sat up. She answered vigorously:

"Yes!"

Seeing Ernesto's bewildered gesture, she added:

"Don't be such a fool as to think it was an accident! I can swim, and I know these rivers better than the boy who saved me."

"Then you. . . ."

"Yes. Because I don't want your son to be born. I don't want an illegitimate child."

She challenged him and held his glance. She saw how her own reflection was distorted in the pupils of his eyes until it became a filthy crawling creature from whom everything else turned with repugnance.

"Why don't you dare to hit me? Are you afraid?"

Ernesto turned slowly on his heels and started to walk away. Matilde was gasping for breath. She couldn't stay like that sitting stupidly on the ground, with all the hate that crumbled away in the unreproaching silence. She laughed indecently, and her laughter accompanied Ernesto's footsteps, and the children and the Indian and the stable-boy laughed too, uproariously, without knowing why.

12

Ernesto pushed the school door. It creaked lightly and gave way. He stopped on the threshold to survey the dilapidated state of the room. The only furniture was a table and a chair of unpolished pine. Splinters were always clinging to Ernesto's garments and tearing them. The furniture was for the teacher. The children squatted on the floor.

There was no blackboard on the wattle walls, no map, nor anything to show what the room was used for. Felipe had cut a photograph of Lázaro Cárdenas from a newspaper. The President did not stand out at all among the crowd of peasants. His portrait was placed very high, almost on the ceiling, and had been stuck with candle grease.

Ernesto bestowed on the chair an irreverently ironical glance before pulling it out to sit down. From his trouser pocket he drew a bottle of home-brewed liquor and placed it on the table. When the children came in and saw what was to them so homely an object, their faces brightened. Without a word or a sign of greeting, they filed past Ernesto and took their places on the floor. They squatted there, silent and gentle, waiting for the man to start talking about all those things they didn't understand. But Ernesto didn't talk. Carefully he began unscrewing the stopper, and when the bottle was open he pulled greedily at it with long, noisy gulps. Then, still holding the bottle, he wiped his mouth with his shirt-sleeve, stretched out his arm, and offered:

"Like some?"

The children looked at one another in hesitation. It was a familiar gesture; their fathers made it often enough in their presence, and some of the boys were already quite capable of accepting it. They were going to acknowledge Ernesto's offer, but he had already withdrawn it. He said:

"We're wasting time in a most paltry way, comrades. What's the use of meeting here every day? I don't understand a jot of your accursed language, and you not a tittle of Spanish. But even if I were one of those teachers who give their pupils the multiplication table and all that, what good would it do us? It's not going to change where we stand. Indian you're born, Indian you stay. Me too. I didn't want to be a donkey-boy, which would have been the natural thing, my walk in life. I wanted to learn a trade. I'd a better head than most. Why shouldn't I be more than the rest? I'm telling you out of experience so you'd better take note of what I say. Better stick your machetes back in their sheaths. Look how you come, all spit and polish. I bet they cut your   ; and plaster you with brilliantine as if you were going to a party. And all to show off in front of me. I can guess what you're saying up your sleeves: it's all the fault of that bastard! How d'you say bastard in *tzeltal*? There must be a word for it. Don't come to me with the tale you're that innocent you don't know. The children of the big house who are younger than you and not exactly full of grey matter, they've learned to call me bastard, bastard! Behind the grown-ups' backs of course. Because if they heard them, they'd be giving them a tidy tanning. Well, so says I. Looking at it fair and square, who knows? The whitest toadstool poisons most. There's Matilde, for instance, no need to be searching further. D'you know her? I recommend her to you. She's a girl . . . well, that about calling her a girl is something we'll concede her, you and I. Because when a girl's breasts hang like a couple of coconut husks it means she's a sight over-ripe. She didn't want me to see them. She tugged at her blouse to cover them up. She wanted to close the window because it was noon and the sun was coming in and it was delicious. I pretended to shut my eyes, and then she was calmer and quiet as a little dove. But I wasn't asleep. . . . I was noticing that about her breasts, like I've told you. Other things too. Such a little lady! So prudish, and scandalized and all, yes indeed! D'you think a lady gives herself like that to the first that says what lovely eyes you have? And I didn't even say so. I'd no need to beg her, or force her. I just kissed her and she went into a fit, quite beside herself. She began tottering backward, all stiff and cold and pale like she was dead. I carried her to the bed and laid her down. I was terrified, I give my word for it. I shook her by the shoulders and I cried 'Matilde! Matilde!' Not a word she answered. She just set to trembling and crying and begging me not to harm her, that she was afraid I'd hurt her. Why should I tell fibs about it? I've got God for a witness that not one evil thought had passed through me, but seeing it was put into my head I began to find all kinds of excuses, such as that Matilde would say I was little enough of a man if I left her just then. Anyhow she began to struggle in self-defence. She even wanted to scream but I stopped her mouth. That would have been a nice kettle of fish if they'd found us there together. I said so to Matilde, to quiet her down. She wouldn't pay any attention. She obeys nobody. They brought her up that spoilt she's only used to doing what takes her fancy. What she needs is a man who'll put her in harness and toast her nice and brown. But it's obvious that man's not me. Well, comrades, this deserves to be celebrated with another drink. Your health!"

Ernesto took another pull at the bottle. A pleasurable warmth enclosed him. He liked this sensation that counteracted his malarial fits. Then he began to move about dreamily, as if walking on cottonwool. It didn't matter to him that he should be saying whatever it was he was saying, because he was sure that not one of his listeners understood. He stared fixedly at his hand on the table and was surprised to find it the size it was. From the weight of it, it ought to have been very much, but enormously much bigger. This discovery produced a bitter laugh. He twitched his fingers and the tickling that ran through his arms made the laughter break bounds. The children watched him with round, indifferent eyes.

"I looked for her again. I didn't want to specially but I looked for her again. In these miserable ranches there's little enough choice. In the village, in Comitán, there things would have been different. Ah, comrades, if you'd seen the dead fly of a thing Matilde was, like she'd never so much as broken a plate in her life. She didn't give me a chance to talk to her. Of course a lady of her class couldn't deign to speak to one that's illegitimate. But then, how did it all turn out? Poor thing, sin had its own reward. It appears she's having a child, and as she's so clever nothing better occurs to her but to throw herself in the river and let the stream carry her off, when the right thing to do's tell the man. I wouldn't have left her in the lurch. I wouldn't have let her stew in her dishonour. That's as things should have been. But after what she did she needn't think I'll go pleading to her. I'm not that shameless. To me it's as if she's dead. By her son will her sin be found out!"

His tongue was scarcely obeying him any more. In his befuddled state he mixed up the words and they came slobbering out like a thick stream of endless spittle. The children, so used to seeing men drunk, hadn't been paying attention to Ernesto's monologue for some time. The boldest of them began prodding his neighbour, who trembled with the pain, and the others laughed cautiously, covering their mouths with their hands. But by now they were shoving each other quite brazenly, throwing pellets of mud and starting noisy squabbles. Ernesto's dilated eyes watched the disorder and didn't take it in. It seemed a very remote event with which he personally had nothing to do.

"One has to swallow one's words. When my uncle César told me he was getting involved with the Indians— and the crowd of half-wild, half-civilized brats one finds all over these parts makes it impossible to be deluded about them—I said, Jese, it'll be necessary to want it pretty urgently and strong. Because, being what I am, in Comitán I'd mix myself up with no little Indian baggage. But here I've had to swallow my words. And d'you know who with? The cocoa-grinder. She's a bit of a doll, more like a clay goatherd, the kind the peddlers sell. But close to she stinks of . . . whatever it is the cocoa-grinders stink of. She's got a smell to heaven on her that a hundred soapings won't remove, a smell of rancid dough. It was only because I needed it bad I went and stuck my nose into her hut. But later I retched like they'd given me poison. The cocoa-grinder just stared at me so, like you're staring now, with idiot eyes. Saying nothing. And my vomit stank there beside us. Then she got up and went to call a dog. Fine. Might as well laugh about it. D'you know why she brought it? To mop up the vomit. The dog, hungry as they always are, poor things, rushed in and licked it all up at a gulp without a trace left. Just a little damp stain on the ground. I'll bet my uncle César would have been pleased as punch. But from that day I haven't been able to eat from the gall it gives me. I have to go away somewhere else. First it was just the stench of the dung when they put a poultice of it on the maggots, but now it's the stink of dough everywhere. I tell you honestly, I can't go on here. I've done my best but it can't be managed. So what am I up to staying here, all in all? I'm not bound by any promise, I told César so since Comitán. And he, oh yes, yes, very agreeable to my conditions, but when he thought he had me cornered he left me tethered to a short rope and without fodder. Why? By what right? Aren't I as much an Argüello as he? There's only one difference, I'm poor, but we're going to be all in the same boat soon."

Banging his fist on the table, Ernesto rose unsteadily to his feet.

"Let them come and end it, for good and all! Let them take the cows and good eating to them! Let them come with their lice and fill the big house with them! Share out all they find and leave not a single Argüello! Not one!"

Ernesto's exaltation broke in a hiccough. He wanted to sit down again but couldn't hit the spot where the chair was and fell to the ground. He made no attempt to rise, but stayed there with legs splayed, snoring quietly. The children were afraid to go near him in case he woke, and they swarmed out, laughing and playing, back to their huts. Round Ernesto's head the insects buzzed. At dusk people from the big house came looking for him. He was still unconscious. His weight sagged over the shoulders of the men who carried him.

13

Quite a number of messages had to be sent before Doña Amantina, the medicine-woman from down Ocosingo way, would consent to come to Chactajal.

Chactajal

"Don César Argüello says that someone's ill at the farm."

"Bring the sick one here I say."

"She's in danger and can't be moved."

"I don't usually go paying calls."

"It's a special case."

"It means leaving my patients."

"You'll be well paid."

So Doña Amantina sent to have her litter prepared, and two sturdy Chactajal Indians—one alone wouldn't have managed that quivering mountain of fat—shouldered it. Behind them a boy in Doña Amantina's confidence carried the locked chest in which the medicine-woman carried her luggage, hidden from the eyes of strangers.

They took the daily stages leisurely, stopping in the shade of the trees so that Doña Amantina could unwrap the food basket and beat up the *posol* and swallow the raw eggs, for she was fainting with hunger. She ate quickly as if she were afraid the Indians—whom she never invited to share it—might snatch the food away. She sweated from the effort of digesting, but an hour later she was asking to stop once more for another snack. She said her work sapped her and that she needed to recover her strength.

They were waiting for her in Chactajal and had spread fresh cypress in the room made ready for her. Doña Amantina inspected it, made signs of approval, and then suggested they might adjourn to the dining-room. There they could talk more at ease. Between one cup of chocolate and the next, with the Argüellos showing signs of impatience, Doña Amantina asked:

"Who's the patient?"

"A cousin of Cesar's," answered Zoraida. "Do you want to see her? She hasn't left her room for days."

"Come then."

She got up solemnly. Gold rings were embedded in her

chubby fingers. Gold and coral necklaces shone against the cloth of her coarse, grimy blouse. From the flaccid lobes hung a pair of large filigree ear-rings.

As they opened the door of Matilde's room a smell of cooped-up air, stale from being too often breathed, hit them in the face. In the darkness they groped toward the bed.

"Here's Doña Amantina, Matilde. She's come to see you."

"Yes."

Matilde's voice was expressionless and far away.

"We'll open the window."

Light entered to show a yellow Matilde, uncombed, with sunken eyes.

"She's been like this since the river carried her off. She won't eat or speak to anyone."

Matilde remained totally indifferent while Doña Amantina leaned over her sick and wasted body. She tapped Matilde's abdomen roughly, squeezed her arms, flexed her legs. Matilde groaned with pain when the two bejewelled hands sank unnecessarily hard into a sensitive spot. Doña Amantina listened attentively to the groans, and kept returning to the painful places while she breathed heavily. Then, saying nothing, she let go of Matilde and closed the window.

"It's water-fear," she diagnosed.

"Is it serious, Doña Amantina?"

"The cure will take nine days."

"Will you begin today?"

"As soon as you provide me with what's necessary."

"Just tell us."

"You must kill me a calf. A yearling bull."

This request seemed to Zoraida excessive. Cattle aren't killed just like that, only on important occasions. And bulls not even on important occasions. But Doña Aman-

159

tina asked with the manner of one who admits no argument, and it wouldn't look well for the Argüellos to haggle over Matilde's cure.

"Let it be a bull-calf yearling. Black. String the marrow-bone on a spit. Oh, and don't throw the blood away, I'll drink that myself."

Next day the bull-calf was carved up in the main corral. The lumps of flesh were dusted with salt and hung on a wooden frame to dry, or put to smoke from hooks in the kitchen.

"Will you have another cup of broth, Doña Amantina?"

(If she accepts, if she swallows one more cupful with that noise that's like water boiling over, I swear to God I'll get up and go and be sick in the passage.)

"No thanks, Doña Zoraida. I've had enough."

Ernesto sighed thankfully. This woman repelled him, he couldn't bear her near him. The more so since he suspected why she'd come to Chactajal.

"About what time did the accident happen to the child Matilde?"

"They went down to bathe about one. Isn't that so, Ernesto?"

"I didn't look at the clock."

They needn't think they could count on him to help in his son's assassination. And was Zoraida an accomplice, or didn't she know? Women are always let in on one another's secrets. They're all birds of a feather, and that's a fact.

"To invoke her spirit the child Matilde must go to the place she got the shock, and at the same time of day."

"But Matilde can't move, Doña Amantina. You know that."

"She must try. If she doesn't go, I can't answer for the cure."

And to make her warning more sinister:

Chactajal

"It's dangerous to leave the cure half-done."

There was no way of opposing her. Very early that morning Doña Amantina had taken from her chest some sprigs of a shrub called *Madre-del-Cacao*, and with them she had "swept" Matilde's naked body. Then she dressed her, leaving the sprigs used for the sweeping between the sheets, because being close like that their virtue would begin to work.

As usual Matilde submitted passively and unprotesting to the cure. When they said she had to return to the river, she allowed them to dress her as if she were a rag doll, and let them carry her, and she never opened her eyes when they laid her in the shanty erected on the beach.

Suddenly Doña Amantina's voice rose in a shout:

"Come now Matilde, Matilde, don't skulk there!"

The medicine-woman's heavy, grotesque body suddenly unloosed itself from the force of gravity and ran agile across the beach. Her arms beat the air with a eucalyptus wand as if she were herding home Matilde's spirit which, since the day it had been shocked, had been lurking thereabouts. The woman seemed to be driving it back to the body it had deserted.

"Open your mouth, let your spirit come in again," Zoraida advised Matilde in a low voice. Matilde obeyed. She hadn't the strength to resist.

Suddenly Doña Amantina stopped her wild dance. She took a mouthful of brandy into which she had already dropped some pounded rosemary leaves. Then she spat over Matilde till the fluid trickled down her skin and seeped through her clothes. Before the alcohol had time to evaporate, she wrapped Matilde in a shawl.

But there was no change in the patient's condition. Nine days later her colour was as bad as before. It had done no good at all that each night Doña Amantina anointed the sick woman's joints with marrow, or that she splashed her spine with cold milk. The evil didn't want to leave the body it had possessed. The medicine-woman tried one more ruse. She put the leaves of the *Madre-del-Cacao* to boil in a tub, and extracted the juices. Then Matilde was made to swallow the infusion, called *chacgaj*, three times. But even after this she showed no sign of improving. She was still overcome with drowsiness, and though they prepared all sorts of dainties to encourage her appetite, she wouldn't eat. It was Doña Amantina who made good use of the choice dishes. Her hunger seemed insatiable, and her good humour never flagged in spite of the failure of her treatment. It was unthinkable that anyone should doubt her ability to exorcise illness. She could see that Matilde was much the same, neither worse nor better, so she said without turning a hair:

"It's the evil eye."

So they had to get the egg of a dappled hen, which Doña Amantina passed over Matilde's body while she prayed the Lord's Prayer. When she had finished she wrapped the egg in a cloth, together with some sprigs of rue and a crisp chile, and bound them into Matilde's armpit so the egg might hatch during the day. That night, careful not to look at it, she broke the egg into a bowl which she placed under the bed. But next day when she inspected the yolk for the two eyes that are the sign of the evil thing pursuing the sick, she found only one: the one yolks normally have.

But Doña Amantina showed neither surprise, discomposure, nor discouragement. After locking herself in her room all afternoon, she emerged to say that undoubtedly Matilde had been bewitched, and that it was her sister Francisca who had done it, and that in order to cure her they would have to take her to Palo María.

"No! I don't want to go!"

Chactajal

Matilde sat up in bed, electrified with fright. She wanted to get up and run away. They had to call in the cocoa-grinder and the other servants to force her to lie down. They gave her a sleeping-draught.

"But Matilde's not fit for the journey, Doña Amantina. And the shock of seeing her sister. . . ."

"Don't worry, *patrona*, I know my job. Things will turn out all right."

Dinner being over and conversation languishing, Doña Amantina got up, said good night, and retired. In her own room she took from her blouse the key to her chest and opened it. But as she was beginning to rummage among her things a very light tap on the door announced someone there.

An almost imperceptible smile spread across Doña Amantina's face, but she went on sorting her things as if she'd heard nothing. The knock was repeated stronger and firmer. Doña Amantina opened.

There was Matilde, shivering with cold, huddled under a woollen blanket. Doña Amantina pretended an exaggerated surprise.

"Jesus and Mary and Joseph, don't stand there, child, you'll catch your death! Come in, silly child. Come in, sit thee down. Or would you rather lie?"

She stressed the familiar *thee* as if insolently mocking. No one had said she might, but that didn't matter to Doña Amantina.

Matilde was quite still. Almost fainting she managed to stammer:

"Doña Amantina, I. . . ."

"Come in, girl, I know what ails thee. I'll get thee out of thy trouble."

Chactajal

14

Felipe's woman Juana gathered the few scraps left from
the meal into a clay bowl; she finished washing the pots
and tilted them on a board to drain. She removed the
griddle-pan from the fire till next day. She picked up the
bowl and went out to the farmyard. There was only one
scraggy pig rooting in the mud.

The pig fell upon the food and devoured it instantly.

"It won't be fatted for All Saints," Juana thought,
"I'll never be able to sell it at the market."

Discouraged, she went back to the hut.

From the clothes hamper she took a blouse. It was the
one she had used on her wedding day. She had kept it
afterwards to wear only on special occasions, but now
she even wore it midweek and she'd had to wash it several
times in the river. However careful she was, gentle and
painstaking, the cloth wore thin and tore in places. Now,
taking advantage of the last rays of sun—for the faint
glow from the embers wasn't enough—Juana set to darn-
ing. Felipe might come home any minute and find her at
her task, but he wouldn't so much as ask her if she needed
money to buy a new length of cloth. Felipe had washed
his hands of house expenses. He came and went among
the farms and villages and never thought to bring something home for his wife. She'd had to give him the little
money she'd saved, to cover the cost of travelling. Because with all this business of agrarian reform the *patrones*
looked suspiciously on Felipe and wouldn't employ him.
As to advancing the cloth on credit, as they once did, it
wasn't to be thought of. When she went to the big house
they didn't content themselves with refusing credit, they
claimed past debts as well. But it wasn't on that account
Juana had stopped going to the house. Sometimes she

used to wander about the cobbled yard with a bowl of beans balanced on her head. She didn't lose hope of being able to speak to the *patrones* on Felipe's behalf and ask them to forgive his cussedness and have patience, because he'd come back to his senses one fine day. Felipe wasn't a bad man, she knew him thoroughly. But the Argüellos walked past her absently as if she were too small to be noticed or heeded. And there were people who told tales on her to Felipe. One day Felipe beat her and told her to watch how she went prowling like that or he'd leave her. And that's how it had to be, that's how it ought to have been for a long time now. Felipe had kept her with him only out of kindness, not because he had to. God had punished her by not favouring her with sons.

"Good evening, *comadre*."

The words were spoken in *tzeltal* in a tremulous voice like one shuddering with cold or just over weeping.

Felipe's wife rose to greet the visitor. It was her sister María with the youngest of her sons.

Felipe's wife bowed and greeted her in the usual way:

"*Comadre* María, what a miracle that you condescend to come to this your humble house."

She offered the log where she had been sitting. It was the only furniture. However much she complained to Felipe, he took no notice, didn't even bring another log from the forest.

María sat down and began casting sidelong glances into all the dark corners. It was a long time since she'd been there and she found the hut more wretched and un-furnished than ever.

Juana chose to interpret the inspection differently:

"Are you looking for your *compadre* Felipe?"

María nodded. Juana chose the smallest and slenderest of the pine branches piled in a corner. She knelt to light it in the embers and said:

Chactajal

"Your *compadre* Felipe isn't here. Was there something you were needing?"

"I wanted to talk to him. They say it's my *compadre* Felipe who knows about the school."

The child let go of his mother's hand and went to Juana. Selecting the spot where he would be full in the light of the pine torch, he raised his face for Juana to see. Juana looked surprised and didn't understand, so he had to point to the bruises—here, and here, and here—because they were so nearly the colour of his skin.

"The teacher beat me."

He had previous experience and knew how grown-ups reacted to statements of this sort. He waited for an exclamation of concern. But Juana just looked on silently and then, with an air of indifference, she turned her face from the bruised child.

In order to gain Juana's sympathy, the boy thought it necessary to repeat the story. He was just going to begin but felt such a severe glance fall on him from his own mother that he decided to keep quiet.

María's severity wasn't due to the child's behaviour but to Juana's incomprehensible attitude. Trying to arouse her curiosity about events, Maria said:

"Don Ernesto got sozzled."

The child, who had been trying hard to keep quiet, abandoned himself to his urge to share his secrets, and began chattering away. For ages now Don Ernesto hadn't been sober when he came to class. Of course ever since he'd started school he'd not stopped talking. But now he didn't say what was in the books as at the beginning but he talked and talked to himself. After that he had drunken visions and fell asleep.

Juana interrupted the child s chatter to ask María:

"Will you have a cup of coffee?"

If María accepted, Juana would give her own share and

go without coffee that evening. María mustn't leave the house saying Juana had treated her badly.

María refused.

The child was glad he'd been interrupted. In his enthusiasm to tell the tale he had almost given the whole thing complete. He wasn't sure how his mother would take that, because he'd told it to her only in bits.

Like all the children, he was afraid to see a man drunk. He'd seen the fury and violence that overtook his own father. But Ernesto got soused in another way. He didn't seize things around him and smash them, he simply became completely disinterested in his surroundings. The children quickly learnt that in such a state Ernesto didn't notice them, so from then on his presence was no obstacle to their games and pranks. One of them had even dared to run and jump on Ernesto's unconscious body as it lay on the ground. The rest merely yelled and threw things. Once a bitter orange hit Ernesto smack in the face just as he was trying with the utmost difficulty to stand up.

Ernesto howled with pain and leapt up with agility to vent his wrath on the first child within reach, not troubling to discover who the culprit was.

"What I say is," said María, "is it for this we make sacrifices to send our children to school? The little brats could be helping us here. They chop wood, fetch water, and take gran'pa's food when he's working in the fields."

Juana shrugged her shoulders as if to rid the complaint of its importance. María went on maliciously:

"Not having sons, you don't know what it's like."

Juana turned her back. Silently she moved about the hut in search of something. María's words pursued her:

"That's why I said I'm going to see my *compadre* Felipe, so that he can advise us, because it was his advice got us into this mess."

At last Juana found what she was looking for, a useless

old brushwood broom she hadn't thrown away till she could get herself another. She dragged it behind her ostentatiously, crossed the hut, and placed it behind the door.

María, who had watched Juana's movements closely, got up, livid with rage. She didn't understand the motive, but she knew what the gesture meant. She left the hut without saying good-bye, and the child ran after her.

When Felipe's wife was alone again she put both hands over her heart because the beat was so quick and strong it seemed her ribs would break. She'd dared do that! The submissive, shadowy, spineless Juana had dared to turn María out of her home! The other women would take their cue how to behave from that. If they had any matters to arrange with Felipe, they'd look for him outside his home.

It wasn't jealousy. Jealousy is a human emotion accessible to everyone, and Juana would have been able to bear it, hide it, savour it. If Felipe had loved another woman, Juana would have faced an equal adversary and could have fought with the same weapons, and could have beaten her, because she was the legitimate wife even if she had no children. Or if she'd been beaten she could have accepted defeat. But it wasn't that, and what it was, was a dreadful thing. Juana didn't understand it, and she beat her head with her fists and asked herself what she was paying for to be so punished.

Juana saw no way out of her predicament but to go to the big house and tell them everything Felipe was doing so that the *patrones* would be so kind as to diagnose whether he was a case of witchcraft and how it could be cured. Because Felipe was by no means the same since he had come back last from Tapachula. He hadn't rested since he'd begun building the school. He was the first up, and went early from house to house waking the others. He worked harder than any. Then when the school was finished Felipe himself felled the pine for the furniture. And the ungrateful cuss never noticed that in his own hut they had to sit on the floor! Then he removed the picture that he'd always had stuck with candlegrease over the cot where he slept, and took it to paste on the school wall. If only he'd stopped at that, all would have been well. Likely as not he was drunk—because it was during the nine-day feast to Our Lady of Health—but he went off alone to the big house to speak to the *patrón* and tell him they'd done their part and built the school and must now insist the *patrón* keep the law and send a teacher. How would Don César regard him except as a lunatic, for he was certainly all of that, and it was out of pity the *patrón* hadn't ordered him to be flogged. Felipe was an ungrateful wretch. Instead of yielding as he should, what did he do? Passed the whole day—since they gave him no work—passed the whole day deep in the forest, and that from sheer laziness. For he wasn't capable of bringing her so much as an armadillo to plaster with mud for baking, or of picking fruit. He couldn't lift a finger to help. At nights he went from hut to hut chattering like a magpie. But it wasn't entirely his fault. The others egged him on, with all their deference. Felipe spoke, and they ran to obey. They didn't give him a single moment's peace at home with his family—with her, for she was the only family he had. Good. She didn't want Felipe there either. Because when he did come home he only pulled a long face and frowned and thought of other things.

"I'm putting up with no more," said Juana, "I'm going with the *patrones* when they return to Comitán. I'll toady to them, and speak good Spanish in front of visitors. Yes, sir, yes, ma'am! And I won't wear a *tzec* any more."

When Felipe opened the door of the hut, his woman lowered her head like a sheep attacked. She was exalted by the daring of her own action and ready to defend it and take the blame. But Felipe didn't speak. Indifferent as usual, he went to the water-jug and drank a calabash full. Then slowly, with the air of a man whose thoughts are elsewhere, he put everything back in its place—the stopper on the water-jug, the gourd—and sat close to the fire to wait. Presently the others turned up.

"We send our children to school so they'll be corrected. If they make a mistake, the teacher's like a father and a mother and has the right to reprove them."

So said the old ones, those who wanted to push prudence to extremes.

"They begin beating the children. They'll end beating us."

"Again!"

"Perhaps it's as it should be."

"Why, if we're equals?"

They always forgot. Felipe had to remind them.

One from the back asked:

"Why go on sending the kids to school?"

"To obey the law."

Felipe couldn't explain more or promise more. But the others were speaking now of the benefits they'd enjoy.

"My boy will know how to read and write. He'll speak Spanish when he's with the *ladinos*."

"He'll be able to stand up for himself. They won't deceive him that easy."

"Once they sold me a single shoe when I hadn't enough to pay for two. When I put it on, the Comitán boys laughed at me."

Felipe went up to the one who had spoken and touched his shoulder.

"They'll not be able to scoff at your son, I promise you."

When Felipe spoke that way those who heard him were afraid. It meant he was going to ask for courage and strength. One, with a question sharp as a knife, broke the expectant silence:

"What do we have to do?"

"We've been patient. How have they paid our patience? With insults and more abuses. So we have to go to the big house and tell the *patrón*: that man you brought from Comitán to be teacher is no use. We want another."

Each looked at the other and nodded approval, solemnly.

From her corner Felipe's woman watched them with enmity. Looking at her husband, she mused:

"Which of them d'you think will have the courage to go and say that? Not one. The only man capable of such impudence is you. They back you up here, but in front of the *patrones* they'll let you down. And they'll kill you, you fool Indian, they'll kill you!"

"No one shall go with me but the father of the lad who was insulted."

Felipe had pronounced judgment. But in Juana's eyes he wasn't to blame, it was *they* who were to blame, all of them, for they had made Felipe mad with their submission and obedience. "Get out of here, you filth!"

Juana made a movement toward the broom. She put out her hand to pick it up and fling it in front of them all and throw it to the door, but her hand was stopped, helpless and trembling, in mid air. Juana felt Felipe's stare upon her and it brooked no nonsense. She became a very small thing before him. Strength left her and she crumpled up till she was on her knees on the floor, shaken like a bush by a gale of sobs.

15

"So that's how things are. So the Indians want me to swop Ernesto for another teacher. The simpletons think they'll benefit by the change, and I'm not going to un-deceive them. I brought Ernesto and I'll stick up for him because he's to my liking. I'm head of this house and I'll show it. Damn it, the principle of authority stands above everything else. Now these poltroons want rope to hang themselves. I've made enough mistakes to please them. Let them go and inquire at the other farms, see how they treat their comrades the other Indians there. Jaime Rovelo for instance. On his farm things went straight to the point. The first that felt like insubordination he gave a good share of whippings and that ended the matter. He's got them where he wants them, gentle as lambs. But I . . . truth to tell I've no stomach for such goings-on. Besides, the thing that weighs against me is that in Chactajal the habit of being severe was dropped some years back. Not that my family was all that Catholic. Mother yes, she used to go to church and pray. She saw to it that the Indians on the farm were baptized. But Father no. He was good by nature. They happened to live in better times, a fact that has to be reckoned with. The Indians were docile and put themselves out to do their duty conscientiously. But I'd like to see that Estanislao Argüello now, the one that was said to be so famous and such a civilizer. I'd like to see him in my place and see if he'd go on preaching tolerance and kindness or whether he wouldn't be fixing his problems the only possible way. I've not yet made up my mind, not quite. I know I can count on some of the boys, but I don't want to. Those white-collar Indians are capable of betraying Judas himself. But supposing Abundio and Crisóforo and that lot's on my side, it's still not much comfort, because we're fewer in any case than those Felipe's been inciting. How can I speak to that fellow Felipe without seeming to be looking for a truce, without cheapening myself? He's not so tough that he wouldn't be bought off with a few cows.

Chactajal

Man alive, maybe things can wait. And let's have no fuss now, not just this moment when the grinding's going to begin. Because all in all, what the devil does it matter to me whether Ernesto's the teacher or not? I wouldn't hand him over when the Indians came to ask it, but that was only so's not to give them my arm to twist. Though this precious Ernesto's certainly turning out a broth of a lad. And a drunkard to cap it. Well, the poor fellow didn't steal that particular quality, he got it by inheritance. If my brother really did kill himself, it was in a drinking bout. And the two of them aren't even drunks with some spunk in them like those that send sparks flying from the horses' hoofs and brighten up the fiestas. Oh no, all alcohol does is make them more lily livered than ever. And they go about nice and foolish slinking in corners, not wanting to eat they're so gloomy. I swear the boy's turned out the spit of his father. Ernesto was my brother, and it's better to let the dead lie, but meaning no offence he was a ninny. All that nonsense about not wanting to live on the ranch, just because it's sad. Naturally, because they're not capable of busting broncos or going to the fields or swimming the river. They shut themselves up indoors all day long and of course it's sad then to see the twilight fade. But after work is done, how pretty it is then to watch the sun set. That's life though, there are people haven't these things in their blood. Zoraida's bored here. She won't admit it because she knows I'll scold her, but she's bored to tears. Well, I can understand it in her case. She was never a ranch woman till she married, not of a ranching family either, and she's happened on bad ranching days at that. She'd like to push one into acting foolishly. She thinks because I've controlled myself and tolerated so much nonsense I'm scared. It's not true. Whatever happens, one must keep one's head screwed on and act cautiously. Of course if it rested with me I'd have told all those rebellious boys long ago what they were worth. But slow and sure wins the race. Just now it's better not to take risks. I'm doing a lot even by just living here. Look at the other *patrones* sitting pretty in the Frontier Casino in Comitán, leaving it to their foremen to fight the evil. Jaime Rovelo himself, very brave he is, beating the Indians and putting them in the stocks! But he's such a weakling he stays in Bajucú and waits for things to happen. My cousin Francisca, now there's a lass to wear the trousers. A real Argüello. But it's a risky business what she's up to. One day those very Indians who have so much respect for her because they think she's a witch will stick a knife into her and it'll be the end of the story. Besides in a woman such tricks don't look so bad, but a man must face things fair and square. And in this place I'm the one who must do it. I'd like to take a trip to Ocosingo and have a word with the Municipal President. He's a friend of mine. I'd explain the situation and he'd help me. But on the other hand he might make out he'd be compromising himself by helping, that orders come from above and that the policy of Cárdenas is all in favour of the Indians. That's what he'll tell me, no doubt, but I'll answer back we're so isolated no one will know what we're doing. That precious Gonzalo Utrilla must be inspecting other districts by now, and one might persuade him to come over on to our side at that. If things don't get worse."

"Uncle César. . . ."

Ernesto had crept silently to the door. César turned and looked coldly and severely at his nephew. Ernesto felt the glance tighten his heart and squeeze the blood out. He knew it wouldn't be easy to speak. César didn't help him with a question or even a reproach.

"I gave no classes today. The Indians haven't been to school."

(Splendid news! Why should they? Just so the teacher should beat them? They might as well stay at home. Ernesto should have stayed at home himself, tied to his mother's apron strings, so as not to go doing harm in other men's houses. But Ernesto was so irresponsible he couldn't even calculate the consequences of his actions. Here he was, his eyes popping out with surprise, hoping a stronger will than his might set things right. César turned on him with deliberate but threatening calm.)

"Good! I'll ask Zoraida if she can't find a job more fit for you!"

César might have left it at that if joy had not crept indiscreetly into Ernesto's eyes, as if he were imagining he'd been forgiven. What right had he to expect forgiveness when he was so stupid he couldn't even measure the extent of his folly? César added disdainfully:

"A temporary job. Till you're ready to go back to Comitán."

"The usual trap," thought Ernesto clenching his fists. "A bit of friendliness, the kind of smile one gives a dog. Then a kick and humiliation. It's no use trying to approach this man. We're not equals. But let's see if he goes on thinking himself so superior when he hears what I'm going to tell him." With perverse satisfaction Ernesto announced:

"The Indians wouldn't let me into the school. They're all there on guard till the new teacher comes from Comitán."

César jumped to his feet, the sudden news clouding his face.

"What's that?"

"They've downed tools. They say they won't budge till the new teacher comes."

"And who the hell gave them leave to play such a low trick?"

Ernesto shrugged.

"I don't know. I didn't ask. I don't understand their language."

It wasn't his words but the insolence of his tone and the threat in it. César took hold of Ernesto roughly and shook him by the shoulders.

"Look what you've done! Now who's going to do the grinding?"

Ernesto's heart skipped a beat. The veins in his neck swelled.

"Let me go, Uncle César, or I don't answer. . . ."

César didn't let go. He gripped harder.

"And you still want to threaten me! Where did you get such nerve? Let's see . . . what does your breath smell like?"

"I've drunk nothing all day."

César let the palms of his hands drop wide open, as if Ernesto had turned his stomach.

"Then I don't understand."

The gesture with which César let him go was so sudden and unexpected that Ernesto tottered a moment, off balance. He was aware of having placed himself in a ridiculous position and shouted:

"It's not fair to blame me now. I told you in Comitán I'd be no good as a teacher. And you promised."

"Shut up! We'll attend to that later. The cane must be ground on time, and that's what's urgent now."

César turned his back on Ernesto and went to the window. He stood there thinking, his chin sunk on his chest. He seemed so far away and inoffensive that Ernesto dared to suggest:

"We might bring peons from Ocosingo."

"What? Go looking for labourers when I've got my own Indians? You'll never set eyes on the day that happens, Ernesto."

"But if the Indians refuse. . . ."

Chactajal

"Who are they to refuse? You're darned wrong if you think I've suffered their impudence out of fear. They're right to insist on certain things, and it's good that they do. But they're as feckless as children. They've got to be looked after so that they don't ask for what's not good for them. Land holdings! The Indians don't work unless they feel the lash. A school! To learn to read. What? To learn Spanish. No self-respecting *ladino* will condescend to speak Spanish to an Indian."

At every phrase of César's, Ernesto felt more gripped by the truth of it, more possessed by enthusiasm to uphold that truth against all attack, at whatever risk. With a voice unsteady from emotion, he asked:

"What are you going to do?"

He wanted to help, wanted to be one of the Argüellos.

César went to the cedar chest in a corner of the room and opened it. In it was a belt and the pistol holster. He took out the pistol. He checked that it was well oiled. Then he opened the case, gathered up a handful of cartridges, filled the pistol, and said:

"I'm going to talk to them."

He made for the door. Ernesto caught up with him.

"I'm going with you."

Together they reached the school. The Indians were squatting against the wattle wall, smoking cigarettes wrapped in cheap yellow paper, They saw the two men from the big house, but they didn't budge.

"Have you no greeting for the *patrón*, comrades?"

One made as if to rise, but another stopped him quietly with his hand. César noticed the gesture and said sardonically:

"We're not enemies, as far as I know."

No one answered. He went on:

"What did we agree? That you'd erect the school and I'd supply the teacher. We've each kept our word. Here's

177

the school and here's the teacher. Why don't we stick to our bargain?"

Felipe swallowed, then replied:

"The teacher's no good. When we went to speak to you at the big house we told you why we wanted him changed."

"Of course. And we all spoke impetuously in a moment of anger, and things seemed much worse than they are. Ernesto behaved like a green boy, but he's promised it won't happen again. That's to say, if you've no more complaint than that he struck a child. If the child also says he'll be respectful in future, everything will be all right again."

Felipe shook his head obstinately.

"Your teacher's no good. He doesn't know how to teach."

César bit his lower lip to hide a smile. He mustn't provoke them. But they looked pretty silly taking seriously their role of savages wanting to be civilized.

"So you insist I bring another teacher from Comitán."

"One who knows *tzeltal* so the kids will understand what he's saying."

"Good. So you can see I really want to come to a settlement with you, give I my word I'll bring you one."

César said this with the air of one offering a valuable gift. But the Indians, apparently not understanding the generosity of his offer, remained quiet, shut in, expressionless. César made an effort to be patient, hoping they would get up and return to work. But nothing happened. In a voice whose friendliness held a slight threat, he said:

"Good, so now we're agreed, we can get to work again."

Felipe said no and the others backed him up.

"No, *patrón*, not till the new teacher comes from Comitán."

Chactajal

César hadn't expected this resistance, and he made as if to stop it. Impulsively he put his hand to his pistol, but controlled his movement before drawing it.

"Come to your senses, Felipe. This isn't a matter that can be arranged just like that. You must realize that I've got to go to Comitán myself and speak to different people till I find the right one. And then the person's still got to make up his mind. The thing takes time."

"Yes, Don César."

"And for the next few days I can't leave Chactajal. It's grinding time."

"Yes, Don César."

Felipe repeated the phrase mechanically and unconcerned, with the air of someone listening to a lot of tall stories.

"And if you don't help me, we'll be delayed still more. Go back to work. It's best for all."

"No, Don César."

Felipe said no in the same tone as he'd just said yes. This caused great delight among his companions, who laughed outright. César decided to ignore the incident, but his tone became more insistent.

"If there's no one to harvest the cane we'll be ruined."

The Indians looked at one another still laughing and shrugged their shoulders to show they didn't care.

"If it doesn't matter to you, it does to me. I'm not prepared to lose one cent in follies like this."

Now they were serious. Their eyes sought Felipe's.

Felipe avoided them.

"Come now! To work!"

He thought his voice would be enough to spur them, but the Indians gave no sign of being inclined to obey. César pulled his pistol.

"I'm not playing. Anyone who doesn't get up at once, I'll clear the matter up here and now with a bullet."

Chactajal

The first to stand was Felipe. Tamely the others followed. One by one they filed past César and Ernesto.

"It's what I've always held," Zoraïda said later. "With them one can only use force."

16

Those who first knew this land said in their own tongue, "Chactajal", which means "The Place of Much Water".

The voice of the big shepherd river sounds from far away as it calls to the little tributaries. At their sources they are hidden, but they turn up later, gliding between the mossy mountain rocks, opening up their beds and ploughing the plain patiently. But even at their sources they have names, long, liquid names—Canchanibal, Tzaconejá —which they surrender and lose so that the Jataté shall be enriched in power and lordship.

Water reflecting the swaying branches of trees, water slowly eroding the stones, water the sun-eater; all the waters are one, this single one with its bitter foretaste of ocean.

Those who first gave a name to this land held it in their mouths as their own. It was the taste of corn weighing down the stalks. It was the thick white honey of the *chirimoya*, and the moon-pulp of the custard-apple, and the oily seed of the sapodilla, and the slow oozing of juice from the lacerated palm. But it was also the cloudy vapour rising betimes to lay on the leaves the footprint of its passing. It was the warm panting of the domesticated animal and the furtive breath of the prowler. And the rhythmic absorption of air by the moors at night. It was a symbol too: of one who traces the pheasant in high flight, and leaves the snake in the sand.

Chactajal

Those who settled first in this land took stock of it as they might have done of a treasure. The extent of the maize fields and other crops. The preserves for the hunting of deer. The cross-roads where the ocelot falls on his prey. The distant cave where the jaguar cub threatens because of his hunger, and the plain that is in league with the cautious prowling of the fox. The beach where the lizard lays its eggs. The thicket where the monkeys play. The thicket where many birds flutter, flying off from the slightest noise. The fierce-eyed thicket of stealthy footpad and rapid claw. The stone beneath which predatory snakes distil their venom. The place where the viper dozes.

They did not forget the tree weeping slow-flowing resins. The tree that casts an evil shade. The tree that splits open its hulls with a pungent scent, or the one that during the dog-days keeps all its freshness inside the wrinkled husk of its fruit, like a tightly closed fist. The tree that burns merrily and crackles on the hearth. Or the one that is loaded with evanescent flowers.

And to all this they added the briar protected by its thorns, and the rotting leafmould breathing out its unhealthy vapour, and the hour of the insect gold with pollen, and the nervous blinking of the fireflies.

And in the midst of everything, deep-rooted, was the silk-cotton tree, keeping guard over the villagers.

Those who came later baptized things differently. Our Lady of Health: that was the name of the feast days, unpronounceable to the Indians because it was just as foreign to them as the big house and the chapel and the sugar-mill.

The *ladinos* measured the land and fenced it, and they set their landmarks as far as it was possible to say, "It is mine." And they set their house on a hill treated kindly by the winds. And they put the chapel there, where they could see it. And for the sugar-mill they measured out a generous distance which year after year the canefields spread and covered.

The sugar-mill weighed down first the back of the Indians and then the earth. Its great bulk squatted there guarded from the elements by a lean-to roof of blackened tiles. In order that the animals could not go near it and the hay of the pastures should be kept within bounds and the grass should not tangle round it, the *ladinos* ordered a fence of four wire ropes.

And the sugar-mill squatted there silently, quiet as an idol, watching how the cane it would later grind in its jaws grew up around it. But on the day when the mill began to work it emerged from laziness with a monotonous creaking, while round it circled the old blindfolded mules, and in the canefields the Indians waved their knives quick as lightning in the sharp cane leaves.

Cramp twisted the Indians' arms and their sweating, sunburned backs, but César's watchfulness, as he rode on horseback through the paths opening in the fields, compelled them to hide their weariness and heap the cut cane higher.

Under the lean-to the juice ran thickly over the great wooden matrices, and the bagasse spewed out by the machine piled up untidily.

There was a pause at noon, the time to beat up the *posol*. The Indians sheathed their machetes and went to the pronged sticks where they had left their nets of provisions hanging. They unstoppered their waterskins and poured the water into gourds. They sought the shelter of the eaves, and there on their haunches they beat up the mass of *posol* with strong, grimy fingers. From a distance, well protected from the direct rays of the midday sun, César watched them.

It was a moment of perfect stillness. The horse blinked

lazily with drooping head. In the pastures the cattle lay curled up, chewing their plentiful cud. In a treetop the sparrow-hawk folded its threatening wing.

And the silence. A silence like many crickets drunk with song, like distant pastures rocked on the wind. Like one single bleating lamb still sucking and looking for its dam.

It was at that moment the first flame leapt in the bagasse. They knew then that all this motionless beauty existed only to be eaten up by fire.

The fire announced its presence howling like a wild beast. Those nearest jumped suddenly up. The mules pricked their ears trying to place where the danger came from. César's horse whinnied. César, once the first confused moment had passed, began shouting orders in *tzeltal*.

The Indians moved first, not to obey but to escape. Behind them their belongings lay scattered higgledy-piggledy: the net of provisions upset, the gourds turned turtle, the empty waterskins rattling scathed against the stones. And the Indians rushed forward terrified, tripping over one another, the large curved scabbards of their machetes tangled between their legs. A stray flame came crawling insidiously over the ground, faster and faster, to bite them in the heels. The sparks were flying, searching for a place to fall and propagate. On ran the Indians till César's horse neighing on its hind-legs, stopped them. César himself stopped them with his words. He lashed them across their cheeks and drew blood. The Indians were forced back to the burning sugar-mill. The wooden matrices fell into the flames. The cane juice smoked with an unbearable stench but didn't put out the fire. The Indians screamed as if they had been in chapel and the ear of God had been listening to their cries. They waved their frayed straw hats as if the fire were a beast to be scared away. The smoke curled in their throats and strangled them. It sought out the tears in their eyes. As long as César was behind them blocking their retreat they stood their ground. But when the horse no longer obeyed the reins, but went galloping off through the pasture, then the Indians, weeping and blinded, their hands gripping at their throats as if to help the process of suffocation, fled too.

No one thought of untying the two mules trotting desperately in a perpetual circle round the mill. The scorching air singed their haunches and the unbearable smell of burning sugar juices suffocated them and made them cough stupidly.

One of them folded its forelegs before the other. The beast fell with lips contracted, its huge teeth bared. The other continued running round, dragging for one more circuit the dead weight to which it was yoked.

The smoke rose thick now with the stench of roasted flesh.

The plain surrendered with a faint crackling, gently, as quickly as paper. First the creeping fire ate the grasses. Then it undercut the taller stubble whose stalks lacked strength, and lastly the big trees, from which flocks of birds went flying away. The branches disintegrated noisily, filling the air with sparks as they fell.

The fire took loud breaths on the moor like a red beast of prey.

The stampede of the cattle was stopped when the wires tripped them. The posts, eroded already by the disaster, put up only a brief resistance before they collapsed, scattering little lumps of charcoal far and wide. A calf tried to squeeze its body through the tangle of wire, and another was held, caught by the barbs, tearing its pelt each time it tried to break free, lowing, with eyes starting out of its sockets, until a sudden leap of flame put an end to its agony.

The cows with full bellies, the bullocks slow from their

weight, wallowed on, leaving their hoof-prints deep in the sticky mud. The fire came up behind and wiped out the traces.

Others, those who could run more lightly, threw themselves down the gullies and lay groaning from broken bones until the fire fell into the hollows too and took possession.

Some succeeded in reaching the water and threw themselves into the river and swam downstream. Many cattle were saved. Others, caught in the whirlpools and dashed against the stones, overcome by exhaustion, were observed by other men on other beaches, as they were swept with the current, swollen and stiff with water, pecked at by vultures in their flight.

Howls of beasts echoed in the mountains. Monkeys swinging from branch to branch. The tiger making the sheep in the fold tremble. The birds jabbering with terror. The ants fanning out over the ground in useless fear, with disorderly diligence and the nervousness of despair.

All Chactajal was speaking now, speaking in a powerful, fear-inspiring voice, regaining its old supremacy under threat.

The Indians inside their huts trembled. They fell on their knees to implore forgiveness and mercy. For somebody, one of themselves, must have invoked the powers of fire, and the powers had gathered in council with red-bespattered faces, their long hair dishevelled, their jaws hungry, and their hearts ignorant of law.

The Indians worked with eyes fixed on César's pistol, as they dug a good deep ditch round the big house.

The women had shut themselves into the drawing-room. As she hugged her children convulsively, Zoraida intoned:

"My soul glorifies the Lord and my spirit shall be filled with joy. . . ."

Chactajal

The confused muttering of the others drowned the words. Only Matilde's voice was clear above the rest:

"Santa Catalina Pantelhó, patron of long strips of dunked mutton flesh. . . ."

The prayer was meaningless, and as she recited it she couldn't resist a mocking, playful tone. She laughed, interrupting her giggles with a painful hiccough. Then, beating her head with closed fists, as the Indians do when drunk:

"Santa Catalina Pantelhó. . . . I can't remember even one more name. God will punish me. . . ."

The door opened and Ernesto stood on the threshold.

"The horses are ready."

Zoraida turned on him angrily.

"We're not going."

"There's still time. Later there's no guarantee."

"What are those damned Indians doing, that they can't finish the ditch?"

"The ditch isn't altogether safe. A spark might fly up into the roof."

But Zoraida paid no attention to Ernesto's reasoning. With her face buried on Mario's chest, she sobbed:

"I don't want to go back to Comitán like a beggar. I don't want to be poor again. I'd rather we all stayed here behind walls."

A joyful clatter burst from outside. Zoraida lifted her face, which was at once all attention. Matilde stopped searching in her mind for the sacred names she couldn't remember. Ernesto ran into the patio and called out:

"Rain! It's started to rain!"

When the rain had stopped it was possible to measure the extent of the disaster: the pastures destroyed, charred skeletons of animals scattered over the fields. Those that survived wouldn't move from the river banks. For weeks they were to go on injuring their muzzles as they snuffed the bald surface of the plain, tasting at each mouthful the burnt flavour of ash.

That night the Indians eyed each other suspiciously, because each one of them might be harbouring some accusation against the other. They ate their food remorsefully. They took strong drink to frighten off whatever it was they feared. And only one of them was capable of thinking that he had acted justly.

The *ladinos* kept vigil all that night, full of terror and resentment.

17

One candle was alight in a corner: the others had already burnt out. Mario was asleep in Zoraida's arms. Now and then she rested her feet on the floor and the wicker rocking-chair in which she was sitting swayed slowly.

"Don't make a sound, César. Mario will wake."

César gave no sign of hearing. He paced the room and the hobnails of his boots underscored the barking of the dogs.

"What about a cordial?" Matilde asked timidly. Her needlework rested a moment on her lap. Her eyes blinked the question, as if the dying light hurt too much. She got no reply, and bent over her sewing again.

Ernesto rose and half-opened the shutters of the window. This atmosphere was suffocating and he wanted to breathe the night air. But the air that blew in was still charred.

The candle flame flickered and nearly went out.

"He's like a tiger in his cage," Zoraida thought as she watched César. "If he'd paid attention to me when I advised him to make himself respected, to treat the

Chactajal

Indians as they deserved so they'd see who was lord and master, they'd be dancing to another tune now. But why cry over spilt milk? We're in trouble up to the neck. Good-bye, Doña Pastora and fare you well. You'll be offering your wares to the farmhouse all in vain. We can't buy anything now. And no one will be anxious to give us credit. Even suppose they did, I wouldn't touch it. I'm not going to hamstring my soul again, waiting for the debt-collectors' knocking. I know where those coral necklaces and filigree rosaries and rings of wrought gold will find a home now: with the women at the brandy-distiller's, those so-and-sos whom I wouldn't even have as nursemaids for my children, though they put on airs now because of the money they have. Who's this Golo Córdova? A miserable guttersnipe who began putting on side from the moment he set up his factory so secretly. The Revenue Inspectors came down on him but he greased their palms and now he stinks of money. César sold him the cane crop. I told him not to unless he got payment in advance. But he said he had to pay off other commitments and wouldn't listen to me. Look at the situation now, a pretty debt we're saddled with. And nothing to set against it. The fat cattle were the first to be roasted on the fence-wires. That Golo's quite capable of walking off with the farm. Not because it would be good business, for what business can there be in owning a seething cauldron full of Indian upstarts? But just to have the prestige of putting his foot where Argüellos have trod before him. I know César though, he's stubborn as a mule. He's the kind that twists his own rope to hang himself. And must I really go on living with him? I don't want to live miserably in Comitán. I don't want them to see me come down a peg where I used to be queen of the walk. It's not that I shirk·work. I know how to work. I used to weave palm leaves and stitch palm hats. I could easily earn a living anywhere I'm not known, and keep the home together. I and the children alone. But not in Comitán."

"Maybe the fire wasn't deliberate," Ernesto said.

"What do you think? It was an accident?" César stopped to answer. His vehemence made him tumble over the words.

"An accident! The fire started in the mill. The heap of bagasse was the first thing to burn. The Indians were all near. I can see it as if I were watching it now. They were sitting beating their *posol*."

"Felipe wasn't with them. He stayed here drawing water for the house. I saw him myself."

"Felipe needn't have done it with his own hands. He could quite well have ordered them. The others obey him as they've never obeyed me."

César believed them perfectly capable of doing what they did, and exactly in the way they did it, treacherously. They were too cowardly to face things fair and square. That's why they came to the big house with their spokesman: they squatted on the veranda to listen to him speaking. And then they'd be putting a knife in one's back or waiting for one at a bend in the road to hunt one like a stag. Because they were cowards. César knew that, he'd known it since he was born. But never till now had he come smack up against it like this, against all the hate and cowardice of the Indians, solid before him, an obstacle that stopped his progress. His blood boiled with fury and impatience. He would have liked to rush out and strangle his enemy by the neck. But the enemy feinted, played with his anger by vanishing away, assuming another shape, annoying him still more with a quality of intangibility like smoke. Then César was forced to hide his fury and act like a fool. Not only had he to run about all day giving orders and struggling to put out the flames.

Chactajal

He was hoarse with shouting so much, his muscles hurt with the effort. But his exhaustion wasn't deep enough to grant him quiet rest. He tried to sleep. He closed his eyes. And the next moment he would open them in confusion and look about him tense and expectant, on the defensive. He couldn't even sit down peacefully. The soles of his feet itched, and the sweating palms of his hands. He had to be on the move. He paced back and forth, from end to end of the room, counting the bricks, trying not to step on the cracks, throwing a grotesque, disjointed shadow. Every time he looked at his wife he caught in her eyes a mute supplication: silence please, have some consideration for Mario, he's sleeping. Consideration! If César had had more, he'd have shaken that frail little boy by the shoulders, he'd have roused him good and proper to let him know just what had happened. "This is your inheritance," he'd have said. "Learn to defend it, because I'm not going to live forever."

César wanted his son to be a man, not a nincompoop like Ernesto. At Mario's age he, César, had known how to ride a horse and go out to the fields with the cow-men and lasso the calves. He would have liked his son to do the same. But Zoraida made a terrible fuss whenever the subject was brought up. She handled her son so gingerly he might have been made of marzipan. Naturally, as she wasn't a rancher, she didn't want Mario to be one. She'd even be getting ideas of sending him to study in the Capital. Of course, so that he'd turn out a broth of a boy like that precious lad of Jaime Rovelo's who comes out now with the brilliant idea the *patrones* are stopping progress and our farms ought to be seized. And we're just going to let it happen, that's all. They think a bit of shouting's going to scare us. They don't know we're bored to tears of holding wakes for the dead. We've survived worse fixes than this one. I know others in my shoes wouldn't hesitate and at this moment that scoundrel Felipe would be rocking on the post of the sheepfold with his tongue lolling. But I don't want to dirty my hands with blood or be martyred to the rebels. Better act cautiously and keep within the law as I've done till now. I suppose they'll accuse me of asking free work of the damned Indians when I took them to the grinding! But I was going to pay them fair, not the minimum wage. The fellow who began to dispute it was off his head. Fair and square it was going to be. But instead of obeying decently they dug in their heels like a lot of stubborn mules. They think I'm by myself and have nobody to back me up, while they've got their pal Gonzalo Utrilla. But I've got friends too. To start close at hand, there's the Municipal President of Ocosingo. I'll only have to call and he'll send me the men I want. Those damned Indians will look a sorry sight when they find themselves tied elbow to elbow and dragged off to jail. Because this fellow that's called César's not going to stay whistling on Do-Nothing-Hill and the cane all burnt. There's got to be an inquiry, and the guilty one's got to be punished. One doesn't lose thousands of *pesos* just at the snap of one's finger. And I'm not going to my creditors with the snivelling excuse I can't meet my bills because there's been an "accident" on my ranch. I've got to pay up or have them throwing it in my teeth I'm untrustworthy, and that's a thing no Argüello, not even Ernesto, has ever put up with. For the present there's only one solution, to go to Ocosingo. But damn it, I can't risk leaving the farm with those savages in the mood they're in. If they dared do what they did when I was here, heaven knows what they'll be capable of when they find there's no man about. I'm afraid for the family too, there have been cases of raping the women. And a general flight's out of the question. This is a man's game. I'll have to go, and get quickly back. What with my luggage and all, I couldn't get to Ocosingo under three days.

"Would you be able to go to Ocosingo and deliver a letter to the Municipal President, Ernesto?"

The question startled him. Before he knew just what he was letting himself in for, Ernesto had agreed. He didn't repent. His uncle had never tolerated the slightest vacillation, and he would tolerate even less now, believing as he did that the cause of the whole trouble with the Indians was Ernesto. If Ernesto hadn't got so drunk as to strike his Indian pupils, their parents wouldn't have protested by refusing to work at the mill. True, Ernesto had not so much as sniffed the bottle since that day, but the harm had already been done. So now he had his tail between his legs, and he could do nothing else but obey. Anyhow, what was being asked was nothing out of the ordinary. A trip to Ocosingo was simple enough. Ernesto began to imagine himself galloping lightly over the moor, his body light as air, without this constant contraction in his stomach, without this persistent stench of manure and creosote, with a freedom he enjoyed only in dreams.

But when he saw César sitting in front of him writing, and heard the pen scratching disagreeably on the paper, he felt himself plunged once more into the painful reality of his position, and a cold sweat wet his shirt.

César directed the envelope, stood up and handed it to Ernesto.

"It's addressed to the Municipal President. It's to tell him the fix I'm in. If he asks you for details of what happened today, give them to him. At least you're well informed as to the cause."

Ernesto felt his ears burn. He turned his face quickly away to hide his shame, and his glance fell on Matilde's bent forehead. He thought he caught a passing look of scorn. How had she the impudence? There she sat, hypo-

critically deceiving them all with a look as if butter
wouldn't melt in her mouth. What would happen if he
began suddenly to scream out that he hadn't got drunk
from vice but because Matilde had been on the point of
assassinating the child they'd created between them? For
a moment Ernesto thought he was going to give way to
his impulse and confess everything. But the words stuck
in his throat. He wasn't such a fool any more as to confide
in these people. He knew them by now. César and Zoraida might not realize what kind of a little worm Matilde
was, but the fact that she bore their name would be quite
sufficient for them to protect and shield her. As for him,
he was just a bastard and could go to the devil.

"I want you to tell him all that happened in detail. And
tell him I won't be satisfied till justice is done. Whoever's
to blame shall pay dear. If they don't punish him, I will."

Now that the details of the journey were settled,
Matilde raised her head. Zoraida was dozing with her
cheek leaning on the wicker rocker. She was as calm as
if nothing had happened. Matilde envied her. Since
Doña Amantina's visit to Chactajal she herself had had no
taste of sleep. If she closed her eyes, the old woman's face
haunted her, with its sullen expression of malice and complicity. She heard her call, and woke trembling with
shame. Her nights passed like that, and her days were no
happier. She knew she had no right to raise her head in
front of Ernesto. She avoided him as much as possible.
But sometimes—the house, the whole world, would not
have been big enough—they met and she had to speak to
him naturally and pretend indifference so that the others
would suspect nothing. Why should they? They trusted
her. Yet she had been deceiving them every day for
months. She had paid their hospitality with scorn and
brought dishonour to a house whose doors had opened to
receive her. She worked for them from sunrise to sunrise,

and had served them on her knees, but that didn't repay them for the trust she had abused. As if to force them to suspect, as if to warn them, Matilde began risking phrases that sounded coarse from a young woman, and made allusions to facts of life that a spinster ought not to know. Zoraida looked at her so suspiciously that she blushed. Together with the rush of blood to her face came terror that she might be found out. Where should she go? Where? This emptiness confronting her kept her on the verge of a nervous crisis. A shadow on the wall, an insect's persistent flight, the sudden neighing of a horse, made her scream and sob disconsolately.

"Get married," César advised her, patting her on the shoulder half kindly, half mocking. "Get married and stop seeing things."

And Matilde would beg forgiveness for having upset them, and force a smile and pretend to be calm. But suddenly she cried again:

"Oh!"

Zoraida woke with a start.

"What is it?"

Matilde had run to the middle of the room. Trembling, with chattering teeth, she stammered:

"There, in the window—a man!"

Zoraida and César looked at each other anxiously. This time they hadn't the spirit to say Matilde was seeing things.

18

Ernesto folded the envelope so that the letter would fit in his shirt pocket. At every breath of his and at each stride of the horse he felt it move with a hardly perceptible rustle. There, on that piece of paper, César had

194

given vent to his fury, accusing the Indians and urging the Municipal President of Ocosingo to come to his assistance. With calculated crudity he reminded the man of many good turns and suggested that now was a good moment to repay them.

When Ernesto read the letter for the first time (it had been handed to him open, but he had licked the envelope himself and had closed it in front of the whole family. Later in his bedroom, however, curiosity, not so much to know its contents as to discover César's true state of mind, had caused him to open the envelope and substitute it for another, addressed in his own handwriting) he had to admire the vitality of that man whom even such circumstances as these had not crushed. He admired his natural aptitude for command and his way of addressing others as if they were by nature his subordinates or inferiors. Ernesto yielded once more to the fascination that this behaviour exercised over him. He felt that to obey César was the only way to grow more like him, and during all the hours of wakefulness, restless in his bed, until a knock at the door of his room announced that it was time to be going, he was making up his mind to support César's written vehemence with his own spoken testimony. His heart was beating hard, burning with indignation, and he imagined himself arriving in the presence of the Municipal President of Ocosingo still aflame like a torch to light the dark cave of injustice.

But now that his belt was beginning to rub him from his constant adjustment to the horse's gait, Ernesto realized that his enthusiasm was waning. His breathing was rapid and difficult because the horse was now climbing Chajib Hill, and his eagerness petered out in mute irritation. How long had he been riding? He had no watch, but could calculate the time that must have elapsed. He had left Chactajal before dawn, and now the sun, still chilly and weak, pricked his shoulders with warm needles.

"And what's it all for?" he asked himself. "The Municipal President isn't going to take any notice, and he's not going to send anyone to investigate the burning of the cane. Nor is it exactly a world-shaking event. The fact is that César himself is the one who's making it impossible for them to meet his requests. He doesn't know how to ask. Suppose I don't deliver the letter?"

Ernesto imagined himself dismounting in front of the arches of the Town Hall, tying his horse to one of the stout plaster pillars. The President would be inside, in the shade of the veranda, shooing off the heat of the afternoon with a flick of his hand. Ernesto had heard that the climate of Ocosingo was sultry and unhealthy. He would go up to the President with hand outstretched, smiling, self-assured, just as he had seen salesmen approach the shopkeepers in Comitán.

The President would smile, won over immediately by Ernesto's charm and grace. The President would know he was an Argüello just by looking at him. The features, the "perfection", as the people of these parts liked to say, all proclaimed it. And then, the air of authority that emanated so easily from his person, without the dryness and coarseness of the other Argüellos, but with a friendliness that made other people anticipate what he wanted, so that they might serve him in any possible way. Ernesto smiled, satisfied with his self-portrait.

"A beer, Señor Argüello?"

Yes, an iced beer because he was thirsty and it was very hot. Ernesto raised the bottle with a toast, and the gesture was reflected in the thick drinking-house mirrors.

Propping their elbows on the same table, side by side, almost intimate, the Municipal President and Ernesto began

to converse. Ernesto was sure the President would begin:
"So what is it you want?"

And Ernesto, letting the cigarette smoke dissolve in the
air (he didn't like to smoke, actually, but they'd told him
it was good for warding off mosquitoes, and as Ocosingo
was in the tropics there'd be plenty of those) would tell
him all that had transpired. He, Ernesto, had been in
Chactajal on an engineering job, merely out of regard for
the family, because he had more than enough clients in
Comitán. Well, so César had called him to survey the
small property because he'd decided to obey the law and
hand their holdings over to the Indians. But one of them,
a certain Felipe, their self-appointed chief, had been inciting them against the *patrón*, making Ernesto the scape-
goat. Felipe had said that, since Ernesto was César's
legitimate nephew, Ernesto wasn't likely to share out the
land fairly. And yet first and foremost, wherever he
worked, he'd never acted from family interests but according to professional ethics. But how get such a notion into
an Indian's thick skull?

So misunderstandings had accumulated to such a point
that the aforementioned Felipe had set fire to the cane and
then, to prevent their reporting the matter to Ocosingo,
had laid siege to the house at Chactajal with the help of
those he'd managed to win over to his side. But Ernesto
had succeeded in escaping, thanks to his own astuteness
and the protection of the cocoa-grinder, a law-abiding
Indian woman.

At this point Ernesto would answer the insinuating
leer with which the Municipal President would receive
this confidence with a knitting of his eyebrows, declaring
that the poor woman had offered herself to him but he
hadn't wanted to take advantage of her situation. Besides,
Indian women—here he would allow himself a picar-
esque wink—weren't to his taste. Poor old thing! They

treat them like animals. So if anyone looks in the least favourably on them (he, after all, had only behaved like a gentleman to a lady, who must always be respected whatever her social position), they respond with eternal gratitude. So thanks to the cocoa-grinder here was Ernesto asking the Municipal President to go back with him to Chactajal and to send a picket of soldiers in advance. No, not to meet the ringleaders with violence. The Indians weren't bad. The most that could be said was that they were ignorant. It might surprise the Municipal President to hear such an opinion from the mouth of one who belonged to the class of the bosses. But Ernesto was a man of advanced ideas, not a rancher like the others. He'd studied engineering in Europe. When he returned to Mexico he had found the progressive policy of Cárdenas worthy of support. As to that, the Municipal President could rest assured. The fact that he had answered the call from Chactajal's owner need in no way be interpreted as disloyalty to Cárdenas's policy. They had called him in only as mediator.

His last scruples gone, the Municipal President would not hesitate to accompany Ernesto. How pleased they would be in Chactajal to see them arrive. He, Ernesto, had saved their lives. Matilde would look at him again with the same longing eyes with which she had greeted him in Palo María, before César had blurted out that about being illegitimate. But now this act of generosity was going to convince them all that his bastard state did not prevent him from being morally equal or better. César would be astonished at the good sense that had made him, Ernesto, realize that the tone of his—César's— letter had had to be softened. From that moment he would never want to take a step without being guided by his nephew Ernesto. Moreover, César would want to reward him in cash, but Ernesto would refuse, not disdainfully, but with calm dignity. César, impressed by this altruism, would send for the best Mexican specialist to examine his mother. At the time she went blind Dr. Mazariegos had assured them the condition was not incurable, that cataracts, when they reach a critical point, can be operated on. And once his mother was well again, what would prevent Ernesto from leaving Comitán to seek his fortune elsewhere, where to be illegitimate was no stigma?

He'd reached the banks of a stream. His horse stopped and began shaking its head, impatient for Ernesto to loose the reins and let it drink. Ernesto had no idea how much longer it would take to reach Ocosingo, and as the long ride had given him an appetite he prepared to eat a calabash-full of *posol*. He dismounted and led the horse to where it might conveniently drink. From his saddle-bag he brought out the gourd and *posol* dough, and he sat himself in the shade of a tree. While the dough was soaking, he pulled the letter from his shirt-pocket, unfolded it, and read it again. One quick movement of the hand would have been enough to crumple it into illegibility. But the paper remained there intact, held carefully between his trembling fingers while a great anguish wrung Ernesto's heart and drained the blood from his cheeks.

Suddenly all his dreams seemed silly and meaningless. Who the devil was he to meddle in César's affairs? Undoubtedly he was going out of his mind. It must be the sleepless night he had passed, he thought.

So he folded the paper again and put it back in the envelope and into his shirt-pocket. He even stuffed his handkerchief on top so that the letter shouldn't be splashed while he was beating up the *posol*.

Ernesto was digging his fingers into the dough. At that moment a shot rang out.

The bullet had been fired at point-blank range. It

hit Ernesto between the eyes. He fell backward instantly. Only a stain of blood marked the place where the shot had entered.

The horse reared in fright and would have galloped off if a man, an Indian hidden in the foliage, had not run forward to catch the reins. He patted the horse's neck, talking softly to quiet it. Then he tethered it to a tree and went to Ernesto's body and without hesitation, for he must have been watching Ernesto put it away, he pulled the letter from the shirt-pocket, tore it up, and threw the pieces into the stream. Then, seizing the arms, limp in death, he tugged and dragged the corpse to where the horse was pawing.

The body left a track like a lizard in the sand.

He laid the body horizontally over the saddle, and tied it with a rope so that it wouldn't slip and fall when the horse moved. Finally he untied the animal, set its head toward Chactajal, and with a shout and a wave of his straw hat brought his whip down on the horse's rump. Off it galloped.

When the sweating horse, its mane plastered to its neck, passed the first Indian huts of Chactajal, it unleashed a furious barking of dogs, and behind these the children ran and shouted. The grown-ups eyed one another with eyes of guilt, and closed the hut doors behind them.

The horse entered the farmyard whose gates were wide open since it was not guarded by any farm boy now. Galloping, it left the big house behind, the kitchen and the granaries, eager to reach the stable. César had to go out there to retrieve Ernesto's body. With Zoraida's help—there wasn't an Indian who would lift a hand—he carried his nephew to the chapel to be laid out. Matilde went in disarray and threw herself weeping on to Ernesto's breast, intact in death. She kissed Ernesto's cold cheeks and still soft, gentle hair.

Chactajal

Zoraida leaned toward Matilde and whispered in her ear:

"Get up. You're going to set people talking if you behave so exaggeratedly."

Matilde still knelt by the corpse. She screamed hoarsely: "I killed him!"

"You're out of your mind, Matilde. Be quiet!"

"I killed him! I was his lover. I wouldn't allow his son to be born!"

Zoraida turned to César:

"Why do you let her tell lies? It isn't true what she says, she's out of her mind."

But Matilde was possessed by a frenzy which acted as her enemy and removed her mask and destroyed her. Turning tear-stained cheeks to Zoraida, she said:

"Ask Doña Amantina how she cured me. I've shamed the name of Argüello."

The three of them were alone round Ernesto's corpse. Steadily, coldly, as if his attention had been elsewhere, César looked at his cousin. The threatening silence ticked on and on. Matilde shivered. In a curiously childish voice she dared break it. She asked:

"Aren't you going to kill me?"

César blinked and came to. He shook his head. Turning his back on Matilde, he said:

"Go."

Matilde kissed Ernesto's cheek for the last time, and got up. She started to walk, under the sun, over the scorched moor. On and on. Under the deep shade of the mountain trees. On and on. Nobody followed her tracks. Nobody knew where it was that finally she got lost.

That same night the Argüellos returned to Comitán.

PART III

"... When We Left the Place of Abundance"

———— ❦ ————

Very soon we shall begin to foretell them the future. When we left the Place of Abundance, an animal called Keeper of the Gorge made plaint at the gate of the Place of Abundance. Thou shalt die. Thou shalt perish! I am thy soothsayer.

From the Annals of the Xahil

1

We reach Palo María in a few hours. The roads are dry today and we are all on horseback. Father has spurred his and drawn blood from its flanks. The pigs are runting in the farmyard. Many nights of ash are heaped where the pine-flare once stood. How distantly the piercing cock-crow sounds, and the noise of work ending in the huts and fields! All the doors and windows of the big house are shut. We dismount in front of the veranda and stand there knocking, but nobody takes the slightest notice of us until presently an Indian appears and asks us what we want.

"I wish to speak to my cousin Francisca," Father says.

The Indian doesn't ask us to sit down. He leaves us standing and goes into the house. After a time my aunt comes out, dressed in black, eyes lowered. She stands still in front of us. We are silent a moment. Father doesn't know how to begin explaining to her what happened. He stammers:

"Your sister Matilde. . . ."

Aunt Francisca stops him.

"I know. The *dzulúm* took her."

Father looks at her disapprovingly and says:

"How can you believe such nonsense!"

"It's not the first time the *dzulúm* has taken one of our family. Remember Angelica. The forest calls us. Some of us have the knack of being able to listen."

Mother has been trying hard to keep quiet, but indignation gets the better of her and she exclaims:

"It's not proper to tell the truth in front of the children,

"... *When We Left the Place of Abundance*"

but Matilde shouted it over Ernesto's corpse, and it's worse than you're capable of supposing."

"I suppose nothing, Zoraida, I'm just a simple woman."

If we had said good-bye at that moment, Francisca wouldn't have prevented us. But Father didn't want to let things stand as they were:

"When Matilde came to Chactajal and told us what was happening here, we didn't believe it. It seemed incredible that you, so level-headed and sensible as you always were, should go in for such a stupid farce as you're playing now."

Aunt Francisca answered like her old self, forthrightly and stubbornly:

"But I stay, and you run away. Chactajal wasn't worth defending. You must know that, César, since you abandon it so readily. We have two different inheritances, you and I. I'll never give mine up. Not even when I'm dead will I let what belongs to me go. They can come, all of them, and break my fists, but I'll not open them to let the handful of earth I'll be taking with me fall."

"You've said it. We don't know each other any more. When strangers come, they are offered no hospitality."

Aunt Francisca reddened. She made a step toward Mario and me, but stopped on the point of caressing us.

"I don't want you to judge me worse than I am, César. We were brought up like brother and sister, and I owe you much. But the Indians would lose confidence if they saw me open my doors for you. It's months since anyone has crossed the threshold."

Father smiled sardonically.

"And where do you brew your magic potions? And where do you give advice to those who consult you? And where do you lay curses on your enemies? It seems inappropriate here in the open air. Witchcraft thrives on mystery."

"... When We Left the Place of Abundance"

Aunt Francisca was trembling with rage.

"You're mocking me. You may not know it but I have more power than you think. Ernesto. . . ."

"Ernesto was murdered. Shot. The bullets were common ones made of lead, not of curses or evil desires."

"Did you find the murderers?"

"Nobody looked for them."

"So much the better. It's useless. I know who killed Ernesto. And I know too that as long as I have the pistol that did it in my possession, nobody can take vengeance against its owner."

Father looked at her in speechless reproof. Turning on his heels, he ordered:

"Come away."

We got back into the saddles. In front of us a hillock unfolded gently. Before passing the last elbow in the road I turned to look back at the house. Aunt Francisca stood there just as we had left her, a tall, silent, black figure guarded by a hundred pairs of slanting eyes.

2

I'm longing to reach Comitán to give Nana the present I've brought her. But Father has ordered that before we unpack Nana herself must go and fetch Don Jaime Rovelo: he wants to speak to him urgently.

Don Jaime arrives, greets us, and asks:

"How was Chactajal?"

"Disastrous," Father answers bitterly. "The Indians burnt the cane harvest and killed Ernesto. It was touch and go they didn't kill us too."

"Cárdenas is asking for it, with his laws. There's already crime and lawlessness; misery will soon follow. It's very comfortable to have ideals when one's tucked cosily away like my son is. But let them come and get a taste of the problems themselves. They'd soon be convinced the Indians deserve no better than pack beasts."

"Zoraida," says Father, "tell them to get us a drink. I'm thirsty."

She goes to obey. Don Jaime pulls out his tobacco pouch and rolls a cigarette. He asks:

"And what do you mean to do now?"

"Fight."

"How?"

"There's only one way. Call in the law on our side."

"Another bright idea like choosing a rural teacher?"

"Don't scoff, Jaime. It's nothing like that now. We've got to ask the Government to send a surveyor to parcel out the land and give it to its rightful owners. In self-protection I've got to know first what the law regards as mine."

"Have we come to this? To ask for arbitration? We're the bosses."

"And you know why we haven't been able to hold on to our properties? Because we're not united. Each of us works only for his own profit. No one thinks of the rest."

Mother appears with glasses of lemonade. She offers one to Don Jaime. Father gulps his down thirstily, wipes his mouth with a handkerchief, and says:

"The small holding can't be touched. As to that, we've got to insist on our rights being observed."

"Insist? To whom?"

"The competent authorities. If we've failed here, then we must go to Tuxtla and speak to the Governor. He's a friend of mine and will help us. Once the boundaries are settled and we all have our title deeds and the demarcations of our land, then we can begin working again."

"Your optimism's boundless, César. Begin working again. With what men? The Indians will be happy enough

208

to sow their own fields and eat their maize. For the rest of the time they'll sit on the ground and scratch for fleas."

"Obviously it won't be like it was. The Indians won't give free work now they're so ill-advised. If necessary we'll pay them."

"The minimum wage?"

Father makes up his mind on the spot:

"The minimum wage."

"As if money meant anything to them! Especially now they're in such a state of mind. Don't be deceived, César, don't count on the Indians for work."

"Even suppose you're right, there are still the *ladinos*. We can rope them in. Of course the wages will have to be higher. And we'd need to add the transport costs to the farm."

"And once they're on the farm, build houses for *ladinos* to live in, cook food for *ladinos* to eat, hand out clothes buckshee for *ladinos* to wear. How long would you be able to meet such expenses?"

Father bends his head and looks thoughtfully at the dusty toe-caps of his boots. The discussion seems over. Slowly and softly he adds:

"All you tell me now I've been repeating to myself day and night on the road. You're right. The sensible thing would be to let the farms go to the devil and look for another way of earning a living. But I'm not of an age to begin or learn anything new. I'm only a rancher. Chactajal's mine. And I'm not prepared to let anyone seize it from me. Not even a President of the Republic. I'm going to stay there, whatever the conditions. I don't want to live anywhere else. I don't want to die away from it."

From the seriousness of his voice we know his words were final. Don Jaime put his glass down.

"And the only road is to Tuxtla?"

". . . When We Left the Place of Abundance"

"The only road. I go tomorrow."

"It's madness. Nobody will help us or take any notice. The bosses, as my son says, are an institution that's out of fashion these days."

"We must fight. We must fight together. You'll come with me, won't you, Jaime?"

"Yes."

In silence they shake hands. They go together into the road.

When they have left us alone, Mother begins unpacking with Nana's help.

"These shirts are soiled from the ranch. There wasn't time to do a thing. We had to escape. . . ."

They sort the shirts. They put aside those Father will want for the journey and those he won't.

"Will the *patrón* be away long?"

"Who knows? Official matters often take a long time."

"Shall I pack these woollen socks?"

"No, Nana, Tuxtla's in the hot land."

Open boxes, trunks half unpacked, beds rumpled. Things in disorder on every bit of furniture. I take advantage of the two women being so busy to look for the present I've brought Nana. Having found it, I go out on to the veranda and there I stand waiting. Presently Nana comes by. I call her in a whisper:

"Come, I've got something for you."

I open her hand and pour into it a stream of pebbles I picked up on the bank of the river. Nana's eyes are glad when she hears me say they're from Chactajal.

3

Mario and I dress in black to go with Mother to see Ernesto's mother.

"... When We Left the Place of Abundance"

She is an old lady and blind. She sits on a stoop of the veranda and in her lap is a calabash full of tobacco. She and a neighbour are crumbling it in their fingers.

"Good afternoon," we say as we go in.

The blind woman stretches out both hands as if by her touch to give shape to the unfamiliar voice.

"It's Doña Zoraida Argüello and her two children," the neighbour explains.

"And nothing for them to sit on. Please bring out the armchair from my room."

The neighbour goes to do as she is told, and the blind woman gets up and leans on her stick. In her hurry she doesn't notice that the calabash has dropped from her lap and the tobacco is spilt over the floor.

"We've brought bad news," says Mother.

But the blind woman isn't listening, she is preoccupied with something else.

"Neighbour, have you found the armchair?"

"I'm coming, Nati child, I'm coming."

"Why didn't you warn us of your visit, Doña Zoraida? We'd have prepared something for you. We're very poor but we mean well. And when it's for people we're fond of we can always find some little thing."

Mother sits in the armchair, while the neighbour begins gathering up the spilt tobacco.

"And what news have you brought me of my son Ernesto? Will he be some time longer in Chactajal?"

"Yes, still some time longer."

"I say he's more than my stick. Such a gentle son, so ready to do his duty. He's the comfort of my old age."

"Don't let Doña Nati speak of her son", says the neighbour, "or a whole day won't be enough."

"He won't have put me in the wrong with you, Doña Zoraida? I advised him so strongly to be obliging and respectful."

". . . When We Left the Place of Abundance"

"We've nothing to complain of," Mother forces herself to say.

"He comes of good stock. I don't say so for myself, but his father, Don Ernesto that was, he was a real gentleman. When I came into disgrace, my name was on everyone's lips. My name was chewed up proper by everyone. They mocked me, they pitied me, they insulted me. But when they knew my disgrace was with the deceased Ernesto, you just should have seen the envy that turned their faces yellow! He wasn't an Argüello for nothing."

"And what good did that do you, Doña Nati? Were you able to feed on his name?"

"It's the honour of it, woman, the honour I laid on my son's head. And the blue blood. Oh, how he was reared, like a colt with fire and nobility. Sundays I used to send my little fellow well scrubbed and in his best clothes to walk about the streets so that his father could admire him. Sometimes, even if he was talking with other fine gentlemen, Don Ernesto—him that was—would call him and would give him his pocket-money in front of everyone: two *reales* or a *tostón*, according. And my little one, instead of spending them on trifles or sharing them with the other little Indian brats, brought them to me to help make ends meet. For poverty's never been far away from this house. Afterwards I began to notice that my Ernesto was reliable and intelligent. So I went to talk to the priest, hoping he'd allow the boy to attend his school. I had to scrape to pay the fees, but how happy he used to come home from his classes! Every day with new words they'd taught him, or with a bit of paper in which they said he wasn't rough, that he applied himself and behaved well. I don't know if anyone gave him advice or if he began to think it out for himself, because he's very bright, but the fact is he started to be ambitious. He wanted to go to

". . . When We Left the Place of Abundance"

Mexico City and continue his studies, to get a degree like Don Jaime Rovelo's son. I didn't dissuade him, and in the meantime I worked harder and harder, so that his thoughts wouldn't turn out to be like if wishes were horses, beggars would ride. Because I didn't want him to be eating his heart out with disappointment. Then I got his first pair of shoes on credit, and shod him. Bless my soul, what a sight he was on the day he wore them first! Such great big blisters came out on his feet. But Ernesto was always one to keep a stiff upper lip and he didn't complain. He went out to take a turn round the park, as if he'd been a dandy since the day he was born."

Doña Nati hides her own bare feet under the hem of her skirt. They are fissured from so much exposure. Mother seems to want to interrupt her, but the old woman pays no heed and goes on talking.

"Then came my illness. A bad air got me. Ernesto had to leave school and go into a workshop. He did his duty, and that's less than the truth, but I knew he didn't like it and I thanked God that if an evil thing had to come upon me, that thing should be that I might go blind, so as not to see my son's distress."

Mother turns to the neighbour and in a very low voice asks her to go and boil a little water. The neighbour looks at us suspiciously, but asks no question and obeys. When she has gone, Mother says:

"Nati, I've brought no letter from Ernesto."

The blind woman laughs, faintly amused.

"And why should he write me? My son knows well enough I don't know how to read and wouldn't be able. Besides, he can let me know anything necessary through you."

"Yes. You know, Nati? Ernesto's a bit delicate."

"Has the fever got him?"

The alarm of it makes Nati feel about her, dully.

213

"Really it was an accident. He set out on horseback for Ocosingo. . . ."

"And didn't arrive?"

"On the road some Indians did him harm."

"Did him harm? Where is he? Take me to where he is!"

The neighbour comes hurrying up to us with a pewter mug in her hand. She wants to put it to Nati's lips, but the blind woman pushes her off roughly.

"What is it you want to make me drink?"

The neighbour gets in ahead of us:

"The visitors are dressed in black."

Nati drops her stick and raises her hands to her face.

"My eyes!" she cries, split to her roots.

4

Mother's just out of the bath and her hair is dripping. She wraps it in a towel so that it won't wet the bedroom floor.

I follow because I like to see her dress. She draws the curtains, foiling the street's curiosity. A discreet, silent warm shadow fills the room. From the drawers of the dressing-table Mother takes the stiff bristle brush, the piebald tortoiseshell comb, the pots of different-coloured cream, the pomades for lashes and brows, the red pencil for her lips. She opens them carefully and uses them one by one.

Ecstatically I watch how her face is transformed, how her nose, eyes, and mouth jump into relief, how this or that feature is stressed, making her very lovely. When the final moment comes my heart is brimming over. She opens the wardrobe and brings out the little mahogany casket and empties the contents on the silk counterpane, asking:

"Which ear-rings shall I wear today?"

"... When We Left the Place of Abundance"

I help her choose. No, not these. They weigh too much and are too conspicuous. These like calabashes, my father gave them to her on their wedding night, are for special occasions, and today's just any old day. The jet ones. Good. Doubtfully she puts them on, sighing:

"Pity! Such pretty jewellery Doña Pastora sells. But now ... nothing doing. I'd be resigned to it if only your papa were here."

I know she isn't talking to me. If I were to answer she'd be cross because someone had overheard. She's confiding to herself, to the wind, to the furniture round her. So I scarcely dare move in case she'll notice I'm here and send me packing.

"There. The ear-rings suit me very well. They match my dress."

She goes to the mirror. She touches her cheeks in the glassy surface, runs over her features with the tips of her fingers, and seems pleased and satisfied. But her nostrils begin to dilate, as if she were sniffing an unknown presence in the room. Mother turns abruptly:

"Who's there?"

Out of a corner comes Nana's voice, then she herself:

"It's me, Señora."

Mother sighs, relieved.

"You scared me. This mania your people have of walking about so noiselessly, lurking in ambush, jumping out when one least expects. Why did you come? I didn't call."

But Mother's attention has wandered and without waiting for the reply she turns back to gaze at herself in the mirror, to stiffen the little crease in the collar, to shake the speck of dust off her shoulder. Nana watches, and as she watches a sob wells up, seeking an outlet, like water breaking through the stones in its way. Mother hears and stops scrutinizing herself. She is annoyed:

"God grant me patience! What are you crying for?"

215

"... When We Left the Place of Abundance"

Nana doesn't answer but the sobs swell in her throat and hurt.

"Are you ill? Have you a pain?"

It's clear Mother doesn't like this woman. Just because she's Indian. During all the years they've lived in the same house, Mother's tried to have as little to do with her as possible. She edges past her as she would circumvent a puddle, with petticoats drawn up.

"Here, have this, it will take the pain away."

She hands her a white pill, but Nana refuses it.

"It's not because of myself, Señora. I'm weeping to see how this house is crumbling to bits because there's no longer the binding cement of manhood."

Mother puts the pill away again. She manages to hide her annoyance and says in a voice even and tight:

"It's only a month since César went. He writes me often. He'll be back soon, he says."

"I'm not speaking of your husband, nor of these days, but of what will come."

"That's enough fortune-telling. If you've something to say, say it at once."

"So far and no farther will the name of Argüello go. Here in front of our eyes it will be snuffed out, for your womb was sterile and yielded no son."

"Yielded no son! There's Mario, the pride of my heart. What more do you want?"

"He's not going to stay the pace, Señora, he'll never reach manhood."

"Why do you say that, you evil-tongued old woman?"

"How should I be saying so, talking against my own entrails? It's others who've said it, and they have wisdom and power. The ancients of the tribe of Chactajal have gathered in conference. For each one of them has heard, in the secret of his dreams, a voice saying: 'May they not prosper or be perpetuated. May the bridge they have

216

thrown into the future be broken.' A voice like an animal's counselled them so. And they have marked Mario for condemnation."

Mother gives a start. She remembers:

"The sorcerers. . . ."

"The sorcerers are beginning to eat him up."

Mother goes to the window and flings back the curtains. The noon-day sun comes in, barbed and strong like an arrow.

"It's easy enough to whisper in a dark room. Speak now. Repeat what you've said. Do you dare offend the face of light?"

Nana's voice when she answers is free from tears. With terrible precision, as if she is carving bark with the blade of a knife, she utters:

"Mario will die."

Mother seizes the tortoiseshell comb and twists it convulsively in her fingers.

"Why?"

"Don't ask me, Señora. What can I know?"

"Didn't they send you to threaten me? I bet they told you: frighten her so she'll open her hands and drop what she's holding, and then we shall share it out among us all."

Nana's eyes open wide with surprise and horror. She can only manage to stammer:

"Señora. . . ."

"Good, then, go to them and tell them that I'm not afraid. That if I ever give them anything it shall be from charity."

Nana pulls her hands back quickly, closing them tight in case Mother should try to put something into them.

"I command you!"

"The sorcerers want no money. They want the male-child, Mario. They'll eat him, they've begun to eat him already."

217

Mother faces Nana resolutely.

"I'm surprised at myself. How long have I been listening to such nonsense?"

Nana takes a step back, begging:

"Don't touch me, Señora. You've no rights over me. I wasn't a part of your dowry. I belong to the Argüellos. I'm from Chactajal."

"Nobody's tied my hands. I can hit you."

With a furious gesture Mother forces Nana to her knees. Nana does not resist.

"Swear that what you've just said is a lie!"

Mother gets no reply. The silence angers her still more. Furiously she begins to smack the sharp edge of the comb down, again and again, on Nana's head. Nana neither defends herself nor protests. From my corner I watch them, trembling with fear.

"Upstart Indian, get out of here! Don't let me see you in my house again."

Mother lets go of her and sits down on the stool in front of the dressing-table. She is breathing hard, and her face has broken up into sharp wrinkles. She passes a handkerchief over it, but can't wipe them away.

Stealthily I tiptoe up to Nana, who is still on the ground, all broken and abandoned, like a thing of no worth.

5

"It's been impossible for us to obtain an audience with the Governor yet. Jaime and I have been to the Palace every day. We sit and wait in a cramped, stuffy room, with dozens of people who have come from all over the State to set their affairs in order. They don't call us by turn, but according to the importance of our business.

". . . When We Left the Place of Abundance"

And judging by the way the politicians of today are thinking, it's much more urgent to patch the peasant-farmer's homespun trousers than to see justice done to the *patrón*. Perhaps that's why a lot of those who were with us earlier, asking for their lands to be returned, have got tired of waiting and have gone away. But I still believe we mustn't give up hope. Chactajal will be ours again. Not under the same conditions as before, we mustn't deceive ourselves about that. But we'll be able to go back there and live. So that Mario can grow up on the land that will one day be his, and so that he'll be able to take care of it and love it.

"The whole thing is to have patience and be sly. We've had dealings with lots of people since we've been here. Of course we try to see that such people are important and influential in the Governmènt. It's essential to treat them well, wait on them, manœuvre them. It's the done thing here to take cool drinks or iced beer because it's so hot. It's not thought beneath one's dignity as it is in Comitán for gentlemen to go into a drinking house. Anyway it's difficult at first sight to distinguish an educated man from a common one. The climate allows only of light-weight garments, and everyone goes about in the same rough dress. The waistcoats you packed for me aren't much use here. I haven't had a chance to wear them even once. But apart from the climate and the clothes, there are really no gentlemen, because practically all the inhabitants of Tuxtla live at the expense of the exchequer and have jobs with miserable salaries. It shouldn't be difficult to bribe them and get them to help us fix our affairs. You know how ashamed I am to resort to such measures, but we have no alternative. I don't propose to stop at anything to gain my ends. I swear to you I won't return to Comitán without the necessary papers guaranteeing that we can live on the farm again.

"... When We Left the Place of Abundance"

"I miss you and the children very much. At nights Jaime and I take a turn round the town because it's impossible to stay shut up in the hotel room. One gets suffocated breathing the hot, stale air, watching the beetles crawl over the walls, the broken ventilator, the shower without water. The streets are a sea of mud or a dustcloud according to whether it has been raining or not. The houses are drab and ugly. Only in the park there's a little breeze. And there are flamboyants always in flower. And music.

"But don't start getting it into your head I'm enjoying myself. I can't grow used to the way the Tuxtlecos live. I belong to the cold land, and I love my home, and to be with you. I'm making this sacrifice just for you, but the result's got to be worth it.

"Jaime's already fed up and has asked for a reprieve. He's going in my name to speak to Golo Córdova, the brandy merchant, to see if he won't have a little more patience with us. Just at the moment I can't meet my obligations to him. I've also asked Jaime to give you this letter."

Mother folded the sheet thoughtfully.

"How do you see the situation, Don Jaime?"

"Bad. César doesn't want to face facts, but actually the Government is deliberately arranging things so as not to listen to our protests. We may have logic on our side, even law, but they've got force and they'll use it to help their favourites. Just now they're trying to ingratiate themselves with the powers that be. They're turning themselves into Bartolomés de las Casas, protecting the Indians and the underdogs. But it's all ambition really."

"So?"

"So we've got to let the world tick on. The vultures will swallow the carrion."

"Don't you intend returning to Tuxtla?"

"... When We Left the Place of Abundance"

"What for?"

"If you're so sure it's useless, why did you leave César there?"

"Do you think I didn't do everything in my power to bring him back? But no one can stop César once an idea gets fixed in his head. He's obstinate, and in a certain way he's right. He's not fighting for himslf alone, but for Mario. I'm old already, and after me, who's left?"

"Don't spit in the face of God, Don Jaime. You have a son."

"Oh yes, a model son. His college career was brilliant. He ends up with a lawyer's degree. Nobody better than him to defend us in this crisis. He'd win our case; and not for me, but for himself, since it's his inheritance. But do you know what he answered when I suggested it? That he'll gladly renounce his share of the booty seized by the ranch thieves. That we go on imagining it's ours, but it hasn't even cost us the trouble of robbing."

Mother was scandalized.

"It's not possible he can have said such a thing! It's disrespectful. It's a lie. We're the owners, the legitimate owners."

"My son doesn't think so, Doña Zoraida. This is the age of ideals. He believes in these new theories, Communist or whatever they're called."

"Oh blessed San Caralampio!"

"It's not his fault, it's mine for having sent him to study. But it's no use complaining now. What's done can't be undone."

They were both silent. After a space Don Jaime advised her:

"Write to César, Doña Zoraida. You write. It'll be long before he's back."

"I'll write. . . . I've bad news to send. Do you remember that Indian, the one that was my child's Nana? But

"... When We Left the Place of Abundance"

you won't remember because one doesn't notice servants, especially in other people's houses. Well anyway this one I'm talking about was brought up by the Argüellos. She breathed the same air we did, and was very much one of the family. But she had to come out with her ha'penny-worth of nonsense."

"What did she do?"

"Making a great song and dance of it, she comes to announce that the sorcerers of Chactajal are eating Mario up, that he'll never come of age."

Mother said this lightly, with assumed frivolity, but beneath her words one caught a tense expectancy. Don Jaime said nothing.

"Do you think it's possible?"

"It's always very painful to lose a child, and there are so many ways of doing that."

"But Mario can't die!"

Don Jaime got up. He was irritated:

"Why not?"

Then he repented of his sharpness:

"Besides, it's better so. I promise you it's better so."

6

The wooden chest with her clothes in it is still in Nana's room: the *tzec* with its many-coloured ribbons; the frilly blouse; the Guatemalan shawl; and, wrapped in a piece of silk, the pebbles I brought from Chactajal. I gather them up and put them in my blouse to keep them warm. Then I go in to breakfast, into the dining-room with its high ceiling and dark furniture, amid the clatter of metal spoons against plates that keep clamouring for attention.

Then the lonely wandering round the house. It's so huge. The garden where Mother has been sowing dahlia seeds; and a patio; and the back yard. And the bedrooms. And the veranda. And the pantry. All empty, even though other people such as Aunt Romelia have come to live with us.

She and Mother sit on the veranda crocheting the never-ending cloth runner for the altarpiece in the chapel. They both like gossiping, and they pass hours crocheting and talking.

"What do you suppose happened to Matilde?"

"If a wild beast didn't eat her, she must be acting as housemaid in some ranch or other."

"Poor thing!"

"Poor nothing. She got her desserts, dishonouring the family. Though strictly between ourselves I'm telling you it was the only way to avoid being gobbled up by the maggots in the granary. Even if she was my sister, I must admit Matilde had gone to seed. Anyhow she was never exactly an oil painting. Francisca even less, in spite of her strong character. She knew nothing at all except how to order other people about. And look where she's landed herself."

"César says Francisca's not crazy, that she's only play-ing at being a witch. It's a trick so she can stay in Palo María. One can see by the result. All the farm-owners except herself have been forced to leave. When it comes to the day of reckoning, Francisca will be the only one to come out creditably."

"Who says she's crazy? What I say and maintain is that she's bewitched."

Mother drops her needlework and sits staring at Romelia in distress.

"Do you believe such tales?"

"Good heavens, dear, of course it's perfectly true. Such things as I've seen on the farm! And after that they want one to go on acting quite calmly. If they'd only managed to cure my jitters then, if they'd only made me forget what I'd seen, I wouldn't be as ill as I am now."

"Did you actually see the sorcerers?"

"A certain man that's my *compadre* lives near Palo María. His cattle were all well fattened and content, and suddenly they began to fall as if a thunderbolt had struck them, tongues hanging out, black as coal. And the corn-fields, you'd have thought the locusts had got them. Not a leaf left, and that was the end of it."

"It must have been some disease. Some pest."

"No. A sorcerer had fallen out with him and had marked the door of his house with ashes. That was how the disaster happened."

"Can sorcerers hurt people too?" Almost in a whisper my mother added: "Children?"

"Children especially, because they're more often out of doors. Newborn babies wake to the light of the sun and they're purple from asphyxia."

"Perhaps there's nobody to look after them."

"And little boys, when they reach puberty, they swell up with poison."

Mother throws her crochet-work aside and stands up. She is breathing fire:

"That's not true. It's only among the Indians! Their threats don't work against us. We're of another race. We aren't in their power."

Aunt Romelia goes on hammering her statements home in a monotonous voice:

"It works for us too. Take the case of Francisca."

Mother sits down again. She is very pale.

"But there must be a way to placate them. If they want vengeance, let them be revenged, but not on the children."

"Oh, Zoraida, I don't know what's in their heads. All I can tell you is I wouldn't go back to Palo María for

"... When We Left the Place of Abundance"

anything in the world. Just think, Francisca might wake
up one fine day in a bad temper and do me some harm.
She's never liked me anyway. She's always thrown it in
my teeth that I'm a bit crazy and my illnesses are all
make-believe. Make-believe! I'd like her to hear what
the doctors in Mexico City have to say about me.
Imagine, they assured me that what I need . . . is, well,
that I go back to my husband. What do you make of
that?"

Mother isn't listening. She looks at her vaguely with
shifting, vacant eyes.

"Oh yes, I know that husband of mine is a useless good-
for-nothing. I didn't leave him without cause. But I've
got to be magnanimous about it, or the one to go crazy is
going to be me."

Aunt Romelia is seeking Mother's approval or disapproval. But Mother's lips are closed, and no words
come. She goes on crocheting very quickly and persistently. She does a long piece and then finds she has to
unpick it all because she's made a mistake.

7

Today Mario and I were up before the sun had properly
risen. Yawning heavily and rubbing our eyes, we let
ourselves be dressed. To get us moving, Mother said:

"Hurry, we're going to visit the crookback."

Mario and I looked at each other in surprise. To visit
the crookback. That's enough for us:

"Stop buttoning up our jackets as if we were dolls.
No, no, we can put on our shoes ourselves."

How quiet the streets are at this time of day! The donkey boys haven't finished yoking their beasts yet, for the
drawing of water. The servants are still preparing the

225

"... When We Left the Place of Abundance"

maize dough to take to the baker. So ahead of us stretches a total stillness which we break with our feet like a thin crust of ice. Our footsteps echo loudly as we leave block after block of the town behind us. Down San Sebastian Hill. Through the park. We leave it by way of Yaxchivol, where the pavement ends and the narrow path winds through the tender green cornshoots tipped with dew.

"These fields belong to my friend Amalia."

Behind the stone fences the trees are nodding: plum trees with bitter yellow fruit. Custard apples, their leaves broad and thick. Avocado pears.

As soon as we see the first shingled house, we know we've reached the poor district. We stop before a door which gives way to a slight push of Mother's hand.

"Come in, Doña Zoraida," a voice says.

We can't make out from which corner of the room it comes, because we are blinded by the daylight outside. But Mother knows the room well and without hesitation goes to the only window and opens it. A cramped and poverty-stricken room is revealed. The woman who spoke is lying very still on a low cot. Her long hair is grey and spills untidily over the pillow. Her face is like a desert plain into which her eyes have sunk like two pools of water.

"How are you this morning?"

"My body aches rather, but it's probably the moon."

With Mother's help the cripple is propped up and sits on the edge of the bed, beside which is a table with some half-empty bottles. Mother picks one up.

"I'm going to rub you with liniment; perhaps it will ease the pain."

She starts to lift the cripple woman's nightshirt. Mario and I turn our faces prudishly to the wall, which is covered with postcards, coloured ones and black-and-white, fixed there with tacks or candle grease.

"... When We Left the Place of Abundance"

The sun here, setting behind a mountain, is the twilight the cripple can look at whenever she pleases. These girls with bunches of lilies in their arms are her constant friends, sharing interminable conversations through the long-drawn days. These doves are always carrying her sealed letters in their beaks.

"Mario, draw up that chair."

My brother does as he is told. The cripple settles herself on the hard wooden seat and waits for Mother to comb her hair.

"Are these your children, Doña Zoraida?"

"Just the two of them. I couldn't have more."

After combing her, Mother goes to the corner where the whitened clay brazier is sitting. She blows on the ashes and fans them, and the dormant embers begin pulsing again, faintly at first, then stronger and redder. She places the coffee-pot on the fire and it soon starts bubbling.

"I brought a piece of salt meat for breakfast."

Mother pulls it apart with her fingers and puts it on a plate. From there she picks up the morsels and slips them between the crippled woman's teeth, who chews slowly, her hands lying quietly in her lap. Her eyes wander over our heads in the direction of the postcards, and there they rest, quiet and content.

When she has finished eating, Mother wipes the corners of her lips with a napkin, then goes to wash the plate in a little wooden bowl.

"How do you like my children?"

"Very well behaved, very pretty. Not frightened to look at me, and they don't make fun of me."

"The boy is six. After him I had no more. He's the only son. He's got to grow to manhood, he must."

"And why not, Doña Zoraida? God will bless the kind acts that are in him."

227

"... When We Left the Place of Abundance"

Mother finishes setting the room in order and goes to sit on the edge of the bed. She bites her lips, hesitantly, then she turns her face toward the cripple and says:

"It's the first time I've brought my children to see you. I wanted you to meet them. Especially the boy, because I'm going to ask you a favour."

"Me, Doña Zoraida? Me? But I'm so poor and help-less."

"I want you to read me the cards."

Mother goes quickly to the table and pulls it closer to the cripple. She removes some of the bottles and lays a pack of playing-cards in their place.

"But I don't know how, Señora. . . ."

"There's no need. Just lend me your hand, that's all, I promise."

The cripple looks down at those hands that for such a long time now have not been hers.

The pack of cards is in the centre of the table. Mother's hand grasps the cripple's and leads it toward the pack. As she lets it go, it drops with a thud on the table.

"Try, woman, you've got to help me."

Mother is breathing hard and her cheeks are burning with fever. The cripple's eyes shift from the twisted face before her to her own fingers, knotted and deformed with rheumatism. She can't imagine how she has done it, but one card falls apart from the rest.

"Which card has come up?"

Mother doesn't dare look. Turning the other way, she waits for the reply.

"Spades."

"Spades, that's trouble. No, we didn't do it right. Let's try again."

She reshuffles the pack and puts it back on the table, seizes the cripple's hand and guides it until one card has been pulled from the rest.

"...When We Left the Place of Abundance"

"Spades."

Mother's movement is so violent that the table shakes and the bottles jostle together with a tinkling sound. The cards fall face up on the floor, their secrets revealed. There are spades, and more spades. . . .

Mother stares at them in horror. She is trembling as she faces the cripple.

"And is this your gratitude? Have I come every day for years to dress your festering wounds and drag you this way and that like a log and satisfy your insatiable hunger, and then to be thanked with this?"

The cripple gazes at her with huge, dry, wounded eyes.

But the sudden rush of strength has left Mother limp, and she is on her knees now, kissing the cripple's feet, begging her with her sincerest and most heartfelt voice:

"Forgive me, for God's sake forgive me. I don't know what I'm saying, I'm out of my mind. In the name of whatever you love most, ask that if someone has to die it shall be me and not him, for he is innocent. Not him, whose only fault is that he was born of me."

The cripple has turned white. Beads of sweat have broken out on her forehead, and her mouth is distended with suffering. She is shaking all over. We run to support her but reach her too late. Her lids droop. Her head falls to her shoulders, broken. Her whole body abandons itself to the current that bears her swiftly away—far, far away from us, our voices, and our sorrow.

8

When I close my eyes I get a picture of the place where Nana and I will be together. The great plain of Nicolocac and the kites like constellations in the heavens. Some are flying close to the ground, because their strings are short.

"... When We Left the Place of Abundance"

Others drop out of the sky with broken props and paper in shreds. But Mario's kite stays there among the highest and the lightest and most beautiful, like a fixed star brightly burning.

Then will come the *marimba*, and the man who jumps on to a box to announce that the circus is coming. From a train that has brought him there specially to meet us, out will get Don Pepe, all twisted into contortions. And the sisters Cordero will perform that trick so difficult we can't even imagine it, called the Irish loop. And so many snakes will uncoil, and so much confetti will rain down on us that it will be quite a job to see the procession of foreigners.

Nana will say: "That one there is Chinese. You can recognize him because of his yellow skin and the way he's riding a dragon. The one going by now is from Mexico City. Just think, the only way he can speak is of *thou* and *your honour*. He doesn't say *ye* even to one like me. That one over there is black. No, don't go licking your finger to rub it on his face, because the colour won't ever come off. And here's one with tattoo-marks on his cheeks and a ring in his nose."

Suddenly Nana will lower her eyes and make me lower mine too. Because there in front of us will be the wind in his best cloak. He'll stroll across the plain until he possesses it all to himself, because everyone will give way before his kingly state. We'll hear his great voice and will tremble because of his strength. Bit by bit, so that he doesn't notice, we'll dare to lift our eyes till they are stopped by the sight of him. And Nana and I will sit there hand in hand and go on looking forever.

9

About seven this evening Amalia, Mother's spinster

friend, came looking for us. She wouldn't wait for us to finish supper but took us straight back to her house.

Lots of people were there, sitting on benches placed in the first courtyard and on the veranda. Poor women covered with *rebozos* and unshod. Snivelling children sweating in their outdoor clothes. Ladies, stiff and withdrawn, trying not to speak to anyone and wrinkling their noses to repel the smells around them.

Amalia asked Mother:

"Would you care to visit Our Lord Jesus?"

We went into the drawing-room from which the old lady and the furniture had vanished. On a table covered with a very white tablecloth stood a reliquary, and, flanking it, two metal candlesticks in which burned tall, fat candles. Hassocks had been placed in front of the table, and there we knelt. Mother closed her eyes and plunged into hard and painful thoughts. Her lips were tight. Mario and I amused ourselves inspecting the room, which looked so different from usual. Amalia leaned toward us and whispered:

"Have more respect, children. You're in the Holy Presence."

Mother crossed herself and got up. We went out on to the veranda.

"Is it certain he'll come?"

"Quite. He told me himself to put everything ready."

"What a lot of people. He won't have time to attend to them all."

"You'll be the first, I promise."

"But can you really manage that?"

"I ought to have some privileges, considering the risks I'm running. Just imagine what would happen if the police should come and search the house."

"May San Caralampio preserve us!"

"We'd all be in jail."

"... When We Left the Place of Abundance"

"Aren't you afraid?"

"Someone must offer to help."

"But why should it be you? You're a woman alone."

"Husbands won't let their wives do it. It's hard for them even to get permission to come here. Look, some of them are going already. They can't be away longer or their husbands will scold them."

"César's in Tuxtla luckily. I can stay as long as necessary."

Hours and hours sitting on the veranda. Mario and I nodded sleepily, propped one against the other.

"Don't go to sleep. He won't be long now."

About ten at night we heard the jog-trot of a horse. It stopped at the door. Amalia hurried to open, very stealthily and cautiously.

"Come in, sir."

Everyone knelt for the new arrival. He was a middle-aged man—tall, stout, and with a manner of one used to being obeyed. He was dressed for the road and carried a whip. Some of the women crawled after him begging:

"Your blessing, Señor Cura."

He made a perfunctory sign of the cross in the air. Using the tip of his whip, he opened a way through the crowd. In the artificial light his face seemed to have been carved with an axe.

"Would you like some refreshment, Father?"

Amalia led him to the drawing-room. Behind her were a number of people anxious to follow him in, but Amalia allowed no one but ourselves.

The curate prayed an *Ave Maria* before sitting down to table.

"Is that how you like your meat, sir?"

"Anything is a feast after those miserable ranches where there's nothing to be had. And mind you, they keep the best for me, but the best is a cold *tortilla* and a cup of watery coffee."

Amalia gave an abject smile, but the curate didn't notice. He was eating rapidly, not lifting his eyes from the plate.

"Father, you know my friend Zoraida, César Argüello's wife."

"By name. She's not one of the devout."

"She's come now because she wants your advice."

Only then did the curate raise his eyes and notice those round him. The way he stared was like a wall, and we came slap up against it.

"I suppose it's a case of conscience."

Mother stepped forward to be closer to where the curate sat.

"I don't know, Father. You're going to make fun of what I have to say. I didn't take it seriously either at first. But now I'm afraid, and I need you to enlighten me."

The curate pushed his plate away preparatory to listening.

"Wouldn't it be better if the children went away, and then you can explain things more freely?"

"It has to do with them. With Mario. This one."

"So small, and already causing trouble?"

"A woman, an Indian from the ranch, threatened me that the sorcerers would eat him."

The curate tightened his fists and, with the whole weight of his body, banged them down on the table.

"That's all. I might have guessed. Witchcraft and superstition. They bring me the little ones to be baptized and it isn't because they want to make them Christians, because nobody thinks of Christ, ever, but only so the holy water can help to ward off the werewolves and evil spirits. And when they marry, it's just to have a nice party. And they go to church only to murmur against their neighbours."

His eyes were glassy with rage. He was trembling as if he had been faced by some vile and crawling insect that he couldn't for some reason squash underfoot.

"I have the Sacraments in my keeping, and yet I can't preserve them or defend them. Every time I place the Host to one of your lips, it's like surrendering it to the flames. I'm always saying the same old absolution for the same old sins. I've never known such hardness of heart as there is in this village."

Amalia was frightened.

"We didn't mean to offend you, sir. . . ."

"It's not me you're offending. And it isn't for you I make sacrifices. Would it be worth putting up with hunger just so as to honour a ranch-man who's up to every trick to avoid paying tithes and first-fruits to the church? To suffer weariness and cold on roads that never come to an end anywhere, simply in order to attend a bunch of rebellious women who don't even know how to do their duty as Catholics? To wear oneself out fighting against the terror of this iniquitous and senseless persecution just so that the children of this heap of perdition, the darling children, shall grow up to be exactly like their parents?"

An artery swelled on his forehead and throbbed as if about to burst.

"No, get this quite clear, it's not for you."

He put his hand to his forehead and flattened the artery with his fingers. After a pause he commanded:

"Open the window, Amalia, we're suffocating."

Amalia obeyed. From the open window she looked stealthily at the curate, afraid yet curious. Mother, who had not received the answer she was hoping for, persisted:

"But the sorcerers can't do any harm, isn't that so?"

"They are men. All men can do harm."

"... When We Left the Place of Abundance"

Mother dropped into a chair, utterly crushed. Almost inaudibly she said:

"Then there's no help for it."

Amalia interrupted timidly:

"I've advised her to let the child take his first communion. . . ."

"Yes, let him, if he's of age."

Mother's fit of faintness passed. She recovered and was on her feet again. With ill-concealed reproach, disappointment tightening her throat, she reiterated:

"Is that all you can tell me, Father?"

"Have faith. And be resigned to God's will."

"Even if God wants to fatten himself on my children. . . . But not on the male child. Not on the boy!"

"Zoraida!"

Amalia threw herself on Mother as if she wanted to knock out of her hands some weapon she was brandishing blindly.

"Not the boy! Not the boy!"

"Quiet, woman. It's blasphemy what you're saying."

The priest stood up and clenched his fists till the knuckles turned white. Little by little he loosed them again, spreading his fingers on the table while the blood flowed in his hands once more and they returned to their usual colour. When he spoke his voice was flat and indifferent.

"Let her be. She isn't blaspheming. Sorrow knows no other way to speak but that."

Mother gave us a shove toward the door. As we passed the curate he made a move as if to detain us, but Mother pushed us on violently.

"No. You're our enemy too."

By the time we found ourselves on our way home through the dark, deserted streets, it was midnight; and all the way Mother wept.

". . . When We Left the Place of Abundance"

10

"Divine Providence never abandons those who trust its power."

Aunt Romelia allowed herself the luxury of a short, ironical laugh.

"Oh, Amalia, it's so obvious you've never lived."

Amalia raised her calm, unreproachful eyes.

"No, I didn't marry or have children, and it wasn't possible for me to become a nun either. For years I've been ashamed of being a kind of stumbling-block, like a stone against which people trip as they walk. But it's different now. Now I'm of some use."

"Of course you are. What would become of your mother if you didn't look after her?"

"It isn't Mother I'm referring to. The poor old thing won't last much longer. I was thinking of something else. Since the persecution of the Church I've been lending my house for services and to lodge the priests."

"Nice priests! Zoraida told me how that vermin behaved to her."

Amalia was trembling with indignation.

"Yes, people want them to be tame and defenceless, so's to finish them off quicker. They want them submissive so as to manage them just as they please. What a hope! The curate can do more than all Comitán put together."

Mother pressed her hands to her forehead and shuddered, begging:

"For pity's sake don't argue any more, my head's splitting."

"Listen to me, Zoraida. Divine Providence watches over us always. Make a sign of confidence and put yourself in its hands. Then it will reward you as it has rewarded me."

Aunt Romelia turned to her incredulously.

"You?"

"Of all the people who have visited my house, not one has come to spy. Not one. The Municipal President's wife assured me so. They haven't received a single denouncement. And it's not because of caution on my part. I've let everyone in. Lots of them I don't even know. But Divine Providence looks after us."

"And what would Divine Providence have Zoraida do?"

"Mario should take his first communion."

"Yes, why not?" Aunt Romelia conceded. "It's like homoeopathy. If it doesn't cure, at least it doesn't harm."

"But you've turned to your husband for your *own* cure, not to homoeopathy," Mother snapped.

Amalia was surprised but intrigued by the news.

"Really? Are you going back to him?"

It was clear Aunt Romelia didn't like her plans being known.

"The doctors from Mexico City advised me."

"But when you left him you said. . . ."

"I've got to swallow my words. Anyway I'd rather live in my own house, however humble, than be imposing myself on others who at every possible moment throw their generosity back in my teeth."

Aunt Romelia got to her feet and strode off. There was a pause.

"She's vexed with you, Zoraida."

"She doesn't matter to me. Neither she nor anyone else on earth. I'm desperate, Amalia, desperate."

Amalia stroked Mother's bowed head.

"I don't know whether to write to César and ask him to come back. I've begun a letter a thousand times, and always tear it up. What's the use of his coming, I think, and then I change my mind because if anything should happen. . . ."

"Nothing can happen. The sorcerers are powerful, everyone says so. They have no respect even for the house of the *patrón*. But before the door of the Sanctuary, there they stop."

"You've been very good to me, Amalia. You're the only one who pays any attention to me or listens to me. The others all think I'm mad. And when I ask advice they refuse it because nobody cares whether they kill my son. But really it can't happen, can it, Amalia?"

"Let me help you. Send your children to me and I'll teach them their catechism."

Mario and I started going that very afternoon.

We had our classes on the veranda, surrounded by the flowerpots and the cages full of chirruping canaries. We sat on little rush stools with Amalia opposite to us in her rocking-chair. She opened her catechism.

"Tell me, children, what are your names?"

Mario and I looked at one another surprised and were too shy to answer.

"Don't be frightened like that. It's the first question Father Ripalda will ask."

She read for a few moments silently, then closed the book.

"It's very complicated for you, the way it goes on. I'd better teach you in my own way. You know nothing about religion, that's true, isn't it?"

We nodded."

"Then you must learn the one most important thing. There is a hell."

This was nothing new. We had heard the word before. But it was only now that we discovered it meant something red and hot and those who had the bad luck to fall

238

into it were made to suffer in all sorts of ways. They were given a bath in great cauldrons of boiling oil. Their eyes were pricked with needles "the way it's done to canaries to make them sing better". The soles of their feet were tickled.

Mario and I had always lived in private worlds, each occupied with ourselves and paying little attention to the other. But now suddenly we became each of us aware of the other's company. Slowly, almost imperceptibly, we slid our chairs closer, so that when Amalia told us that in hell the demons danced at Lucifer's command, we were able quite easily to hold one another's hands, sweating with cold and fear, especially at this hour when the shadows had taken possession, one by one, of the bricks on the veranda wall, and we were caught in their power. Especially at such an hour when the old lady would be sobbing to herself by the window and there would be no one to comfort her. Especially now when the birds had fallen silent and the climbing tendrils assumed such terrible, wayward shapes.

"Children who behave badly go to hell."

What did behaving badly really mean? An example might be if one disobeyed one's parents, but it wasn't all that easy to do. Mario and I had sometimes tried, but never with much success. From now on we shan't try again. It might be stealing candies, but they're not all that good to eat after all. Or neglecting to study, but we don't go to school now. Or quarrelling with other children, but which? They always shut us up at home and we're not allowed to go out and play. What then? It looks as if the chances of a trip to hell are fairly remote after all. Mario and I relax the pressure that keeps us hand in hand, because it's six in the evening and the lights have just gone on.

". . . When We Left the Place of Abundance"

11

> *Hippity, hoppity!*
> *What did Hippity hoppity cry?*
> *He cried to you to let me go by.*
> *But how shall we pay, oh tell?*
> *With a white egg shell.*
> *And how shall you span the gulf so high?*
> *With little and big planks the lumbermen hew.*
> *But how shall you pack them, how shall you?*
> *In little bags and big ones too.*
> *And what will you give me my way to find?*
> *The little grey donkey that lags behind.*

We were playing in the back yard. Our two nurse-maids—one's called Vicenta and the other Rosalía, but in this game of Crossing-the-Frontier Rosalía has given herself the name of Guatemala and Vicenta is Mexico—our two nursemaids locked their arms to stop Mario and me from passing. They questioned us closely until we told them which of them we wanted to go with.

"I'll go to Mexico."

"And I to Guatemala."

Then as a rule it happens that one of us grasps the one we've chosen round the waist and the side that tugs hardest wins. But today just at the wrong moment Rosalía let go and stopped pulling, and Vicenta and Mario nearly fell over backwards. They laughed. This novelty in the game made it more fun.

"Again, Vicenta, again!"

But Vicenta huddled in her shawl as if she were cold, and shook her head.

"It's very late. It's getting dark. We'd better go in and play 'Dry Monkey'."

". . . When We Left the Place of Abundance"

I put up a solemn opposition:

"Mother doesn't let us play like that."

"Why not?"

"Because. . . ."

"How very obedient you are! It's obvious you're going to catechism classes."

I didn't want to annoy Vicenta because she threatened she wouldn't tell me any more stories. She's been working for us only a few days. She's supposed to look after me in Nana's place. But I didn't want to disobey Mother either because it's a sin and I'll go to hell. So with exaggerated eagerness I suggested:

"Let's play colours!"

Vicenta seemed as shocked as if I'd suggested something dreadful. She crossed herself quickly:

"Colours? God forbid."

"There's nothing wrong in that."

"Don't you know what happened to Límbano Romano's two sons for playing colours? Where I was working before I came here?"

Beginning to feel afraid, we said we hadn't heard.

"Shall I tell you the tale?"

Mario turned his back so as not to have to answer, because Vicenta's stories frightened him. Finding myself left in the lurch, I answered in a tiny thread of a voice:

"Yes."

"But not in this gale that's blowing. Come on, let's go into the kitchen, because such stories as these have to be told between walls."

Vicenta and Rosalía went ahead of us, chattering and smothering their laughter under their shawls.

In the kitchen we lit a candle, and when we were all settled round the hearth, Vicenta began her story.

"Well, so here you have it. There were two children who went by the names of Conrad and Luis. Every night they got into a gang with other little Indian kids and played in the back yard. And bless my soul what a fright we used to get! In the back yard it was dark as dark, what with there being no light and the thick leaves of the shrubbery. But the little boys, who were all for skulking about in queer corners, discovered this place because nobody ever troubled to keep an eye on them there. Well, so one fine night the boys decided they were going to play colours. They sat down there under a peach tree and the boy Luis, whose turn it was to be the angel with the golden ball, went a little way off to wait while the others chose their colours. But quite a time went by and everyone had their colours and the boy Luis didn't turn up. They all began shouting and at last they heard a sound like footsteps among the leaves and a hoarse voice like an old man's said:

" '*Ton-ton.*'

"The little Indian kids asked:

" 'Who's that?'

"And the hoarse voice answered:

" 'The devil with seven cords.'

"It was odd the boy Luis should be saying he was the devil with seven cords seeing it had been arranged he was the angel with the golden ball. But boys being boys and apt to be careless they never stopped to find out why but went on playing.

" 'What will you have?'

" 'A colour.'

" 'Which?'

" 'Leadwort.'

"Conrad didn't want to get up because he was feeling kind of jittery, but the rest pushed him because he'd chosen that colour. So putting a brave front on it he went groping his way to the place where the voice came from. There behind the tangle of briars was a little boy. Conrad

242

couldn't see his face very clear because, as I said, the back yard in that house was mighty dark. And suddenly—goodness only knows by what kind of devil's trick it was —the light went on. And there Conrad found himself, face to face with a little boy, and it wasn't his brother Luis at all. The face was like a child's face but all hairy and wrinkled. It was the devil with seven cords that goes by the evil name of Catashaná!

"The boy Conrad wanted to run away but he tripped over a body lying heels-up on the ground. Catashaná grabbed his hand to stop him, and pointed to the body saying:

" 'Look what you've done to your brother Luis, beating him so hard.'

"Catashaná is father of lies so he has to talk that way. But the boy Conrad got such a big fright that his teeth chattered and he couldn't answer. He was that much upset he didn't even get round to calling on San Caralampio or to making a sign of the cross or anything. Then Catashaná said:

" 'From now on you belong to me and you're going to do all I say.'

"And he didn't let go of the boy Conrad's hand, which was burning as if he'd been gripping hold of a live coal.

"Then Catashaná said:

" 'I want you to bring me a sacred Host to eat.'

"Next day off went the boy Conrad and told the curate he wanted to take his first communion, and he began learning his catechism. But instead of attending to what they taught him, he was only waiting for a chance to be up to his tricks. He was so badly brought up and cheeky that he'd become like the tail of Judas, and that's a fact. Scoldings, threats, nothing did the least good. But Catashaná arranged it so that the curate wouldn't notice and would think Conrad a very well-behaved boy and

243

tell him he was ready to take communion. And so, with
his mouth all stuffed with bad words, up he went to the
altar rail. But the moment the curate put the Host into
his mouth, God punished the boy Conrad. The Host was
turned into a bullet of lead. The harder Conrad tried to
swallow, the less he could. And just as he was making an
extra special effort the ball of lead stuck in his throat and
he fell down dead there and then—choked."

Vicenta's story ended. Mario ran out of the kitchen,
blowing out the candle as he went. I pursued him and
caught him up on the veranda.

"I don't want to take communion," he sobbed.

12

Mother weighed the turkeys in her hands and pinched
their breasts.

"They're very skinny, little Merchant."

"But between now and the holiday they've got time to
fatten. They're well worth their twenty *reales* each."

The market woman took her money and went. Ever
since then the turkeys have been in the back yard, spreading their tails and gobbling with a noise that's like a jug
pouring out water. They peck greedily at the grains of
corn Vicenta and Rosalía scatter for them, and they sleep
wherever night happens to catch up with them. Mario
and I go running after them waving dusters and clattering
saucepans to frighten them and make them fly. But the
turkeys cling close to the mud wall, trembling, and they
don't fly because they are weighed down by the daily
increasing fat of their bodies. When the woman arrived
whom they've called to make *tamales*, and she took a
peek into the yard, she stared at them appreciatively and
approved them—from a safe distance.

"... When We Left the Place of Abundance"

Mother sent for Chepe de Todos, the gardener, to prune the plants. He's been pulling up the weeds, sweeping them, and heaping them in a corner of the garden. But every time Chepe isn't looking, Mario and I go and take handfuls of the rubbish and sprinkle it on the beds so Chepe has to start his work all over again. But he hasn't noticed. Up on a ladder he's decorating the trees and pillars with all kinds of orchids, and he's got to hurry because he's promised that the orchids shall be flowering by the first-communion morning.

All the doors and windows of the house are flung wide and all the rooms dismantled. All but the one, that is, where the chocolate-grinder works, and we're forbidden to enter there. Vicenta and Rosalía are busy in the other rooms, shifting the furniture, hanging new curtains at the windows, cleaning the looking-glasses with damp paper that squeaks and gives us gooseflesh. Mario and I follow behind. We upset the chairs for a joke, streak the walls with paint, and leave ink blots on the floor. Seeing their efforts all going to waste they rage and swear at us under their breaths. Mario and I run to Mother's side for protection.

Her eyes are bloodshot. She's been crocheting day and night to finish the cloth for the chapel altar. She's doing it all alone because Aunt Romelia, who was helping her, went back to her husband over a month ago. The altar cloth was finished only today. They've starched it, and it is now drying, stretched with pins on the ironing-table so it won't go out of shape. While she is waiting for it to be ready to lay out, Mother has been cleaning the chapel. She shakes the dust off the statues and puts them back in their places: the Holy Child seated on a rock whose sharp edges are spiked with cottonwool clouds; bearded San Caralampio kneeling in a niche; the Trinity in friendly conversation.

Vicenta and Rosalía bring in the ironed altar cloth.

245

"... When We Left the Place of Abundance"

Against the light we look at the garlands of flowers interlocked with bleeding hearts and cabalistic letters. They
cover the altar with it, and straighten it out, stretching the
edges and patting it smooth. They're satisfied at last.

Mother orders the chapel windows to be closed, and
the door double-locked. Vicenta and Rosalía obey. They
leave the key in the lock and go away.

Mario and I seem to be hypnotized. We stare at the
little bit of iron that separates us from the chapel and
from the day of our first communion. Moved by some
irresistible impulse, I go and pull the key from the lock.

Mario beats a frightened retreat.

He doesn't want to be my accomplice, but stays behind
while I go off unnoticed to hide the key in Nana's chest
among the clothes and the pebbles from Chactajal.

13

Amalia took a little sip of coffee and replaced the cup
delicately in its saucer. Then she announced:

"God is in Heaven, on earth, and everywhere."

She has told us that this is one of the last catechism
classes. She has already let Mother know that Mario and
I are ready for communion, and she's advised us to take
advantage of the curate's next visit to Comitán.

"Is God with us here now?"

Mario wants her to explain properly and settle the
matter once and for all.

"God is watching us, saying: what a delightful pair of
children they are! They attend to their lessons, don't get
into mischief, tell no lies, and don't disobey the grown-
ups. And he must be saying too: I wasn't so far off the
mark when I put life into that poor woman. She's served
her purpose if she's helped them to know me."

". . . When We Left the Place of Abundance"

"Is God watching us?"

"Always. When you were still tucked away in Dr. Mazariegos's bag, God was watching you. And haven't you noticed how the stars have been blinking ever since? Those are the little holes the angels make in the sky so as to watch us and tell God everything we do."

"But in the daytime the stars go out."

"In the daytime the angel is even closer to us."

"The angel with the golden ball?"

"And at night the devil with seven cords. But that's enough for the moment, children. You're tired. Your minds are wandering off to your games."

Amalia gets up, and before we leave she gives us some candies from the glass jar. Mario and I clutch them in our damp hands, and there they melt and spread a sticky mess over our palms. Escorted by Vicenta and Rosalía, we walk primly home with downcast eyes.

Mother is at the head of the dining-room table. On her right sits Mario, and I'm on her left.

Vicenta and Rosalía come and go, serving dinner: a piping-hot pot full of corn patties folded into leaves, with a delicious smell; boiled plantains and runner beans.

Mario and I refuse everything as fast as it's offered.

"Aren't you hungry?" Mother asks with a trace of concern.

Mario and I say we aren't.

"Goodness knows what you've been pecking at between meals. Have some bread at least. I've ordered the kinds you like."

She lifts the starched napkin. There are rolls with their sesame seeds like hail-stones; rusks of interwoven chocolate and white; spongey yellow cakes; bran cakes with hollow centres that are good with honey; *mille-feuilles*.

We throw up our hands in disgust. Mother uses her last ruse to get us to eat:

". . . When We Left the Place of Abundance"

"It's holy bread."

Mario pushes the basket as far away as he can.

"For God's sake, Mario, don't be cruel to me. Eat. Just a mouthful."

"I'm sleepy. Tomorrow."

"Don't you feel well? Have you a temperature?"

She passes the back of her hand over his forehead and cheeks.

"You feel cool enough. Tell me what's the matter. Have you a pain?"

"I'm sleepy. Leave me alone till tomorrow, Mama."

Vicenta and Rosalía undress us and put on our long flannel nightgowns, wrapping us well up. Then over Mario's head and mine they untie the mosquito-net canopy.

"Leave the candle alight. I'm afraid of the dark."

"All right, Mario dear. Good night, little *patrones*."

They leave us alone. I close my eyes because I don't want to see the shadows the candle-flame throws on the wall. The noises that reach me are muffled by the cloud of tulle: Mario's restless breathing, footsteps, far-off voices in the house and in the street, crickets chirping. My breath rises and falls rhythmically. Sleep fills my eyes with sand.

Suddenly a slight, almost imperceptible noise wakes me. I open my eyes and, blurred by the folds of tulle, vaguely outlined against the trembling candle-flame, I see my mother, wrapped in a woollen scarf, with her shoes off so as to make less noise. She is leaning over Mario's bed and it looks as if she were trying to pry into his dreams. It is only a moment, and then she goes out as silently as she came.

The town clock strikes the hour. I begin counting, one, two, three, four, five. . . . But I'm asleep before the last stroke.

248

"... *When We Left the Place of Abundance*"

Mario's scream splits the night in two.

He screams with pain and anguish, fighting some monster in his sleep. In the midst of his delirium he keeps saying:

"The key. They saw us when we stole the key. If we don't put the key back in the chapel lock, Catashaná's going to carry us off."

Unexpectedly the electric light switches on, and Mother appears in the bedroom door. There she stands, still without her slippers, her hands gripping the wooden door-frame, her eyes unnaturally wide and fixed on Mario's bed.

14

Dr. Mazariegos is a short, stout, childish-looking man with an innocent smile and chubby cheeks, furry as peaches. He wears leather leggings and rides a faded old mule that has done him service ever since he first came to Comitán with his shining new diploma under his arm.

The mule knows the house of everyone of the doctor's patients. Unerringly he stops at ours.

"Here I am," shouts the doctor from the big street-door. Hearing his voice, so gay and fresh, I run to greet him. He seizes me in his arms and spins me madly in the air, then deposits me back on the ground. I'm dizzy and happy. He offers me a stick of chewing-gum.

"Good morning, Señora, here I am, at your service."

Mother comes out. Her face is swollen. She throws herself on the doctor, crying:

"I've been trying to get hold of you ever since yesterday."

He interrupts:

"I couldn't come earlier. A proper epidemic of births

there's been in this village. It's the lack of other things to do."

"But this is urgent."

Dr. Mazariegos goes up to Mother and pats her shoulder in a fatherly way, saying:

"Easy, easy, there's no need to worry. Every ill's got a cure. Let's see now, what's it all about?"

"Mario. . . ."

Her words break and she can't stop trembling.

"Let's see what the little fellow complains of. You come with me, Doña Zoraida, and I'll examine him."

Together they enter Mother's bedroom, and because they are so preoccupied I manage to slip in behind. Mario is lying on his back on my parents' broad bed, covered with a sheet. His eyes are closed, his nose pinched, and sweat has plastered the hair to his forehead.

Dr. Mazariegos brings up a chair and sits down. He pulls a stethoscope from his bag.

He takes one of Mario's hands, which lies limp in his.

"His pulse is normal. Has he complained of pain?"

"He keeps talking about a key. He was carrying on about it all night."

The doctor lowers the sheet over Mario's tummy and runs his hands over it, feeling him briskly with his rough fingers, while Mario groans feebly.

Dr. Mazariegos gets up, frowning thoughtfully. He doesn't go near the patient again, but says:

"Let's see your tongue."

Mario's pupils are dilated and he stares as if trying to stab through the images in front of him. He doesn't obey the doctor and his jaws stay firmly clenched.

"Why doesn't he do as you say, Doctor? Can't he hear?"

Dr. Mazariegos signs to Mother to keep quiet, and tiptoes into the passage. She follows.

". . . When We Left the Place of Abundance"

"What's wrong with him, Doctor?"

Mazariegos shrugs his shoulders, baffled. Then, repenting of having shown his ignorance, he says reassuringly:

"It's too early to diagnose. We must wait for the symptoms to be clearer. To put the matter in a nutshell, we've nothing to go on yet. No temperature, no pains, no. . . ."

"But it isn't natural he should be like this! He won't eat, and can't sleep. He doesn't speak, and doesn't understand what's said to him."

"It's certainly odd. But it may be a passing phase. Perhaps by tomorrow he'll be back to normal."

"We've got to help him, Doctor," Mother says urgently.

"Of course we'll help him. But calmly, Señora. It's just as well you called me. If this case had fallen into the hands of a young doctor, one of those full of long words and not very thorough, he wouldn't have had the least hesitation in giving the condition a name, one of those outlandish new names we've never heard tell of. He might even have advised an operation. They'd rather eradicate the trouble at its root than have the patience to attack it with other and slower remedies that are more effective and less harmful in the long run. Experience shows, you see, that surgical intervention always has its risks, and then too, the consequences are unforeseeable. For instance it's been calculated that a high percentage of patients who have their appendix removed go deaf."

"So it's appendicitis Mario has."

"I haven't said so, Doña Zoraida, please don't jump to conclusions. I'm merely giving you the general picture."

"But, Doctor. . . ."

"And now I'll explain the particular case. It's not critical of course, far from it. But even if it were, here in

Comitán we lack the facilities for practising that sort of cure. It's a delicate business managing the anaesthesia and it's a job that ought to be entrusted to a specialist. You know well enough there isn't such a person here. As to the surgeon. . . . Naturally I did take the course at the medical faculty and passed very creditably indeed, but it's a long time ago and as I've had no chance to exercise that branch of my profession I'm a bit rusty and. . . ."

"Don't say more, Doctor, we'll go to Mexico City at once."

Dr. Mazariegos cut the ground from under Mother's feet:

"How?"

"By car, by train, anyhow."

"It will take five days. In the weak state the boy's in, it's doubtful he'd last such a trying journey."

"It must be possible. There are aeroplanes in Tuxtla. I'll wire my husband to get us one."

"When they've got one free, they'll send it. Aeroplanes are constantly in demand. It will arrive in a week or a month. By that time the crisis will have been resolved one way or the other."

Mother seems very tired, unkempt, pale, wasted, her shoulders bent by many exhausting days. Again Dr. Mazariegos gives her a protective pat.

"Besides, think of the expense. Judging from what I've heard, it seems your husband's business has suffered certain reverses."

Mother's eyes flash.

"I'd steal if necessary."

"It isn't. Who says Mario has appendicitis, or that an operation is indicated?"

"I've known all along. There's nothing we can do. Neither you nor anybody, Doctor. My son is being eaten by the sorcerers of Chactajal."

"... When We Left the Place of Abundance"

"You surely don't credit such superstitions, Señora. . . ."

"Can you tell me what's wrong with Mario?"

"I don't want to complicate matters by using technical terms. But we have plenty of resources within reach and I'll use them all. I promise to study the case thoroughly. You can count on me at any hour of the day or night."

From his inside jacket pocket he pulls a prescription pad. Slowly and meticulously he writes something down, saying as he does so:

"By the way, about that key the boy's been mentioning. . . ."

"He was delirious. I don't know what it's about."

"Pity. It would just be as well if we could humour him, it would contribute to his recovery."

He rips off the top leaf of the pad and gives it to Mother. She reads it, and her eyes search the doctor's:

"Quinine?"

The doctor evades her gaze. Not very convincingly he answers:

"The authorities haven't bothered to drain the marshes, though they've been advised to. They are a breeding-ground for mosquitoes, so malaria is the endemic disease in these parts."

"But Mario. . . ."

"Mario must obviously be infected, there's no reason why he should be an exception. Quinine helps Nature to react against it."

Mother stares at Dr. Mazariegos with such intense reproach that he can't bear it. As he leaves, he begs her:

"Forgive me."

When mother is alone again she crumples the prescription in her hands and throws it on the floor.

15

"What do you suppose they called me for, Amalita? To scare away the evil spirits that are tormenting the boy. Before long I'll be a sorcerer too, and that's a crime that has set evil tongues wagging against me, and evil tongues never tire of inventing calumnies. It's no secret what I am. I'm a hunter, an honest one, a hunter of quetzal-birds to be more precise. If misfortune caught up with me, that still doesn't mean I'm a sorcerer. It was just bad luck. Nobody's immune from bad luck. Besides, when I first went into the region of Tziscao they omitted to tell me. . . ."

"All right, all right, Uncle David. Nobody's saying anything to the contrary."

"But it makes me wild that now Zoraida, whom I've known since she was so high, a little bit of a thing, should come out at me with that stuff and nonsense about witchcraft. Just because since she married César she's become ever so smart and thinks she's got a right to insult the common crowd. But I knew her since she was so high, a little bit of a thing."

"Forgive her, Uncle David. The poor creature's dreadfully upset."

"Yes, and she's reason to be. The boy's dropping like a quetzal-bird when it gets a bullet plumb in the heart."

"Mercy on us, Uncle David, don't say such things! They might hear you."

"Yes, I know one isn't supposed to make a sound. That's why I didn't bring my guitar."

"In these sad times who's got the spirit to be singing?"

"The times are well enough! If I'd waited to be in the mood for singing, I'd never have sung. Who says I sing because I'm happy? I sing to amuse people who invite me to dinner . . . or to a glass of wine."

"... When We Left the Place of Abundance"

"Oh, Uncle David, it's just as well you reminded me. Your meal will be ready in just a jiffy."

"I thought I hadn't deserved it."

"Not a bit of it. But with such goings on I don't know if I'm on my head or my heels. But now I'll get your meal in just three shakes of a lamb's tail. Just as soon as I've boiled some tea for the boy."

Uncle David went to the fire where Amalia had been fussing about for some time. He wanted to see what she was up to. He bent over to sniff the bubbling cauldron, but raised his face in disappointment:

"There's no smell."

Amalia blushed and pulled the pot off the coals. She wanted to avoid Uncle David's scrutiny, and turned her back to him, but he peered over her shoulders while she began pouring the infusion into a cup. Before Amalia could stop him, Uncle David had seized the cauldron and was pouring its contents on to the fire.

"What's this?"

Between thumb and forefinger he held up a little, slender, dark-coloured cord.

"Give it back, Uncle David!" screamed Amalia trying to grab it from him.

"Aha, so that's how it is, you crafty woman. So you're preparing tea."

"There's nothing wrong in that," Amalia answered vehemently. "It's water from Lourdes, and this scapulary is the Virgin of Perpetual Succour."

"Well, good health to you, Amalia dear, and be quick and take the drink to the invalid before it gets cold. May God perform a miracle and the child be cured."

When Amalia had left the kitchen, Uncle David turned to me, who'd been sitting quietly in a corner, and beckoned me to him.

I'm always disgusted with Uncle David's appearance,

so unkempt and dirty. I'm disgusted by the smell of mulled wine that always hangs about his mouth. But my parents have told me to be respectful to the old man and treat him kindly and call him uncle, as if he belonged to the family, so that he won't feel so lonely. Dragging my feet in order to delay approaching him for as long as possible, I obey.

Uncle David sits me on his knees, strokes my head, and says:

"Wouldn't you like to make a trip with me? We'll go to the forest, to the very heart of Balún-Canán, to the abode of the Nine Guardians. You'll see them all, just as they are, with their real faces, and they'll tell you their real names. . . ."

I shake my head and very definitely refuse. Almost on the point of weeping, Uncle David insists:

"Come on! Don't stay here, don't make the same mistake as me. You see the house is falling in ruins? Let's go away before it crushes us!"

I shake my head again. But gently now. So that Uncle David won't suspect I'm saying no because I don't want to go, because his arguments frighten me and his appearance disgusts me, I add—which is a lie, because I don't in the least want to give back what I hid:

"I can't go. I have to return a key."

16

"They invited me to a barbecue party on a farm near Tuxtla. I went because I was told the Governor would be there and I thought there might be a chance to talk to him. A friend introduced us. I thought the Governor wouldn't even remember my name, because though we met and spoke several times when he was in Comitán on his political campaign, it's the way of the world and a person such as he can't keep all the things people ask him in his head. But I was surprised when he questioned me about Chactajal. We talked for a while in the middle of interruptions from other people. In that party atmosphere it didn't seem to me the appropriate moment to explain my problems. I merely said I'd been in Tuxtla several weeks trying to obtain an audience with him. He promised to see me on the following day. But next day when I presented myself very formally at the Government Palace they told me he'd had to make an unexpected trip to Mexico City, because they'd sent for him to settle some business with the President of the Republic, but that I should await his return. So here I am, waiting. I'm satisfied now because I'm sure that when the Governor returns and receives me and understands my problems he'll do everything to settle them favourably. He's a most attractive man, very simple and friendly. One of those rough diamonds from Chiapas but with a big heart.

"As to what you tell me of Mario's illness, I can see no reason to be alarmed. You know how children's symptoms flare up. But if Dr. Mazariegos has told you they're of no moment, it must true. You know very well that he's a most capable doctor and very conscientious, and that you can trust him.

"So don't get so impatient. I'm coming back. But not quite as soon as you ask. I've got to speak to the Governor first."

Mother handed the letter to Amalia.

"Read this."

Amalia read, shaking her head disconsolately.

"But, Zoraida, it isn't César's fault. He's so far away, he can't understand the seriousness of the situation. But if you send a telegram explaining Mario's condition. . . ."

"... *When We Left the Place of Abundance*"

"It won't get there in time."

"Don't talk like that, Zoraida, you're mistrusting Divine Providence! We haven't tried everything yet, we've got to fight to the end."

"This is the end."

"No, we can do something yet."

"What?"

"The priest. Listen to me, please, Zoraida. The priest is the only person who can save Mario. He'll pray and exorcize the devil from this house. Because it's the devil, everyone can see that. Even Dr. Mazariegos. Why do you suppose he wouldn't even try to operate on the boy? Because he knew it would be useless."

Hope came struggling into Mother's eyes.

"And do you think the priest will consent to come after. . . ."

"After what you said to him that night? Do you know, he asked me himself to beg your pardon."

'Then run, Amalia dear! What are you waiting for? Go and call the priest."

The priest! I'm not going to give back the key. When they come they won't be able to open the chapel. They'll punish Mario thinking it's he who's the culprit, and they'll surrender him to Catashaná.

"Don't let the priest come, don't let the priest come, I shan't let him enter!"

Mother turned to me impatiently:

"That's enough from you! Amalia, please take this child with you, she's not giving Mario a chance to sleep the way she's shouting."

Amalia took me by the hand, imagining I would go along quietly. But when she felt my resistance her fingers closed hard and strong like grappling-irons on my wrists. Tugging, she forced me to move a few steps, but I let myself go limp to the ground. Amalia had to drag me

because I was too heavy to carry. With Vicenta's help she
got me as far as the big outer door. My dress was torn and
my legs, grazed against the stones, were skinned. I yelled
all the harder, and louder, because now I was further
away:

"Don't let the priest in! Don't let him in!"

17

They dumped me on the sofa in Amalia's drawing-
room and went away, she and Vicenta. I stayed there,
with my hair tangled, sweating from the struggle, covered
with dirt because of the way they'd dragged me. It
hadn't been any use. Amalia and Vicenta had left me there
in front of a mirror that was not to be gainsaid and an old
woman who paid no heed to the commotion of my entry.
There she was as usual, sunk in contemplation of the
little square of street the window allowed her to see.

And Mario was there alone in his bedroom, quivering
with pain, and the priest coming nearer and nearer.

"*Tilín-tilín*, now I'm turning the corner. *Tilín-tilín*,
now I'm knocking at the door. *Tilín-tilín*, now I've got
you! We'll take communion in the chapel. Where's the
key? You've hidden it! God will punish you! Catashaná
will carry you off!"

And Mario clenching his teeth, resisting in spite of his
suffering, thinking I've betrayed him. And it's true. I've
let him writhe and suffer, and I haven't opened Nana's
box. Because then the witches would eat me, God would
punish me, and Catashaná would carry me off. Who
would come to my rescue? Not Mother. She only pro-
tects Mario because he's the male child.

The old woman sobs, muttering that she wants them to
take her to Guatemala. Mechanically I get up and go to

her chair. I push her as hard as I can but the chair won't budge. And all the time her sobs grow more urgent and disconsolate. The old woman keeps repeating: "Guatemala, Guatemala." And suddenly the name penetrates into my brain. Guatemala? Yes, it's the place one goes to when one runs away. Not so long ago Doña Pastora promised she would sell the secret to Mother and tell her at what place on the frontier there wasn't a guard. You could get through, and nobody would stop you. Once on the other side, nobody could reach you. Not Amalia, nor the curate, nor God, nor Catashaná. Because nobody knows the road, it's Doña Pastora's secret. It's a secret she sells for money. I haven't any money. But warm in my blouse I've got the present I brought for Nana from the farm, which she didn't take with her. A stream of pebbles could drop into Doña Pastora's hands. She'd look at them surprised, like Nana looked at them first. She might even say she didn't want to do business. But when I tell her the pebbles are from Chactajal she'll be pleased and the secret will be ours. And we'll run away, far away, until we're out of reach of persecution and nightmares.

But Mario can't run; he's ill. And I can't wait. No, I'll go alone, I'll save myself alone.

Quickly, quickly. Where can Doña Pastora be? I've got to go and find her now, there's not a moment to lose. I don't know where she lives. But I'll go into the street and ask person after person until somebody tells me: "Walk straight ahead for two blocks; then, when you come to where seven roads meet, turn left. In front of the horse trough. . . ."

I peep furtively into the passage. There's no one about. I advance on tiptoe so as not to wake an echo. But just as I'm about to raise the latch on the street door, a tremendous voice falls on top of me and roots me to the spot.

"Where are you going?"

"... When We Left the Place of Abundance"

Slowly I turn. There stands Vicenta before me in her grease-stained apron. I'm frightened. But something stronger than fear supports me and I say:

"I want to get out."

"There's no getting out, girlie. Back to your place. In the drawing-room."

"I won't be long. I'll be back in a moment. Please. . . ."

"I obey the one I'm supposed to obey. They ordered me to look after you, and what tale shall I tell if I let you out? Come on. Back to the drawing-room."

I can't scream any more. I'm hoarse. My arms are bruised from the way they pulled me here. And that enormous rough woman is blocking my way. If I explain perhaps she'll give in.

"I've got to talk to Doña Pastora, the woman who smuggles. Tell me where she lives."

"Of course, girlie, with pleasure. She lives in the drawing-room. Go and look for her there."

"I'm not fooling, Vicenta. It's true."

"I'm not fooling either. And if you don't go back to the drawing-room at once, Mr. Justice Reason'll be after you."

I tremble, terrified at this name that I've never heard in my life before and that must be something powerful and very bad if Vicenta invokes it. I let myself be led back without further protest. Before me the two panels of the door close well and truly. I stand still a moment in the centre of the room. The portraits wink mockingly at me from their velvet frames. The fans open and close, flashing their teeth in cruel laughter. The looking-glass. . . . No, I don't want it to catch sight of me! I run to the chair where the little old lady is sitting and bury my face in her lap, and together we sob for our never-to-be-realized journey to Guatemala.

"... When We Left the Place of Abundance"

18

Amalia wakened me, shaking me hard. My eyelids were heavy with sleep and the exhaustion of weeping.

"She's behaved very badly," my nursemaid says. "She wanted to run into the street, and when I locked her up...."

She's going to tell the whole story. Yes, it's true I rolled on the floor and threw a fan at the looking-glass, hoping to break it.

But Amalia paid no attention to Vicenta's accusations. She drew my face close to hers (a pucker between the eyes, which were all inflamed, and there were wrinkles gathered round the corners of her mouth, and her hair was turning white) and she said:

"You've got to be very brave, little girl. Mario's just died."

"Did the priest arrive?"

"He got there just in time. But the military stopped him as he left the house. He's a prisoner now."

The priest got there just in time. So he managed to find everything out. He was in time to punish Mario. And the key is well hidden in the box among Nana's clothes, and I'm safe.

"You must be quiet now, child. You must be very considerate."

I put up no further resistance. I allow them to change my dress that's all in rags—Amalia and the nursemaid between them. They put me on a black one for mourning, the same dress I used when I paid the visit of condolence to Doña Nati. A black dress like vulture's feathers.

We go back home. The street door is wide open at this hour of night. In the yard, on the verandas, in the garden, are little groups of men and women in mourning, whispering and gossiping, making a noise like water simmering. Sometimes a gust of laughter rises, but it is soon dissolved beneath the gurgling voices.

Amalia and I pass among them. When I come within reach of the gentlemen and ladies they stroke me, rubbing their faces, damp with saliva and tears and sweat, against mine. They contemplate me with sad, benevolent eyes from their grown-up heights. They speak, and break what they say with sighs.

Don Jaime Róvelo leans toward me and takes me in his arms, murmuring:

"Now your father has nobody to go on fighting for. We're in the same boat. Neither of us has a man-child any more."

Amalia separates us, to take me indoors. All the bulbs of the main chandelier are alight. And there are flowers, flowers everywhere. On the furniture, round the white coffin, spilling over the floor. Their scent mingles with that of burning wax from the four big candles.

Raising the coffin-lid Amalia says:

"Would you like to see your brother for the last time?"

I turn my face away in disgust. No, no, I couldn't bear it. Because it isn't Mario, but my naughtiness, that's rotting in the bottom of the box.

19

"This death is a punishment from heaven. Why should a little boy die like that, before he's begun to flower? And he so gallant and gay."

It's Rosalía who is speaking. Then she wipes away her tears with the edge of her shawl. Uncle David agrees:

"They say the sorcerers on the farm ate him up as a revenge because the *patrones* had treated them badly."

"... *When We Left the Place of Abundance*"

Uncle David is warming his hands by the kitchen hearth. He came here because the men attending the wake think themselves above him and shun his company. Vicenta hands him a cup of coffee.

"Who's going to look at them, proud as they are! Just because they wear waistcoats and gold braid. But these families have a lot of crimes to account for."

"If you think it isn't so, ask Doña Nati, the blind woman. Why, except for the Argüellos, did they kill her son, Ernesto that was?"

Vicenta offered Uncle David a glass of home-brew.

"It's to lace your coffee."

Then, turning to Rosalía:

"But Doña Nati got her little nest-egg of cash. I've seen her out in the street. She's putting on such an air, and just because she's got shoes."

"Money!"

"And what more should she be wanting?"

"As if her son's life can be repaid with money. Now Doña Zoraida knows. Now she's got the taste of it too."

Vicenta laughs long and with relish.

"What a simpleton you are, Rosalía! I know who made the boy Mario die, and it wasn't Doña Nati nor the witches of Chactajal as Don David would have it. I know who let the boy die."

She must have opened Nana's chest, she must have seen the key hidden among the clothes, she must have seen the guilt in my eyes!

Before she can say any more, before she can point at me, I run into the patio, out into the dark.

20

It's light, and then it's dark again. Faithfully the town clock marks the hours, but I have no idea how long has gone by since I've been wandering about the house, opening and closing doors, weeping.

Dully and slowly I walk, taking one step and then, a long, long time later, another. So I push on through the unbreathable air, as of a star recently exploded. In the garden the day spreads out thinly, untidy, and without any scent.

In the patio the hens are feeding the chicks, who know nothing else but how to chirrup and be yellow.

In the stable the animals are pawing and neighing, tormented by an invisible horsefly. And in other patios in other houses distant dogs are barking as if they had scented the disaster.

I go into the kitchen. On the hearth is a cold crust of ash. On the sideboards the mugs are sleeping an irrevocable sleep. The pots have great paunches like overfed grannies. The cups are grinning broadly. The forks with their prongs long as herons' legs: all are dead.

In the dining-room frigid order rules. On to the defenceless drawing-room furniture falls an imperceptible rain of dust. The chapel door is locked.

I reach Mother's bedroom. There she lies on her bed, in which her son died. She is twisting and groaning like an ox when the cow-man throws it and its hide steams under the branding iron marking its slavery.

At the bedside Amalia, in an even, expressionless voice, is chanting:

"It's good to live on the banks of a river. Memory is cleansed as one watches the water go by. Hearing the water go by, pain sleeps. Let's go and live on the bank of a river."

21

Amalia and Vicenta are in the nursery sorting out

Mario's toys and packing them, because they're going to be given to the poor.

"Zoraida wanted to keep them, but I said to her, what for? Memories are always painful."

"The *patrona's* very sad. She doesn't leave her room. She doesn't want to see anyone."

"She'll have to learn to accept it. Time is the great healer. God knows better than we do what's good for us. And when in His mercy He takes something away, it's for our own good; though we may not be able to look at it that way, we ought to suffer in patience and gratitude."

"You speak so pretty, Amalia dear! Is it true what they said, that you nearly became a nun?"

"Yes. From the time I was a girl I wanted to enter a convent in San Cristóbal, but Mother opposed it and disinherited me, so to save money for my dowry I had to set to work. I sewed, made candies, and did anything that came along. I saved everything to the last penny. First of all I bought my habits and put them away in a cedar chest so they'd soak up the sweet scent."

"And then?"

"A month before the date when I was due to go, Mother fell ill. She never recovered, but is just the same to this day, like a little child. She can't even cross herself alone. And she confuses everything—places, people's faces—poor thing."

"Poor thing! You couldn't have been so hard-hearted as to leave her."

"Don't you believe it, Vicenta. I'm very ungrateful. I wanted to go to the convent in spite of everything, but my confessor didn't allow me to."

Vicenta was wrapping the cardboard horse with its mane of pig's hair, long and yellow, on which Mario used to ride.

"So I didn't leave home. Have you noticed, Vicenta,

266

that the houses in Comitán are very gloomy. In mine we didn't have flowers even, or birds. And we went about all shrouded and spoke secretly and didn't open the windows so as not to disturb the invalid."

"We all have a cross to bear, child Amalia. They disowned me when I was still a bit of a thing."

"No postulants are admitted after they're thirty—that's the rule of the convent. And Mother was so feeble I thought. . . . I had everything ready for when Mother should die, the coarse silk dress, a linen kerchief I embroidered myself, everything. And look now how my hair's turning white already."

"Perhaps it was your fate to be a left-over girl."

"My confessor advised me to offer this sacrifice to God. But how could I do that if I did it with distaste and impatience, as if it were the fault of my poor little mother?"

"Are you going to give away Mario's clothes too?"

"Yes. But don't let Zoraida know. Her sorrow is still very fresh. Things soften with the years. My whole heart's given over to Mother by now."

They finish the job and get up to go. But before they can do so I beg Amalia:

"Take me to the cemetery: I want to see Mario."

She doesn't seem surprised by this sudden desire. She strokes my head and answers:

"Not now. We'll go later, when it's time to eat the Holy Bread on All Saints."

22

November. A sad and tenuous wind howls over the moor. From the ranches and nearby villages come great droves of mules heavily laden for the feast of All Saints. When they arrive they spread out their produce on

"... When We Left the Place of Abundance"

Market Hill, and the women go to buy with their heads covered in mourning veils.

Orchard-owners cut huge pumpkins and chop them up to boil them with sugar; and they split the faded custard-apples with their soft pulps, and they pile into baskets the *chayotes*, protected by their prickly husks.

Vicenta and Rosalía have prepared everything for our outing, because the day has come for Amalia to keep her promise and we are going to the cemetery to eat the bread of All Saints.

"Your mother doesn't feel well enough to go with us, but she's asked me to look after you and see you're a good girl."

We go into the street. Along the pavements troop families who greet each other with much ceremony and give way to each other on the sidewalk: they are those who always eat with their dead on this day of the year. Ahead walks the man of the house in his waistcoat and gold braid. Beside him his wife wrapped in a black woollen scarf. Behind the children clean in their Sunday-best. And last of all the servants, balancing on their heads the pumpkins and food baskets.

It's a long way and we arrive tired at the cemetery. The cypresses rise solidly in a single impulse of growth. On either side of the narrow, winding paths, invaded by the lawns, are marble monuments: sobbing angels with their faces buried in their hands; broken columns, tiny niches with shining golden letters and numbers in their depths. Here and there are piles of damp soil only just dug up, with makeshift crosses on top.

We sit down to eat on the first step of a heavy, massive edifice with lettering on its façade announcing: "Belonging to the Family of Argüello in Perpetuity." The servants spread cloths on the ground and pull out slices of pumpkin dripping with honey; and they peel the *chayotes* and season them with salt.

". . . When We Left the Place of Abundance"

Sitting by other tombs, other people whom we know are eating too, and Amalia greets them with a smile and perfunctory wave. There is Don Jaime Rovelo; Aunt Romelia leaning on her husband's arm; Doña Pastora, hot and flushed; Doña Nati led by her neighbour and wearing a new pair of shoes.

When we've finished eating Amalia pushes open the door of the monument, and a whiff of dense, dark, imprisoned air rises from the depths our eyes can't yet measure, and hits us full in the face.

"The steps start here. Go carefully."

Amalia helps me down, indicating the distance between the treads, and the place where my foot can rest most comfortably. We go forward slowly because of the dark. When we are down below, Amalia strikes a match and lights the candles.

Several minutes go by before we get used to the dark. It is cold and damp.

"Where's Mario?"

Amalia raises a candle and directs the haze of light to a point on the wall. Bricklayers have been at work there recently. The cement isn't even dry.

"They haven't written his name yet."

Mario's name is missing, but on the marble plaques covering the rest of the wall are others: Rodulfo Argüello, Josefa, Estanislao, Abelardo, José Domingo, María. With dates, and prayers.

"We must go now, child, it's late."

But first, here by Mario's grave, I drop the chapel key. And then I pray to all those who sleep beneath their stones that they shall be good to Mario and look after him and play with him and keep him company. Because now that I've tasted solitude I don't want him to taste it too.

269

"... When We Left the Place of Abundance"

23

Outside a far-away chill sun is shining. Amalia and I
move among the scattered groups, saying good-bye.
Good-bye, Doña Pastora, to whom I'll never now give
the pebbles from Chactajal; good-bye Doña Nati, walking in her new shoes in the dark; good-bye, good-bye,
Don Jaime.

Away in the distance Comitán is waiting for us,
crested with that yellow air made of the droning daytime and the bees. Away over there are the towers resting
with folded wings; the houses the size of doves.

We walk through the poor district. I remember that
this door leads to the crookback's room. Who'll visit her
now that Mother doesn't any more? Who'll take her
breakfast?

In the suburb of San Sebastián live rich people—brandy
manufacturers, silversmiths, shop owners—but they are
not considered to be of good family. Their houses sur-
round the park with clashing colours. They are very careful not to let their children pull up the flowers or break
the branches of the trees. Sitting on an iron bench,
Amalia and I see Señorita Silvina walking by. She's
looking about her suspiciously. Under her woollen shawl
she carries a sheet of cardboard.

"What are you doing in these parts, Señorita, and on a
feast day?"

She stops, confused, as if caught in a naughty act. She
explains:

"Since they closed my school I've been giving classes
in private houses. Don Golo Córdoba's family's sent for
me. They none of them know how to read."

"It's scandalous that such people should have the money
now," Amalia declares.

"... When We Left the Place of Abundance"

"And what's the cardboard for?" I ask, for I'm jealous of the privilege that other people are now enjoying.

"It's . . . just in case."

We say good-bye to Señorita Silvina and start walking. We leave the rustling shadows of the ash-trees behind, and the noisy flight of the magpies. Tottering, dragging his guitar on the ground, Uncle David comes toward us. He bows comically in greeting. Amalia looks at him disapprovingly.

"Aren't you ashamed, Uncle David? To offend people's susceptibilities like this?"

"And what have I to do with people? I'm a lonely man. I have no dead of my own!"

Amalia drags me quickly away. As we pass the Frontier Casino we see through the windowpanes the figure of Dr. Mazariegos, sitting in a chair, dozing.

Now we go down Main Street. On the opposite pavement an Indian woman is walking by. As soon as I see her I let go of Amalia's hand and run toward her with open arms. It's my Nana! But the Indian watches me quite impassively, making no welcoming sign. I slow up—slower and slower till I stop. I let my arms drop, altogether discouraged. Even if I see her, I'll never recognize her now. It's so long since we've been parted. Besides, all Indians look alike.

24

When I get home I search for a pencil, and in my cramped and halting handwriting I scribble Mario's name Mario on the garden bricks. Mario on the veranda wall. Mario in the pages of my copybook.

Because Mario is far away, and I want to ask his forgiveness.

Glossary of Unfamiliar Indian and Spanish Words

ATOLE: a thick drink made with maize flour and chocolate.

CHAYOTES: a Mexican fruit, *Scisyos edulis*.

COMADRE, COMPADRE: the dictionaries will give these words as "God-mother", "Godfather"; but in fact the meaning is much wider, and anyone who has befriended or patronized one in a definite way may be called *comadre*, *compadre*, also relatives. Sometimes a special ceremony makes a person *compadre* to another.

GRINGO(A): an American from U.S.A.

LADINO: a half-caste, sometimes even an Indian, who speaks Spanish, dresses like a townsman, and has adopted western customs.

MARIMBA: a kind of xylophone, but very much bigger, often played by four or more people.

PERRAJE: a shawl made by the Guatemala Indians, woven in brilliant colours with geometrical designs.

PICHULEJ: palm from which hats are made.

POSOL: maize dough which may be fresh or allowed to go rancid. It is kneaded into a ball and wrapped in a banana leaf. The Indians carry it as food on long journeys because it is easy to keep. The dough is soaked in water before drinking, and sometimes as a luxury a little cocoa or almond is added.

REAL: an old Spanish coin no longer used.

REBOZO: long narrow shawl like a stole used by Mexican women for warmth, to carry their children, etc.

SAN TAT: a respectful greeting.

TAMAL: a mixture of maize and meat or vegetables boiled and wrapped in the outer leaf of the maize.

TATA: a word used affectionately for parents or grandparents or for elders of the tribe.

TORTILLA: a basic Indian and Mexican food, a flat pancake usually made of maize, sometimes of wheat.

TOSTÓN: formerly half a *real*; now half a *peso* or fifty *centavos*.

TZEC: a skirt of coarse blue cloth used in Chiapas. The skirt is very ample, and it is wound round the waist with heavy pleating in front.

TZELTAL: one of twelve indigenous languages spoken in Chiapas, and one of the three most common. *Tzeltal* is spoken in the highlands, in the mountains about San Cristóbal, and on the high plains of Comitán. It is a dialect derived from Maya, to which it bears about the same relation as Spanish does to Latin.